Help Me Remember

Give Me Love

Keep This Promise

Give Me
LOVE

NEW YORK TIMES BESTSELLING AUTHOR
CORINNE MICHAELS

Give Me Love

Copyright © 2022 Corinne Michaels
All rights reserved.
ISBN ebook: 978-1-942834-78-6
ISBN print: 978-1-942834-79-3

This book is a work of fiction. Names, characters, places, and incidents either are products of the author's imagination or are used fictitiously. Any resemblance to actual events or locales or persons, living or dead, is entirely coincidental and beyond the intent of the author or publisher.

Cover Design: Sommer Stein, Perfect Pear Creative
Editing: Ashley Williams, AW Editing
Proofreading: Julia Giffis, Michele Ficht & ReGina Kay
Photographer: Nicole Ashley Photography

Dedication

To the DIY influencers on Instagram who provide me with projects that drive my husband crazy and allow me to procrastinate when I should be writing. I can't wait for more ideas of things I can't do but will spend hours watching.

Dear Reader,

It is always my goal to write a beautiful love story that will capture your heart and leave a lasting impression. However, I want all readers to be comfortable. Therefore, if you want to be aware of any possible CW please click the link below to take you to the book page where there is a link that will dropdown. If you do not need this, please go forth and I hope you love this book filled with all the pieces of my heart.

Click here to find any CW for this book

https://corinnemichaels.com/books/give-me-love/

CHAPTER

One

EMMETT

This isn't happening.

No way is Blakely Bennett in Rose Canyon. Not at Brielle and Spencer's wedding reception. She is supposed to be in Washington DC, not in Oregon.

This is a dream—or a nightmare, depending on what she's here for.

"Great," I grumble as I watch as the woman who haunts me stalks across the room as if she owns it.

"Who is that?" Brielle asks Spencer.

That is a world of trouble and a whole lot of things I tried to forget. I run my fingers through my hair. "Fuck."

"Umm, Emmett?" Spencer grips my shoulder. "Is that—"

"Yup."

Brie snorts. "Can you clue me in?"

"That's Blakely Bennett. She was in the military with Emmett."

"Oh? Are they friends?" Brie asks, but I can't stop watching Blakely. I can't stop the wheels from turning as to what the hell this woman is doing here.

I did what she asked.

I am not being difficult.

Her dark brown hair that feels like silk sways with each step she takes. I can see the warm brown eyes with flecks of yellow watching me.

"I guess. She was his captain and the medic for the unit."

I turn to him, needing a second to get myself under control. Staring at her is like looking into the sun. It hurts and leaves an impression long after you've glanced away. "No, we were the same rank," I clarify. We were both captains, and she did not outrank me, contrary to whatever she thought.

"She totally was his boss," Spencer says softly to her.

I'll kick his ass later for that.

Then she's here. Right in front of me, and I swear to God, I can't fucking breathe. She's so beautiful, so everything, and I still don't feel as if I'm good enough to be in her presence. I never have.

I still want to fall at her feet, which pisses me off.

"Hello, Maxwell." That soft, sweet voice of an angel falls around me.

Only I know better because there's nothing angelic about Blake. She will kill you in your sleep, which is why I never should've trusted her.

"Bennett," I get out in one breath.

Blake turns to Spencer, her smile never faltering. "I thought it was you, Cross. You look wonderful and so happy."

They embrace, and I clench my jaw to stop from saying something stupid. Spencer is happily married and has zero interest in Blake. I don't either. Not at all. She's just . . . Blakely.

Spencer pulls back, holding on to her arms. "It's because I am. It's good to see you, Blake."

She keeps talking to him as though I'm not here. "You too, and I hear this is your wedding celebration?"

"You heard correctly." Spencer nods. "This is my wife, Brielle."

Blakely pushes her hair behind her ear and then takes Brielle's hand. "It's lovely to meet you. I know your husband from one of the training exercises we did. I wish you both much happiness."

"Thank you."

Enough with the chitchat. Blakely didn't come across the

country without a phone call for nothing. She wants something from me, and I would like to know exactly what that is.

"What are you doing here, Blakely?" I ask.

Blake tilts her head to the side, batting those long, dark lashes. "I came to see you, darling."

Unreal and a lie. I'm going to assume she has the divorce papers and this is some kind of ploy to piss me off. "I sent you paperwork months ago."

She waves her hand. "I'm not here for that. I came for something else."

Spencer clears his throat. "What paperwork?"

Blakely shrugs. "Divorce papers."

Instead of screaming like I want to, I groan, running a hand down my face. "Jesus Christ."

"You're married?" Brielle practically shouts.

A horde of nosey people turn to look at me. Great, this is really going to be all anyone talks about.

I look to Spencer and Brielle. "Yes, Blakely Bennett is my wife. And if you'll excuse me, I need to speak with her outside."

I grab her hand, pulling her toward the large glass door. My wife doesn't seem fazed at all as she waves a quick goodbye to everyone currently staring at us. "I'm sure we'll see each other soon."

The hell she will. I'm packing her ass back onto a plane and shipping her home as soon as I can. Whenever she's around, things go badly for me. I forget who I am and become the man she needs but will never want.

Or she wants but won't have.

I had to put distance between us, and apparently, I miscalculated just how much distance would keep her away.

When we get onto the deck, the cool air helps to clear my muddled mind. "Out with it," I say a little more forcefully than I intended.

"Be nice, Emmett, you aren't usually a dick."

"And you aren't here because you missed me."

"You're right, that's not why I came, but I do miss you." She smiles. "How are you? I heard you're the sheriff of this tiny town."

I close my eyes for a beat and sigh. "Yes, I am. Well, technically, I'm a sheriff of the county, but this is where I'm contracted to work."

"Okay, and how are you?"

"I'm great," I lie.

"Good to know."

"Why are you here, Blakely?" I ask through gritted teeth. "I sent you divorce papers, I am ready to be done with it all, and you haven't sent your copies back. So, what else would bring you out here if it wasn't to give us both what we want?"

"As I already said, I'm not here about the divorce, which I also never said I wanted."

No, she never *said* she wants a divorce, but she did make it abundantly clear she didn't want me when she left me that night. I release a heavy sigh through my nose. "You're killing me."

"No, I'm here to make sure that doesn't happen by someone else."

This woman confuses me. "Okay . . ."

"You'll thank me later."

"Or you can tell me who you think is going to kill me."

Which no one is. She's full of shit.

"I plan to, but first, aren't you going to ask about how I'm doing?" Blakely changes the subject.

"Not until you answer the original question."

She shrugs and then moves toward the railing. "This place is beautiful. It's literally like you described it. Super quaint, and the people are all very nice. I was able to find you in just a few minutes."

Sometimes the people in this town are out of their minds. They have no sense of danger or concept of just how much damage can be done with something as basic as a person's location, but she and I do. Years of military training caused us to be cautious of everything and everyone.

"So glad my descriptions lived up to your ideas," I say, not feeling like making small talk. "Bennett?"

"Yes, sweetums?"

"Seriously?"

"We haven't seen each other in two and a half years. I've missed you. Can we please catch up a little, and then I promise to tell you why I'm here and for how long I plan to stay at your place, which you're going to have to agree to since there are no hotels anywhere around here."

"No."

"No to which?"

I tilt my face heavenward and pray for divine intervention. "No to all." A deep rumbling sound emits from my chest. No one makes me as crazy as she does. And the worst part is that all I want to do right now is pull her into my arms and kiss her until she melts.

She grins. "I missed that growl."

I miss feeling in control, and I don't around her. "I am on the last thread of my patience."

"Then play nice and ask me what I'm up to. Who knows, maybe you'll get that answer."

Of all the things this woman is, manipulative is not one. She and I have always valued each other enough to be honest. When you're commanding a team of soldiers, you have to be able to trust the person who has your back. Blakely and I were instantly a team. I ran all the logistics, and she was our medic. She made sure the soldiers were cared for, and I made sure she was safe.

At least I tried.

We got married for all the wrong reasons, or maybe they were right at the time. We were both single, wanted to bank some extra money, and more because I didn't want to lose her from the unit.

It was strictly paperwork—that was, until I started to fall in love with her.

How could I not?

She's perfect, other than the fact that she refuses to love anyone.

That part is not so damn perfect.

"What are you up to, my beautiful wife?" I ask, forcing the frustration to stay out of my tone as I stand in front of her.

"How sweet of you to ask." Her hand moves to my chest, and a familiar current runs through me. Her eyes meet mine, and when her breath hitches, I know she feels it too. She steps back, shaking her head. "I am running a private investigation company out of DC."

There's a shocker. "Really? When did you get out of the army?"

"After you were discharged, I took a desk job with the FBI. I was going to head up a medic training program for them, but I ended up working on their task force for missing people. Once I was discharged from the army, I decided to stay in DC, leave the FBI—way too much bureaucracy—and start my own company since I really enjoy the investigating side."

"You what?"

"No big deal, I left two months ago."

"Why did you leave?"

"Because I've had enough of the government owning me. The politics and the drama . . . it's ridiculous. I got a few clients recently, and I've been able to use my Bureau contacts to get information."

"Illegally?"

She huffs. "Please, I'm not bound by the same rules as someone who works for an agency."

"Okay, so now you're a PI, but why are you here?"

Blakely leans against the railing, her long legs crossed at the ankles. "I've thought about you, Emmett."

The admission stuns me. Not that we weren't close. Not that our friendship ever wavered, not until she walked out on me that night. Not until I realized that I couldn't be around her because I was going to fall even more in love with my wife.

"I've thought about you too." The admission slips out so easily.

She pushes up and walks closer. "Then why haven't you called?"

"The phone works both ways, love."

She grins. "You owed me a call first, and you know why."

Because the only response she's gotten from me in two and a half years is a one-line email after the countless ones she sent and then I filed for divorce. "I should've warned you."

"That would've been nice."

"I didn't think much of it since we were basically roommates with a higher pay rate."

Blakely steps closer, her dark hair shimmering in the fading sunlight. "It still hurt, Emmett. Not a note or a text. No responses for years to how many emails? Nothing other than some guy showing up, handing me the paperwork, and saying I got served. We won't even talk about the shit leading up to that."

I feel like an ass, but I needed to get it done. We are both living in the past that is built on lies. I need to be free to live my life and move on. Because, when I realized that I was falling for her . . . that I wanted to be married in every damn sense of the word, she reminded me why that wasn't possible.

"I thought you weren't here for that."

She shrugs. "I'm not, but you were the cherry on top for this trip. I'm here because you stepped in some shit, buddy, and being the loving and doting wife I am, I came here to get you out of it before you end up dead."

CHAPTER
Two

EMMETT

~Two and a half years earlier~

"**D**o you need anything else, Major?" the nurse asks as she places another blanket over me. Major, I still haven't gotten used to that. I got promoted two days ago, finally outranking my wife, and instead of a ceremony, I am in Germany recovering from a bullet wound.

"Someone who has information on my unit would be nice."

"Sir?"

"Can you see if *anyone* has a status update on any other injuries in my unit?"

I figured, by now, I would at least know something.

She gives me a sad smile. "I'll see what I can do."

I nod, knowing nothing will come of it.

I look around the cold room, hating that I'm here instead of out on that field with my men.

Three days ago, I was shot and sent here. Three days I've been here, worrying and wondering about what is going on with the unit. I don't know if they're safe or even who survived.

Murphy was pinned down with me, and then Hunt moved to higher ground, trying to get our location to the evac crew.

I'm pretty sure Dunegan didn't make it. His wound was deep, and . . . God, I need to find out. The one bright spot is that Blakely was moved to another unit three weeks ago. I don't know that I would be able to breathe right now if she had been with us. I would be out of my mind and out of this bed looking for her.

There's a knock on the door and in walks the surgeon. "Major Maxwell, how are you doing today?"

"I'm fine. I will be a lot better if you're here with any information on my team."

"I wish I could give you that, but I can't."

"Captain, if this were your men, your team of doctors and nurses, exactly how would you feel?"

"I'm not saying I don't empathize with you, but I can't break the rules, not even if I want to."

No one will say anything. Not until Colonel O'Brien gets here. I thought he'd be here when I woke from my four-hour surgery, but no.

"Any idea when Colonel O'Brien will get here?"

"He is in the hospital today, so I imagine he'll find his way here at some point."

I huff. "I just want to know if my guys got out and who didn't make it. I need to make calls to the families as their commanding officer."

Captain Hulse places his hand on my shoulder. "I understand. If I see him, I'll remind him to come here."

I let out a long sigh, resting my head back against the pillow. "Thank you."

"Let me take a look at your wound."

I nod, and he pulls the blanket up, removes the bandaging to expose my thigh. The bullet went through the back muscle, shredding everything in its path. They feel confident that I'll have use of my leg again, but it's going to be a hard recovery. I don't care about that, though. I'm not afraid to work hard and prove I am able to get through it.

"Everything looks as expected. There is a small amount of redness around the wound, which I want to watch. The sooner we get you up, the better, so today we'll start with some light exercises and see how—"

"Where is he?" I hear someone yelling in the hall. "Where the hell is my husband?"

I know that voice. I turn to the doctor, who is watching the open doorway.

"Ma'am, please calm down."

Wrong thing to say. "I am not a ma'am. I am Captain Bennett, and I am looking for Captain Maxwell, who was shot. I am here . . . where the hell is Captain Maxwell?"

"We don't have a Captain Maxwell here, Captain."

"Oh God! Oh God! Is he . . . is he dead? No! They said he was sent here. I came. I came as fast as—"

"Blake!" I yell to her.

"Emmett?"

Captain Hulse looks at me. "Your wife, I presume?"

"Could you save the poor nurse from my wife? She may lose her mind if someone doesn't help her."

He laughs and walks to the doorway. "Major Maxwell is in here."

I hear a loud sigh, and then the doctor is being shoved out of the way and her fear-filled eyes find mine. "Emmett." She breathes my name.

"I'm okay."

She shakes her head, moving toward me. "I came. I . . . they pulled me and said you were injured. No one would tell me . . ."

Tears fall down her cheeks, and I force myself to sit up a little and reach for her. "I'm okay, Blake. I'm okay."

"I didn't know."

"I'm sorry."

"I didn't know. They just said you were shot and in surgery."

Her hands cup my face. "I should've been there with you."

"No. Absolutely not."

Her forehead rests on mine, her tears falling onto my face. "I would've known. I didn't know, and—wait! You're a Major?"

I smile. "Yes. I'll explain everything. Just be quiet for a second if you can manage it." I softly brush my thumbs against her cheeks.

"I was terrified, Emmett." It was two years ago that she held Dylan in her arms as he died. Over eight years' worth of war where she's held countless other men who she tried to save even knowing she couldn't. Each day, Blakely struggles to open her heart to anyone because she never knows if she'll have to save their life the next day.

And once again, I thank God she wasn't with us a few days ago. I'm glad it was some other medic who held my bullet wound and not her.

She sniffles again and then straightens. "What about the team?"

"I don't know."

"What happened?"

I recount most of what I remember. How we entered the town where the target was suspected to be. The intel was sketchy, but it was all we had. We made the decision as a team to move in but be cautious. From the moment we stepped foot off the convoy, I felt like something was off. Everything was too quiet, too tense, but I often feel that way when we're going into a place like that.

I should've trusted my gut.

As soon as we went into the center, all hell broke loose. Bullets were flying from every angle, and there was nowhere to hide.

"Dunegan was shot. I was with him, and . . . I tried to get them to render aid to him first," I tell her. "I think a few others were hit. I don't know. It was a shit show. Everything was fucked from the start."

Blakely's fingers tangle with mine. "If I were there . . ."

"You could've died, Blake. Don't start saying how you should've been there. If you were, I would've died a thousand times trying to get to you. Do you understand?"

I never would've been able to focus if she had been with us. I would've fought and probably been killed attempting to protect her, the whole team would've.

"And your wound?"

"They were able to repair most of the damage from the bullet. I didn't think it was that serious. I still don't. I should've stayed, fought with them until we got back to the base and then went to the hospital."

"I didn't realize you were a doctor now."

I shrug. "That's what they said."

"I'll talk to the doctor myself."

Of course she will. Blakely will have my entire rehabilitation plan worked out before she leaves, that's for sure.

"How long do you have?" I ask.

She must've been distraught for them to have allowed her to leave her unit and get here this quickly. I can only imagine the hell she raised. We both know they aren't going to grant her more than a week, not when she's needed out there.

Blake leans in, pressing her hand to my cheek. "Until they drag me away from you."

CHAPTER
Three

BLAKELY

"D o you need another pillow?" I ask as I arrange Emmett on the couch.

"I'm fine, Bennett."

He's not fine. He's so not fine, but I don't have the heart to tell him everything I know. Like how he almost lost his leg a few days ago. Like how the infection the doctor thought was cleared up, wasn't. Or how the muscle loss he now has means that he will most likely never be a Ranger again.

He's not fine.

But he's alive.

"All right." I pull the blanket up and kiss his forehead.

The last two weeks have been hard for him, having to rely on me and also finding out he lost two men in the ambush. He's not himself, and I understand it.

How many times has it been me dealing with it? Knowing that I wasn't good enough or fast enough to save a soldier. I've watched people die in my arms while I tried so hard to save them but couldn't.

Immediately, my mind takes me back to Zabul two years ago, where I went from happy, to utter despair as my brother was killed before my eyes.

"Emmett . . ." I start because I want to share with him what the Colonel told me. My time is up. I have to leave soon. My unit is heading back out, and I have to be with them. They need me more than I need to be here. "You know I have to—"

"I know, I'm aware of all of it."

I don't think he is. I sit on the edge of the couch, and he scoots a little to give me more room. "You are?"

"Yes. I know I have more damage to my leg than they thought. I know I lost two men. I know I failed as their leader. I know that I have to pay penance for it."

That isn't what I want to tell him, but I am not going to say it now. He needs comfort more than anything. "Do you think I have to pay for it too then?"

Countless times he has told me the opposite of what he just said. When my guilt was overflowing, it was Emmett who said there was no place for it. That I did everything I could. That I have saved hundreds of people and to stop counting the losses and start focusing on the wins.

Of course, that is never going to happen. It's my job to save people. I go out to make sure they go home, and when I fail, it kills me.

"You didn't lead people to their death."

"You didn't either."

He shakes his head. "I can't seem to make myself believe that."

And I understand that better than anyone. "I wish I could tell you it gets easier."

"I wish you could too, but we don't lie to each other."

I smile. "No, we don't."

It's why this arrangement works so well. Not only is Emmett my best friend, but also, he and I know exactly what this is and what it will stay as.

Just this.

My father left when Dylan and I were babies, I lost my brother to the war, and my mother died less than a month later. Since then, I've had to somehow find a way to live with myself, my failures, my pain, and not fall apart. Knowing that if I had to endure one more loss, I would no longer be able to keep the fractured pieces of my soul intact.

"How long before you have to go back?" he asks.

Tomorrow. "Soon."

For some reason, I don't want to admit that to him. I don't want to think about leaving. I want to stay here with him, which terrifies me.

These last two weeks, we've been closer than normal. More . . . spouse-like than friends. Emmett and I have always been close, but helping him clean his wound, shower, get dressed, and generally care for him has felt more intimate than before.

I need to leave and put the distance between us in every way.

"I'm assuming you've arranged my life?"

"I have."

His deep laugh fills my heart. "No one organizes and sees things the way you do."

"I'm going to take that as a compliment."

"It is one. It's what makes you so good at your job. You see everything as a puzzle, and no one can fit the pieces together as fast as you."

His praise warms me. "Are you trying to romance me?" I ask jokingly.

"Is it working?"

I laugh. "No."

"I'm off my game. I blame the meds."

"I'll let you have that then."

"You know all of this has made me think about life." He looks to me, his eyes swimming with emotion. "How stupid I am. How I've lived this half-life. We don't get normal, you and I. We don't get to have the things we want."

Releasing a breath through my nose, I force a smile. "No, we don't even get to have a dog."

Emmett's eyes find mine. "What?"

"A dog. We will never be able to have a pet. We can't have

normal because our lives aren't. There will never be a home with a picket fence, kids, and a dog. We can't love things outside because they aren't for us."

We have both learned that loving something is not in our cards. When we give our hearts to anything, we run the risk of losing it or making someone else suffer. Keeping distance from others protects everyone.

He shifts, staring back at the ceiling. "And you said my romance game was weak."

I laugh and get up to grab the notebook that has his schedule for the next week. "Well, romance is for suckers."

"What's that?" Emmett asks.

"Your life bible. I have everything in here that you'll need, including a list of emergency numbers in case you need medical help, the doctor's contact information, the address for your physical therapy, and the dates and times you're scheduled. Private Montgomery will be here forty minutes before each appointment to make sure you get there on time, and he'll drive you home. If you need anything, he can get it for you as well. I've set up two nurses who will rotate cleaning your wound each day."

Emmett's hand rests on mine. "Blake, stop."

I look over at him with confusion. "What?"

"I don't want to spend whatever time we have left going over my schedule or whatever else. I'll read it . . . I promise."

"What do you want then?"

"Just . . . lie here with me. I'm fucking breaking."

And that statement breaks me with him. I put the book down and do as he asked, lying on my side so I'm facing him. His blue eyes are filled with a sorrow I know he has seen in mine many times.

"It's not your fault," I assure him, brushing my fingers along his jaw. "It's not your fault," I repeat several more times.

His eyes close as his head rests next to mine. I can feel his pain as though it's my own. I continue to caress his face, moving my fingers to his hair. Emmett's arm wraps around my waist, and he pulls me so our bodies have no space between them.

"Blake . . ." His voice cracks. "I need you."

"I'm right here," I promise.

He shifts, rubbing his nose against mine. I know I should stop this, but I want it so bad. I want to kiss him, touch him, and feel the power that simmers around him in every way. We may be best friends, but he's more than that. We're married, and . . . we . . . shouldn't, but I can't force the words from my mouth.

"I need you," he whispers against my lips.

My heart is pounding, at war with what's right and what I want. "I need you too."

And that confession feels like the last breath before he robs me of the need for air.

Emmett's lips are on mine in a heartbeat, and his strong arms are around me, holding me to him as he kisses me deeply. Our tongues slide against each other, desperate for more. The soft caresses are now rough and needy.

He moves his hand down, gripping my ass and then pulling my leg up onto his side. I moan into his mouth, wanting this kiss to never end.

When his fingers slide over my stomach, I shiver. Emmett adjusts us as his hand slides to my breast.

It's been so long. Years since anyone has touched me. Years since it wasn't my own touch giving me pleasure. It is nothing compared to this, to him.

"You are so perfect," he says as his finger moves around my nipple. "You fit in my hand as though we were made to be this way."

My head falls back, and then his lips are at my neck. The heat of his mouth warms me everywhere as he keeps kneading my breasts. "Emmett," I say, wanting him to give me more and stop at the same time.

We shouldn't do this. I know he's in pain, and I am in that state perpetually. He is my best friend, and we are going to regret this.

"I need to taste you, Blake. Please, just a taste."

Yes, I can do a taste. Just one. There's nothing wrong with that, right? I'm helping him forget his pain and he's making me feel good.

"Just a taste," I give him permission.

He pulls my shirt and sports bra up and over my head. My chest is bare to him, and the growl in his throat turns me on even more. Emmett moves me as though he's not even wounded so that his mouth can find my nipple. His tongue swirls around the tip before he takes it into his mouth and sucks.

I could fucking come just from this. It feels so good, and I want more. My hands are at the back of his head, holding him as he moves from one to the other, licking, sucking, and kissing.

I need him inside me. I need him to take my pain as much as I want to take his.

That thought causes me to tense because I have never thought that before. I have wanted him to kiss me, sure. Who wouldn't? Emmett is fucking hot, and we live together, and I've had to help him shower. I know what his cock looks like, and I have spent a few nights imagining him, but this . . . this is nuts.

This is a line that we shouldn't cross.

"Emmett, we should stop," I somehow manage to get out.

"Should we?" he asks as his mouth goes back to my breast.

Yes. No. Jesus that feels good. "I-I think . . ."

"Hmm?" His mouth doesn't release me, and the vibration travels to my toes. Yeah, no, we should *not* stop.

Not only because I want this but also because we are both adults. We know that this means nothing. It doesn't change the fact that we are married on paper and not in our hearts. It's Emmett, and he knows how I feel. There's no confusion here.

And this is sex.

This is about us being so goddamn broken and needing something to soothe the ache.

That is fine.

It has nothing to do with the fact that I almost lost my mind when I found out he was injured. Or that I cried when they took him back in for surgery. It's not about how my heart has this permanent ache when I think about him.

No. None of that.

I lift his face to mine. "We have to be careful."

"I'll be careful, but if you want to stop, now is the time, Blakely. I want you, and I want to fucking lose myself in every way. I want to make you scream my name and forget all the shit we are both feeling. I want to bury myself inside you and never come back. Do you want that, or do you want to get up now and walk away?"

My breaths are coming in short bursts. I look into his blue eyes, knowing that there's not a chance in hell I could get up right now. Everything he wants is exactly what I need. "No looking back," I say.

"Never."

I kiss him, shutting off every part of me that is screaming that I just made a mistake and allowing myself to feel instead of think and remember.

The noise that's always there goes silent, and all I focus on is Emmett.

His lips don't leave mine as he moves to tug my pants down. Emmett parts my legs, sliding a finger between us. When he brushes my clit, I nearly lose it. I'm so wound up from everything, so achingly desperate for him to take over my senses again, that I can't hold back.

"So fucking wet for me. You want this, huh, Blakely?"

"Yes."

"You want me to touch you here?"

He does it again. "Yes."

"Good girl," he praises as he rubs my clit. "Can you do something for me?"

I'll do anything. "What?"

"I want you to come on my tongue, but I have to stay on my back. I want you to sit on my face and let me make you scream."

Yup. I'm dead. I have never been so turned on and afraid at the same time. Not because I doubt his ability to get exactly what he's asking for, but because this is Emmett. My Emmett. My very sexy best friend and marriage-of-convenience husband.

He removes his hand. "Or we stop."

"No!" I yell in protest, causing him to grin.

Arrogant asshole.

"Then climb up here and let me have what I want."

I do as he says, getting off the couch and sliding my pants off. "I'm naked."

"Thank fucking God for that."

"But you're not."

He smirks. "I need help with that, beautiful."

My pulse jumps at the endearment, but I tamp that shit down as I pull his shirt off first and then his shorts. "Emmett?"

"Yes?"

"Are you sure?" I ask. The loaded question means a thousand things. Is he sure about this, about his injury, about what we're going to do?

He removes his boxers, letting his incredible dick free. I've seen it so often in the last two weeks, I shouldn't be impressed, but I am.

"What do you think?" I stare at him, not sure how he got them off without screaming out in pain. I inhale slowly, and he reaches for my hand. "I'm sure, Blakely."

I move as he pulls me, arranging myself as he asks. I look back to make sure his leg is still propped up to keep his injury protected, and he pushes my hips forward so I'm hovering above him. "Hold on, and whatever you do, don't fall back."

Oh God. He lifts his head while pulling me to him and starts. His tongue laps at my clit, flicking it with varying degrees of pressure. I am already close, so it doesn't take much longer before the pleasure is close to cresting. I lean forward, using the arm of the couch for balance. He moans against me, licking deeper and moving his face back and forth. The whiskers he normally doesn't have scratch against my thighs in the most delicious way.

"Emmett . . . I'm close," I warn.

He flicks faster and harder, using his fingers to keep me open, and I want to fall apart. I want to let go of everything other than this—him.

I close my eyes, my breathing growing harder to control. "Fuck!

I can't . . ." I say, panting as it looms to the edge. He doesn't relent, and I can't hold back.

I scream his name, my body going tight before releasing everything. I murmur his name over and over, and he still doesn't stop, teasing out every bit of pleasure he can. I move to the side, unable to take any more.

"I don't think I've ever come so hard," I admit as I struggle for breath.

"We're not done."

"No, we're not."

If all we have is this, I want everything. I move off the couch as the last of my climax ebbs and kiss down his chest, over his solid abs, and down the strip of hair that leads from his belly button to his cock.

"Blake, you don't . . ."

"I want to."

He puts his hands behind his head. "Then by all means."

I don't waste time playing games, I take him deep in one motion. His hands fly to my hair. I give it my all, trying to remember all the tricks from when I actually . . . had a man. From his response, I seem to be doing something right, though.

"Fuck! Blakely, stop. Please, beautiful. I don't want it to end like this."

I lift up, wiping my mouth, feeling quite proud of myself but also apprehensive.

Medically, this is a very, very bad idea. Emmett had a second surgery not even five days ago. This is the last thing we should be doing.

"Your leg," I say.

"It's fine."

I chew on my lower lip. "I'm not sure this is the best idea."

"I don't fucking care. I want you, and there's nothing that's going to stop me."

Stubborn man. "Then . . . we have to take precautions."

"Done to all."

I roll my eyes. The bed is no bigger than the couch. This is a barracks room in Germany, and it's not meant for two people. Our best bet is the floor. "I'll be right back."

A few seconds later, I'm dropping his bedding on the floor and pushing the small coffee table to the side. Once I get everything situated, I help him up. It's slow and slightly awkward since we're both naked, but we manage.

The two of us struggle to get him on the floor, and I realize how stupid this is since I'm going to have to get him back up, not that it really matters at this point. He gets comfortable and rolls a condom on.

We look at each other for a moment, so much passing between us, but then his hand moves to my cheek. I straddle him, searching for the courage to take this step.

He moves his thumb across my lips. "Let's get lost in each other, Blake, instead of all the pain. Let's feel good for once."

That breaks the spell. I sink down on him and allow him to fill the cracks in my soul.

Emmett's hand moves up and down my spine as I lie against his chest.

Now that it's done, I'm not sure how I feel. I'm numb in some ways, but I'm also angry at myself for doing this.

It was selfish to take from him, to allow him to ease the ache, because it's all back now. I had sex with Emmett and have to leave tomorrow, which is only going to hurt him more.

"Are you okay?" His deep voice echoes in the silence.

"I'm not the one who was shot two weeks ago."

"My leg is perfectly fine. You were very careful."

Yeah, I was very stupid too. I lift up to look in his eyes. "Now what?"

"We get married."

I snort. "Funny."

"I thought so." Emmett lets out a long yawn. "I'm beat."

"You took your pain meds not too long ago, so I'm surprised you were able to keep your eyes open through it all."

Emmett opens one eye. "Like I would ever sleep through that?"

"My point is that of course you're exhausted."

"And men love to sleep after sex."

"And that."

"Lie down, Blake. We can cuddle until I pass out."

And then I have to leave . . .

I do as he says, wanting the closeness to smooth the raw edges of my emotions that are trying to slice me. "I am going to miss you," I confess.

"I always miss you when you're gone."

"We are best friends."

He chuckles, but I can tell he's already drifting. "We're more than that. You're everything . . ."

My heart stops for a second. "What?" I ask softly.

"I love you." He breathes the words. "I love you, and I'm going to keep you . . ."

I don't move. Every warning bell is flashing.

No, we're not more. We're friends. We're . . . married friends. We are not more. We can't be more. More is bad. More is death. Death is all that happens to the people I love. My mother. My brother. My friends. How many more folded fucking flags do I need to own?

No. We're not more.

I can feel the panic rising, screaming at me to get the fuck out of here now. No waking him up before I go. No kiss goodbye, because he wants to keep me and that can't happen. He knows my rules. No feelings beyond friendship.

My throat is closing in.

I slip out from under the blanket, careful not to wake him. He looks so sweet when he sleeps, and while I dress, he doesn't stir.

My bag is in the hotel, and I have to leave in a few hours anyway. This is better for him if I go now.

Dressed and with way too many feelings simmering at the top, I grab the notebook, tear out a page, and write a note.

> This is better for both of us.
> It was a mistake, and I have to go back to my unit.
> Schedule is in the book. I'll email soon.

And then, like the coward I am, I leave.

CHAPTER

Four

BLAKELY

~Present~

I replay the last bit of our conversation in my head, trying to find a way to explain the situation without giving away my true reasons.

"I thought you weren't here for that."

"I'm not, but you were the cherry on top for this trip. I'm here because you stepped in some shit, buddy, and being the loving and doting wife I am, I came here to get you out of it before you end up dead."

The lie rolls off my tongue effortlessly. I am here for that, of course, but I'm mostly here because I missed him.

I could've had someone out here look into Bill's death, but when I saw Emmett's name attached to his file, nothing could stop me.

I wanted to see him, which scared the fuck out of me. It's been two and a half years since the last time we were together. That message he left after I walked out on him. I was so afraid of feeling things. So sure that I would've tumbled into love, unable to walk it back, that I lashed out. I hurt him because I knew that was the only way we could be safe. I had to push him to hate me and walk away from me.

I didn't know he'd never forgive me.

Emmett always understood me. He knew I was a mess and he vowed he'd always come back for me.

His sapphire-blue eyes find mine as the sun sets around us. "What shit did I step in?"

"I'm getting there," I say, giving myself more time. I feel disorientated around him, and I'm trying to get my bearings.

"Blakely, the last three months have been fucking hell. If you could, maybe, not be the pain in the ass I know you like being for just once, I'd appreciate it."

And I would have appreciated it if my heart hadn't skipped a beat when I saw you.

I sure as hell won't admit that, though.

I take one more step, making me close enough to feel the heat coming from him, to inhale his deep musky scent that I have craved and see the indent of the dimple on his right cheek that only comes when he smiles.

His hand twitches, and that small movement is victory. He feels it too. The spark isn't dead in him either, and as much as I celebrate that, the fear comes on its heels.

"What happened in the last three months?"

I should know this. I should've been here with him, helping him through whatever pain he was in. As I look closer at him—the bags under his eyes and the worry lines on his face—I hate it. I hate myself for being weak.

His lids lower, and he lets out a long breath. "Isaac died, Brielle lost her memory, and I couldn't fucking do a damn thing to fix it."

There is a heavy knot in my stomach that tightens. Isaac was his best friend. He was the glue of their quad, always making sure that their friendships never faltered.

"I'm so sorry." I shift to him, placing my hand on his chest. "Emmett . . . I would've come. If I had known, I would've been here for you."

And I would've. In a heartbeat. No matter what the status of our relationship is, I would never hesitate. Never for him.

"And saved us all?" he asks with a smirk.

"I always saved your ass."

He laughs a little as his hand comes to my shoulder. "I think you forget just who did the saving."

"Maybe you need your memory refreshed," I challenge.

"Maybe we saved each other."

"I know you saved me—at least once."

The warmth in his eyes causes my pulse to spike. My hand is on his chest, feeling the steady thrum of his heart, and his big hand settles on my back. "And is that what you're doing now, Blake? Are you here to save me only to push me away when you're scared?"

The words cut, exactly as he knew they would. "Em—"

"I was joking."

"Okay." I allow him the lie. "I have information on Bill Waugh that I think you may want."

"Bill Waugh is dead."

"Yes, but his secrets aren't."

He steps back, and the loss of his heat sends a shiver through me. I hate that I want him. I hate that he is the one man who makes me desire more. All this time, I've done just fine without needing anyone but myself. I know loss and pain. I saw firsthand what loving someone does. I don't want it.

All I want is to be amazing at my job and go on with my life.

But then that part of me that knows the lie reminds me that, if that were true, I'd have signed those divorce papers instead of burning them.

"And what secrets have you uncovered on a case that you aren't even familiar with?" he pushes back.

I sigh dramatically. "I have been working Bill Waugh's case before you knew it was one. Which is why, when he died, I was alerted."

He crosses his arms. "I don't remember you being this exasperating."

"Really? I feel I've really grown into it over the years."

"Well, it's a good thing I don't intend to deal with it in the future."

That was mean, but I smile to keep him from knowing it stung. "You're going to get a lot of me in the present, darling. As your case and mine just intersected."

"My case is closed. He's dead."

"That may be, but why do you think Bill was so anxious to keep his life out of the spotlight? Why did he kill himself? In your reports, you stated he threatened Spencer and his bodyguards. Do you think those threats died with him?"

Emmett moves closer, taking my shoulders in his hands. "How do you know any of that?"

"I read the reports. I know everything about Bill Waugh and what happened here."

Well, not everything, but for dramatic effect, that seemed to be the better answer.

"So help me God, Bennett. If anything happens to—"

"I came to make sure it didn't. Because Bill was a person of interest in another case I've been working on that involves a runaway named Keeley. I called my friends in the FBI and asked them to flag his name."

He scoffs. "For what? The FBI doesn't just do those things because a former employee has a hunch."

"Of course they don't, but they will when it makes sense to. I don't call in my favors over stupid things, which is something they are very aware of. I research, and I'm damn good at it."

I may not be great at relationships, but I am at my job.

"I never doubted that."

"Then you have to trust that I wouldn't have flown out here if I didn't believe there was more to this story."

"Then tell me what you know," he commands.

And God help me, I am excited by the edict. Emmett and I usually fought for dominance, and every now and then, he'd give it to me, but I loved when he didn't.

"You have a much bigger problem going on in this town than a guy who hit his wife and kid. He was working with someone else, and I have a photo showing him meeting up with an unidentified male roughly twenty minutes before I can place him at the same location he met with my missing person. My guess is that person who Bill met with is involved as well, considering the threat Bill made."

"I think you still have an overactive imagination. This is Rose Canyon. The biggest crime before Isaac's murder was a shoplifter."

I shake my head, instantly wishing I could wring his neck. "Yes, because criminals only operate within city limits. You are better trained and much smarter than that."

From the outside, Keeley's case looks like any other troubled teenager who ran off. She was struggling in school, quit cheerleading her senior year, started doing drugs and partying. According to anyone I asked, she was in decline, but her best friend was the only one who said different.

She agreed that Keeley was a mess, but she insisted that her friend planned to go back home after the breakup with her boyfriend. They talked every day, and she wanted to get clean and get her life together. Then the calls stopped and she seemingly vanished.

Her parents clung to that, and the police did a piss-poor job investigating it, if you can even call the half-assed, single-page report an investigation. They heard drugs and alcohol and wrote her off as a runaway, just like all the other girls like her.

But when Keeley's parents hired me, I started digging. Her best friend told me all about the guy Keeley met online. When I went through her private messages on a dating app, Bill was there.

Then we found the address of the meeting location where I was able to get a few photos from the proprietor around that time.

"Fine, then I will do my due diligence, which I've already done, and I'll look into it again. Go home, and if I find anything, I'll let you know."

Yeah, like that's going to happen.

"Not a chance in hell. You botched the murder investigation, and I won't have you screw up my case."

Emmett's eyes turn to steel, and I know I struck a nerve. Then I remember that the case was his best friend, and I wish I could take back the words.

"Go home."

"I'm sorry, Em. I really am. I shouldn't have said that. I can't go home, though. My loyalty is to this case, and I have to follow any trail that could lead me to who might have Keeley—whatever that may be—and then I'll be out of your hair."

He looks up at the sky. "You can't stay in this town."

"Why?"

"Do you have anywhere to stay?" he asks me.

"I'm staying with you."

"No."

"Why not? We lived together for years. We're married, and—"

"We are not married, Blake. We are in the process of ending our ridiculous marriage. There is no more military. No housing allowance or unit to keep together. We don't have a single reason to keep pretending."

I hate that statement. They're the truth, but I always thought of us as more than just a financial transaction. "We were friends, too. Weren't we?"

"Of course we were."

I move to him, wanting us to be like we once were and hold his hand, but I know I can't. I lost that right when I walked out on him.

"And we're not friends now?"

"You will always be my friend, Blake, but you can't stay with me."

Before I can say anything else, Brielle pops her head out. "I don't mean to intrude, but people are way too invested in the two of you, and your declaration was heard by—everyone. So, you need to do some damage control, Sheriff Maxwell."

"Sorry to ruin your party." I was too anxious to see him to wait, though. "I will find somewhere to stay, and we can talk later."

"Find somewhere?" Brielle asks. "Why can't you stay with Emmett?"

Emmett sighs. "Because she can't."

Brielle raises a brow. "Fine, then you can stay in my apartment."

"What?" I say quickly.

"I am moving into Spencer's house, and I was going to rent my apartment out while we decide if we want to sell it. It's a great place, and it's directly across the hall from Emmett."

Oh, this is too perfect. "You are so sweet. Thank you."

"She can't stay there either," Emmett says with a grumble.

"I didn't realize you had a say in what I do," Brie challenges and then turns to me. "Blakely, please stay for the rest of the party and get to know all of Emmett's friends. We are nosey as fuck, but we're all fairly normal. My husband said you helped him and for that, we owe you. Afterward, we'll get you settled in my place."

I look at Emmett, who is silently pleading with me not to do it. He should know better. I never could resist irritating him. I turn to Brielle with a smile. "I would love to."

And I walk away, leaving Emmett fuming behind me.

CHAPTER

Five

BLAKELY

"Your home is beautiful," I tell Brielle as I walk in. The apartment is industrial with a modern feel. I love the brickwork, open ducts, and clean lines. It is nothing like the townhome I live in where everything is dated and almost feels dingy, doesn't matter that you could eat off the floors with as much as I clean.

It's just what I can afford in the greater DC area.

"Thank you. I was going to rent it out, but you're welcome to stay for a month or two. It'll give me some time to figure out what I want to do with my furniture."

"Are you sure?"

I feel like a mooch, but I'm not going to turn down a free place to stay since my husband isn't having it.

"Of course. I wouldn't have offered if I wasn't." Brielle smiles, but there's something a little off about it. "I would take payment in the form of an explanation, though."

And there it is. I expected it, but I hadn't thought she would be so direct about it.

I chuckle. "Emmett and I are married more on paper than anything."

"I saw the way he looked at you, those weren't paper feelings."

I refuse to feel any hope, which will only cause further conflict for me. I want and don't want him to feel something for me. I want and don't want to be married to him. Emmett has always made me think I am losing my mind. Two parts of me are always at war when it comes to our relationship.

He is one of the best men I know. He's kind, ungodly hot, protective but also respectful of the fact that I don't need to be protected. I know that I'm safe around him, but my heart isn't.

And my heart isn't what's needed in this situation.

Some things never change . . .

"No, that was anger."

"Which is a very thin line to the other side."

I shake my head. "It's not like that. We got married for the benefits, and now that time is over."

"If it was, you wouldn't be here," Brielle says with a lilt to her voice.

Yes, I would. No matter what, this case led me here, and I will do what I can for Keeley. Emmett is just icing on the cake.

There is a quick knock and then the door opens, revealing Spencer. "Never thought I'd see you again," he says as he enters.

"I hoped." I glance behind him to where Emmett fills the doorframe and return my attention to Spencer. "I assume you interrogated him?"

"Fuck yes, I did. You have no idea the shit he gave me about dating Brielle behind everyone's back. He was all, 'Oh, my feelings and you lied to all your friends.' Look who is the liar now," Spencer notes.

Emmett huffs. "I think our situations are a little different. I don't love Blakely. We were supposed to be a marriage of convenience, seems I misjudged that."

I grin. "I'm happy to be your inconvenient wife."

"You would be."

I fight back the urge to stick out my tongue.

Spencer looks like the cat that ate the canary. "You know?" he says to Brielle. "I don't think Blakely can stay here."

"What?" Both Brielle and I ask at the same time.

"Yeah, I have the place being renovated, and the contractors start tomorrow."

"Renovate what?" she asks, looking around.

This place is in no need of any work.

"This and that."

Emmett snorts. "Who is doing the work?"

Spencer shrugs. "You wouldn't know him."

"I know everyone."

"Not this guy," Spencer says. "Sorry, Blakely, you will need to stay somewhere else because the work is going to be really intense. Probably toxic gas leaks and no running water."

He is the worst liar. "And since there are no hotels anywhere, I am to sleep where?" I ask, with my brow raised.

Brielle looks to her husband with a smirk. "Hmm?"

"You can stay at our friend Holden's house. He has a spare bedroom."

Emmett takes two steps forward. "Holden?"

"He's all alone in that house."

My husband's jaw ticks.

Oh, this is too easy. I reach for my bag and smile. "That would be great. I'd much rather stay with someone whose place isn't possibly about to be exposed to toxic gas . . ."

"You're not staying with Holden," Emmett says with authority.

I laugh once. "Right. Like you have a say?"

"I do, and you're not staying in my best friend's house."

"Are you worried about something happening with your friend?"

Emmett's eyes narrow. "Of course not."

I turn to Brielle. "Is Holden good-looking?"

She grins. "He *is*, and he's a doctor."

"You think Holden is hot?" Spencer asks her.

Instead of answering, she rolls her eyes.

"If that's the only option . . ."

"You'll stay with me," Emmett says, moving closer. "Hand me your bag."

"Please," I finish.

"What?"

"Please. You forgot that word."

He grumbles. "Please."

I hand it over with a triumphant smile. "Thank you. I'd love to stay with you, pookie."

The sad part is before we crossed a million lines, my staying with him never would have been a debate. I would've gone to his house, and we would have snuggled on the couch, watching war movies and laughing at how out of touch Hollywood is. We would eat fattening foods while laughing about some inside joke we had on a deployment.

Emmett was my safe place, my home, until I ruined it all.

He turns toward the door, and I follow him out, expecting to be heading toward the car, but he walks across the hall and throws the door open. Brielle and Spencer smile and I follow him inside, closing the door behind me.

"She wasn't kidding when she said you live across the hall, huh?" I ask.

"Nope."

"Okay then. Hope the toxic gas doesn't waft over here."

He walks into the kitchen, grabs a beer from the fridge, and starts to drink. Once he's downed about half, he looks at me. "What?"

"Nothing."

"You're staring."

"I just . . . you're different."

Emmett places the bottle down. "What were you hoping for, Blake?"

So much more than this. "I don't know. I just hoped for a little less hostility, maybe."

Not that I deserve it completely.

Emmett walks toward me, and I have to tilt my head back to keep eye contact. The man I knew before isn't here right now. Sure, he looks the same, blue eyes, dark hair pushed back, the scar under his eye, and that dimple that never really goes away totally, but the warmth is gone.

"You want less hostile? Then maybe you should've let me know you were coming instead of crashing my friend's party."

"I explained why I came. I had no intentions of crashing anyone's party. I asked where I could find you, and they said there."

He drinks the rest of the beer before saying, "I'm not buying that you think we're in danger. You said you're here because of a dead guy, but that doesn't explain why you showed up unannounced and walked into that party as if you'd been invited."

"I'm here because there is a missing girl, and your dead guy was the last one who saw her. Your dead guy made a threat, and I have seen enough to know there's something more here."

"So you say."

"If you hate me so much, why would you demand I stay here?" I ask.

He turns, gripping the counter with his back to me. "I don't know."

Those three words explain exactly how I feel about everything. I don't know what I feel or why. It's as though I'm on a roller coaster with the ups and downs. Emmett makes me want things—he always has—and that has terrified me more than anything. I can't handle the idea of loss when it comes to him. He is the one thing in this world that I don't want to live without. Even though we haven't spoken, I knew he was okay. That was enough for me.

But when I got those papers, it wasn't.

It was as though the house of cards I built started to shake, and each day, one more card shifted until I was on a plane to come here.

I move to him, placing my hand on his back. "Emmett?"

He turns, forcing me to step back. There's a storm raging in his eyes, and I want it to come to a head. Then we can talk. We can air it out and go back to the way it was. I need my friend back.

Emmett runs the backs of his knuckles down my cheek to my chin before letting it drop. "It's late, and I have to go to work early."

I take the out because I am exhausted too. Right now, it's almost two in the morning on the East Coast. "Where can I sleep?"

"In DC," he offers.

"Funny."

"I thought so. You can have my room."

"And where will you sleep?"

"In my bed."

I want to say so many things, but I settle on, "Okay."

He shrugs. "It's not the first time I've been uncomfortable around you."

I don't take the insult to heart. He's trying to push me away, wound me the way I did him, and I deserve it.

"No, it's not."

His head jerks back a little. "Right. Bathroom is the first door on the left. Bedroom is right after it."

I lift my bag, slinging it over my shoulder. "Thanks."

"Hey, Blake?" Emmett calls to me, stopping me from getting to the door. "You have a week to prove there's something more that Bill was hiding when he died that ties him to the case you're working. I am not going off your bullshit gut feelings shit. Find irrefutable evidence or . . ."

"Or what?" I ask.

"Or we're done and you go home, sign the papers, and we see each other at the next team reunion."

My heart aches at that idea, but it also makes me more determined to find what I need because I don't plan to leave here without closing my case and fixing what I broke between Emmett and me.

CHAPTER
Six

EMMETT

O ne hundred thousand forty-four.

One hundred thousand forty-five.

One more fucking second and I'm going to lose my mind.

I stare at the ceiling, willing myself to fall asleep, but it evades me. I could fall asleep on a rock, with no blanket, standing up, so it's not my bed or lack of covers. It's just her.

It's Blakely lying next to me, long brown hair fanned out on my pillow case as she breathes softly, getting the sleep I'm in need of.

No, fuck that, I'm not going to make her out to be some sleeping goddess. Her hair is all over the damn place, including in her mouth, as she snores and looks like a mess.

She makes a choking sound, which causes me to sit up before she snores again.

I huff, flip over to face the wall, and throw one of those stupid pillows Brielle bought to make the apartment cozy. As much as I wish I could fall asleep, I'm not sure it would be worth it. I have to be at work in an hour, so there's no damn point.

"Fucking hell!" I grumble.

"Huh? What? Emmett?" Blakely sits up ramrod straight, staring at me as well as one pert nipple.

Her gaze moves around the room and mine stays fixed on her breast. "Blake," I say slowly, my hands in the air.

"What? Are you okay?"

I am very, very okay. In fact, I need to be a little less okay and let her know that she's having a wardrobe malfunction. "I'm fine."

She lets out a sigh through her nose. "Oh, thank God."

"Blake, you should fix—"

"I know. Myself. I should, and I tried. I went to see a doctor, did this electrode therapy that helps with PTSD, and nothing really works. I refuse to take medication because I'm terrified of becoming dependent. Dunegan has been fighting his addiction for years."

Jesus Christ. At this rate, she's never going to shut up long enough for me to tell her. "Your breast!" I yell.

"My . . .?" She looks down and then tugs her shirt up quickly. "Oh my God. Why didn't you tell me?"

"I tried . . ."

"Not hard enough! I have been sitting here for a full minute with my tit hanging out and you couldn't just point or cover me?"

I laugh at that. "I was enjoying the view. You're lucky I said anything."

Blake rolls her eyes. "Yeah, so lucky."

I snort. "Well, that is my reward for staring at the ceiling for hours."

"I guess you're welcome. I want to know what my reward is since I couldn't sleep either."

I blink a few times, wondering what world she's living in. She passed out and has been playing instruments in her sleep. "The hell you didn't."

"I'm awake. Clearly, I'm not sleeping."

"Clearly."

She pulls her hair to the side, draping it over her shoulder. "So, you didn't sleep at all?"

I shake my head.

"That sucks."

"Yes, yes it does. And I would've at least been comfortable if I wasn't blanket-less and Blakely-less."

She tilts her head and smirks. "You're so funny."

"I'd like to think so."

I'm also not lying. Her warmth, the smell of her shampoo, the soft little noises, not to mention the very loud snoring, all attributed to my lack of sleep.

Blake rubs her eyes and yawns. "I'm so tired. I am exhausted with this time change and lack of sleep."

"Yes, I can see how you'd be this exhausted. It's hard when you take over someone else's bed."

She turns toward me. "Whatever. I don't sleep much, but it seems worse lately."

It's probably wrong that I'm happy about that, but . . . she deserves it—a little.

"I usually sleep fine," I admit. "But not tonight."

Not when she was this close.

"I could go in the living room," she offers.

"No, that wouldn't help. Then we'd both be uncomfortable."

Blake laughs. "Yeah, we're winning there. Does your leg keep you up?"

"No, I worked hard to be back to where I am. It barely pains me anymore."

It had become my sole focus after I woke up to find that fucked-up note and a schedule of my life. I poured myself into healing, working nonstop to defy the odds. It didn't matter, I was no longer fit to be a Ranger. The muscle loss had been too extensive, and I couldn't handle running long distances anymore. So, I was medically discharged and came home where my world was Blakely-less and I could start a new life.

She smiles, pushing against my chest. "I knew you would. Captain Hulse said that he never saw someone put as much work into rehab as you did."

"You talked to him?"

Blakely's eyes widen for a split second. "Just to see how you were. You wouldn't return my emails."

She says that as if she really expected me to. "Well, it is what it is. We make our choices, and those choices have consequences, right?"

"Yeah, they do."

The two of us fall silent, and this bed is starting to feel like it's shrinking. "Emmett?"

I meet her eyes. "Yes?"

"Do you think we'll ever be able to move past this awkwardness?"

I laugh. "You think *this* is awkward?"

"Just a little."

More like a lot. "What could possibly be making it that way, Blake?"

She sighs. "Well, we have this elephant in the apartment."

It's more like a herd of them.

I love this woman. I love her like I've never loved anyone else. I thought we were on the same page. I gave her my fucking heart, and she broke it. I'm not about to make that same goddamn mistake.

"It'll leave when you do," I reply.

"Are you saying that I'm the elephant here?" Blake asks, moving to a sitting position as she tucks her legs.

"I would never be that stupid."

She smiles. "At least you still have that going for you."

"At least there's that."

She grabs the pillow and wraps her arms around it. "We used to talk about everything. I miss that."

I put my hands behind my head, trying for the appearance of ease. "It's been a long time, Blake."

"It hasn't been that long, and I'm here now. I want to talk about things."

"And that's the problem." There. I said it. I'm done with this and dancing around it. She will never change.

Blakely pulls her lip in, releasing a breath through her nose. "You know why I didn't want more. You were there, Emmett. You know how I felt."

Watching her brother die in her arms will haunt me forever. She couldn't save him. I couldn't . . . fuck. Nothing about that day was right, and I tried everything I could, but Dylan was gone and Blakely was never really the same.

She became a shell of the woman I knew. Sure, she became even more of a crazy medic, taking risks she never should've taken, but she needed to save everyone. Her grief was eating her alive, and then I got shot.

After I was released from the hospital, I thought that maybe we finally had come to terms with the fact that we were a lot more than just friends. That, yes, life is fleeting, but it needs to be lived and is better with someone by your side.

I held her. Touched her. She took all the grief and guilt away like an angel. Like a fucking dream.

And then I woke up and she was gone.

"I saw a lot, Blake. I saw you broken and sad, but I never thought you would fuck me and then disappear. Not a fucking goodbye or explanation other than your bullshit note about a mistake, and you were right, it was."

She flinches. "I had to leave, Emmett," she says, shifting forward. "I had to go."

I run my hand through my hair. "It doesn't matter."

"I think it does."

"No, it doesn't. You are who you are, and so am I. I want more. I want a family and a wife. I want to love someone who will love me back. I see what Spencer has and what Isaac had, and I want it. Sign the papers so we can be done and I can marry someone else."

Her eyes widen. "Are you . . . dating someone?"

"Why do you care?"

Blakely places the pillow back. "Because I do."

I could lie and say I am. "I'm not." She opens her mouth to say more, but my phone alarm saves me from having to hear it. I stand, silence it, and turn to her. "As much as I'd love to keep talking, I have work, and you need to find whatever it is you think is here. You're on a deadline."

"Yeah, yeah. Have fun investigating who took someone's plants off their steps. I'm going to do real work."

I flip her off as I walk into my bathroom, ignore all her shit on my counter, and get ready for any issue that will be a welcome distraction.

"So, you're married?" Holden asks as he enters my office.

When I said *any* issue, I meant other than this fool.

"Are you here to report a crime? If not, leave."

He smirks. "I am actually."

"What? Leaving?"

"Here to report a crime."

I put the pen down and lean back. "What's the crime?"

"Forgery."

I keep my face blank because I'd like to surprise him when I choke him. "What was forged?"

"A marriage certificate for a friend."

I huff. "I don't have time for your shit, Holden."

He shrugs. "I'm a citizen of this fine town, and you're the police. So, you kind of have to make time seeing as it's your civic duty."

"I don't. I have real police work to handle."

He looks at the papers on my desk. "Riveting. I see that you're up to your elbows in complaints about the noise from the repaving of Main Street?"

We had seven calls last night regarding it. All seven from Mrs. Baker, who is also the person who filed sixty-two complaints about the road having two potholes. According to her, they were responsible for giving her a flat as well as caused her son's sprained ankle because he stepped in one. So, at her request, they upped the paving schedule to get it done faster.

"Don't you have a life to save?"

"I do. Yours. Because once the town gets over their shock of you being married, they're going to want answers."

"I didn't realize the town had a right to that information."

Holden just gives me a look. We all know the town doesn't care about what rights it has. Hell, if this were someone else, I would want the information too. There are perks to a small town, but privacy isn't one of them.

"So, I've had to listen to you and Spencer give me shit about Jenna, and here you are, harboring your own nuptials."

"I didn't give you shit."

His eyes narrow.

Okay, maybe I did.

He leans back. "Right. She's pretty, I'll give you that."

She's more than that, but if I let that slip, I'll pay for it. "I appreciate the gesture."

"All right, we know she's pretty, her name is Blakely Maxwell—"

"Bennett."

"Nontraditional? I dig it." I would like him to dig his way out of here, but that's not going to happen. I lean back in my chair, doing my best to ignore Holden as he continues talking. "Spencer filled me in about how you two were stationed together, and now you're living together in your apartment."

"Spencer's doing," I note.

"Where did you sleep?" Holden asks.

"In my apartment."

He grins, clearly enjoying himself. "Yes, but did your wife take the couch, or did you spend it reuniting?"

"I didn't sleep."

Holden's face lights up as he extends his fist. "Proud of you, man. I was worried over the last few years you broke your dick when you got shot."

I do not extend my fist for a bump, as I might punch his face instead. "Go away."

"You're going to leave me hanging like that? Rude."

"Know what's rude? Coming here and wasting my time."

"If you hadn't spent the last however many years lying about being married, I wouldn't have to have this conversation."

Between the lack of sleep, the conversation this morning, and the memories that seem to be on repeat in my head, I'm about to snap. I take a few breaths before I answer him because as much as Holden is pissing me off, I would be doing the same thing if this was him.

"Here's the story, we married for money and to stay stationed together. We were best friends, so it made sense. She was a medic with my unit. I thought we both started to feel differently, and things escalated, then they quickly imploded. I filed for divorce a few months ago, and now she's here."

"Escalated how?"

I deadpan. "How do you think?"

"You started catching feelings . . ."

I didn't catch feelings. I fell like a brick to the ground in them. I fell so goddamn hard I broke every bone when I slammed into the ground, and then she ran me over with her car to ensure I couldn't get up.

"None of your business. We weren't really married anyway. It was all paperwork, nothing else. No love or sex or feelings."

He chuckles. "You were married without any of the benefits?"

"I didn't care about benefits."

"You love her," he says, watching me.

"I do not."

I do. I love her, and she's made of fucking stone. I am not going to make the mistake of believing otherwise again.

"The hell you don't. If you didn't, you'd have laughed, thrown me out, or told me I could fuck her if I wanted, but none of those things have happened, and it's because you love her."

"I would love to choke you to death."

Holden grins. "But you won't. So, I can keep going."

I get up, tap the papers on the desk, and smile. "By all means." I walk out of the room, hoping he'll take a hint.

Holden's right on my heels, though. "I have the ability to follow."

"I really do have work to do, so unless you're here to report a real crime, I am busy."

"Well, lucky for you, I am, in fact, here to do that."

I'm sure he is. "You're full of shit. We just had this exact discussion five seconds ago."

"Yes, but I was kidding then."

"What's the crime?" I ask.

"I'm not sure how to describe it."

I stare at him, waiting for the punchline. Holden doesn't say anything, he just grins. I hate my damn friends. "You're here to report a crime, but you don't know what it is?"

"Exactly."

"Go away."

He opens his jacket and pulls a piece of paper from the inside pocket before handing it to me. "I got this yesterday. I didn't think too much of it because people often send me gifts for saving their lives or a family member."

"And what's strange about this one?"

"It was delivered to the hospital, which I have only been working at for a week. So, not enough time to do superhero things."

I roll my eyes. "Yes, yes, the famous doctor who cures all. Get to the crime, Holden."

"I got a gift. It was a box with a replica of the Eiffel Tower in it, which . . . whatever. But the note was a postcard of the Grand Canyon."

"The crime is that someone doesn't understand geography?"

I wish I could say that I don't have time for this, but I really don't have anything other than the noise complaint to deal with. And so long as he's not talking about Blakely, I'll entertain his insanity.

He shrugs. "That could be it, but read the back of the postcard."

I glance at it.

Dr. James,

I look forward to working together in the future. You'll be receiving a new patient in a few months. There are a few loose ends that need to be tied up prior to her arrival, but I will send further instructions and information soon.

Sincerely,

T

8675300183

"What is that at the end? A phone number? Also, I thought the song went 8675309," I say, amused with myself.

"No, it's my medical license number," he replies.

"Is that normal to have on a letter?" I glance up at him before flipping the card over and taking a closer look at the front.

"Nothing about this is normal. Doctors don't notify other doctors of patient referrals via postcard, nor do they send souvenir-shop trinkets along with it." Holden runs his hand through his hair. "As for my license number, if someone asks for it, I'll give it to them, and it's on the internet, so anyone who knows where to look can find it. What's bothering me is, why would they put it there? That isn't standard. On top of that, who the hell is sending me a patient? Why? I don't even know the name of who to look for."

"Postmark?" I ask, already knowing there aren't any official stamps on the front of the postcard.

"The staff threw the box out."

Of course they did. "Well, wanting you to help someone and knowing how to use Google aren't crimes."

"So, you're going to do nothing?"

I laugh once. "What do you want me to do, Holden? Search for a crime that isn't a crime and arrest someone we don't know for sending you a poorly written note with your public license number? I am all for a good mystery, but this isn't really one."

"And if something weird happens?"

"You're what's weird."

"We could always talk about your wife," he says. "I'd love to discuss that mystery with you."

Not a chance in hell. The dispatcher walks over, clearing her throat. "Excuse me, Sheriff Maxwell?"

Thank God. "Yes, Shelby?"

"We have a problem."

I have never been happier to hear that. "What is it?"

"Deputy Sheriff Holman responded to a suspicious person peeking into windows," she explains. "He was able to detain the suspect but said he needs you to come on the scene immediately."

Finally, something to do that doesn't involve stupid friends, my wife, or a noise complaint for paving a road. I turn my radio on and make my way toward my office. I need my hat and keys. "Of course, is anyone hurt?"

"No, sir. No one is hurt, but the suspect is extremely irate and will only speak to you."

This town and their craziness. "Okay. Is it someone I know?"

I grab my hat and put it on as she follows behind me. "Umm, yes. It would appear that way."

"Okay, who is the suspect in custody?"

Shelby bites her lip and then straightens. "She says she's your wife."

So much for a day of no Blakely.

CHAPTER
Seven

BLAKELY

"When exactly will Emmett get here?" I ask the deputy who's standing by the open car door.

"A few minutes, then we'll straighten this up and bring you to be evaluated by a doctor."

"I am not crazy," I reply.

He laughs. "Sure you're not. You're peeking in people's houses and claiming you're married to the sheriff, who we all know isn't married."

I roll my eyes and slip out the paperclip I keep in my back pocket. "He is, in fact, married—to me."

"If you say so," he says back.

"What did he say over the radio?" I ask, keeping him talking as I straighten the clip and adjust it to the right angle. I was playing nice until he implied that I was crazy. Now, I am going to get out of these damn cuffs and teach him to make sure the person he arrests doesn't have anything on them.

"Just to keep you here until he arrived."

"Don't you think that means something?"

The deputy leans in the car. "It means you're about to meet the man who isn't your husband."

They really need to work on protocol here. First, he put me back here and didn't close the door. If I really were crazy, I could run or hurt him. Second, he has spent most of the last ten minutes leaning against the side of the car, enjoying the sunny day instead of actually watching me—the "criminal."

I move my wrist and feel the clip catch. Well, this is going to teach him.

I sigh deeply to cover the sound of the right cuff unlocking. "If you say so."

He straightens again, leaning against the back of the car.

I twist my wrist, rubbing out the tightness, and move to the left one. "What's your name, Deputy?"

"Holman. First name is George."

"It's great to meet you, Deputy George Holman. I'm Blakely Bennett," I say, adjusting the paperclip again. "I was in the US Army for a long time."

"Good to know."

"Just like your boss was."

"He was special forces. You don't look like special forces since you're a girl and all."

I hate men some days. "No, I guess I don't, and I'm so glad you noticed my female parts."

The cuff unclicks, but I leave my arms behind my back as the lights from another cruiser come into view as it pulls to a stop.

Emmett unfolds himself from the car, putting on that ridiculous hat that only makes him look sexier. His eyes find mine in the backseat, and he shakes his head as he walks over.

"Is she cuffed?" he asks Deputy Holman.

"Yes, sir. Exactly as you showed me. I think we could bring her over to Doc Dehring, the new shrink at the hospital. She's losing her grip on reality."

"She never had a grip," Emmett mumbles.

He ducks his head in. "Blake."

"Hi, darling, are you having a good day at work?" I ask.

"I was."

I grin. "Well, we both were until your deputy got a little paranoid. You should do some training on how to handle a woman."

His eyes turn to stone. "What happened? Are you hurt?"

It seems he doesn't like that. "Oh nothing, just said I didn't look like special forces."

He laughs. "You don't."

"What do I look like?"

"Trouble."

I shrug. "It's true. Anyway, I was at the house to conduct an interview, and then suddenly, I am handcuffed in the back of a police car."

He looks to my arms and extends his hand. "Give me the cuffs."

I have to fight back the smile as I pull my hands out, dangling them. "You mean these?"

Emmett grabs them and hands them to Deputy Holman without breaking my gaze. "Get out of the car, Blakely."

Once he moves back, I do. "Next time, check for any paperclips, bobby pins, or anything else that can get someone out of cuffs. If she wanted, she could've hurt you once you got to the jail or the hospital."

George looks at me, eyes wide. "How did . . . you?"

"Practice. See, us special forces girls, we have to be stronger and savvier than the big strong guys. Isn't that right, husband?" I ask Emmett, batting my eyelashes.

"Wait, you're really married? She wasn't lying?" George asks him.

"No, I wasn't lying, George."

He sputters and then turns to me. "I honestly thought you were lying."

"Hence the handcuffs?"

The blush on his face is almost cute.

Emmett claps him on the shoulder. "Did you frisk her before you cuffed her?"

"No, sir. She's a tiny woman."

"Who could've killed you," I inform him. "I have just as much training as he does. I'm actually a higher belt than Emmett in Jiu-Jitsu. I took down men his size and bigger. Just because I have tits, it doesn't make me less lethal. Right, pumpkin?"

"Blake," Emmett warns.

"I actually got my brown belt last month. What color are you now?"

"I'm about to be red if you keep this up."

I burst out laughing and continue on, this is fun. "I'm sorry, but your officers should be aware that women can, in fact, kill people."

I'm a little disappointed in him, to be honest. I understand this is small-town USA, but criminals are criminals, no matter their gender. No one gives a fuck about your feelings when it comes to staying out of jail.

He ignores my comment and goes back to George. "I know you've only been on the force a few weeks, but we treat every suspect the same—man or woman. You happened to get my insane soon-to-be-ex-wife here, who isn't lying when she says she's just as skilled in combat as I am. Always use your training and don't take risks."

Emmett turns to me. "Seriously? Peeking in windows?"

"I knocked first." I shrug because I will go to any lengths necessary to help my clients. Keeley is missing, and if Bill's widow knows anything . . . anything at all that can help me locate her, then I want to know.

"So, then you proceeded to skulk around?"

"I don't skulk."

"What the hell do you call looking in people's windows?"

I smile. "Investigating, which you'd know if you did it at all."

His jaw clenches. "So help me God."

"Listen, I need to talk to the Waughs."

"They clearly don't want to talk to you, seeing as they called the cops on a weird woman looking in their house."

Interesting. "If they'd answered the door, I wouldn't have to look in the windows."

Emmett's voice drops low. "Did you ever think they've been

through hell? Their lives were turned upside down, and maybe, just maybe, a strange woman knocking at their door would send them into hiding."

I step closer, our noses almost touching. "Did you think that maybe I already considered that and announced who I was? I'm not stupid, Maxwell. I know how to do my job. You"—I poke him in the chest—"are who put me on a deadline. I'm doing what I need to do."

"That's great, but trespassing or breaking any other law isn't happening."

"Are you going to arrest me?" I ask.

"You know I'm not."

I step to the side. "Then, if you'll excuse me, I'm going to knock on the door again."

Emmett groans and walks beside me. I ring the bell, and after a second, the door opens. She matches the photo of Sonya I studied. "You must be Sonya."

She looks to Emmett and then back to me. "I am."

"My name is Blakely Bennett. I am a longtime friend of Sheriff Maxwell. I'm also a private investigator out of Washington DC."

"Friend is a loose term," Emmett mumbles, but I hear it.

"I'm here investigating the disappearance of a teenage girl."

Sonya's eyes widen. "I don't know anything. There's no one else here. My son is at school."

"No, no, I don't think she's here, but your late husband's name came up when we were tracking her whereabouts. I was hoping we could maybe talk a bit?"

Her arms wrap around her middle, and she nods. "Fine, but I'd like it if we could maybe cause less of a scene? My neighbors already treat my son and I differently."

I glance at Emmett, who is already in motion. He gestures to George, who straightens and heads to the driver's side of his cruiser. Then Emmett opens his door and leans against it. "I'm going to park around the block, and then I'll be back. Try not to cause trouble while I'm gone."

"I make no promises," I say with a smile. "Don't get lost, honey."

Sonya watches us and then tilts her head to the side. "Are you a couple?"

What a loaded question. "We're not. We are. I don't know. Do you want to talk outside?" I shift the topic back to her. Whatever Emmett and I are isn't going to be solved here.

"No, we can go inside."

She leads the way into the kitchen. The house is small and dated, but it's clear Sonya takes great pride in what she does have. Everything is clean, organized, and well cared for. Her decorations appear to be carefully chosen to go with the furniture.

I look at the photos on the wall, some look as if they go back a few generations, but most are of a little boy. "Is this your son?" I ask, already knowing his name is Myles.

The look in her eyes shows her love and devotion to him. "It is. He's a wonderful boy."

"How old is he?"

"Almost ten."

I give her a warm smile. "That age is full of surprises."

"Do you have children, Ms. Bennett?"

I shake my head. "No."

And I never will.

"I'm sorry, you just said that as though you knew from experience."

"I have—had a younger brother. My father left the day Dylan was born, so I took it upon myself to become his second mother, much to his dismay." I laugh, remembering Dylan's constant complaints about how I was not, in fact, his parent.

"That must've been hard for you."

"At the time, I didn't think so. I was six and thought he was a great baby doll."

She grins. "I'm an older sister as well and my sister was treated the same."

There's nothing I wouldn't do to have that back again. I miss my friend. I miss the man who would make me laugh until I had tears streaming down my face. Who could turn any situation around. Who joined the army because he was worried about me and wanted to be close in case I needed him, which was dumb because you don't get to decide that.

And yet, he found me. In the desert, in a sea of soldiers, he found me.

And then I lost him.

Sonya reaches out, resting her hand on my arm. "Are you okay?"

I force the emotions down. "I'm fine. Sorry. Jet lag."

She nods. "Have a seat, would you like some coffee?"

"There's never been a cup of coffee worth saying no to," I reply.

I already downed three cups at the coffee shop in town. I figured the best gossip would be there, so it was as good of a place as any to start making friends.

Too bad it was empty.

There are two brief knocks on the back door before it opens and Emmett walks in as though he owns the world. God that man is hot in a uniform. There is nothing frumpy about him in it.

"Sheriff Maxwell," Sonya says, relief flooding her voice. "Would you like a cup of coffee?"

"No, thank you, Sonya. I appreciate the offer."

She brings the cup over to me and the three of us sit at the table, an awkward silence falling around us.

Well, I didn't come here for coffee, so I might as well get to it.

"I'd like to ask you a few questions."

"Of course, but please know Bill always kept me in the dark. He was abusive, manipulative, only out for himself, and didn't care who was hurt in the process. I always suspected things but had enough intelligence to never ask questions. He would've killed me or Myles if I did."

"I understand, but sometimes, it's not about allowing you the secret. Sometimes they give it but don't mean to, so they get enraged."

She shakes her head, looking at the cup. "He was often enraged."

"I'll walk you through it and you give me anything you remember, okay?"

Sonya looks at Emmett, who nods, and then to me. "Okay."

"Let's get to it then."

CHAPTER
Eight
BLAKELY

"The hours are ticking away, future ex-wife."

I flip him off and go back to looking at my notes. "I came here to escape you."

He laughs, taking the seat directly across from me at the only eatery in town—The Diner. It's a picturesque place with old leather covered stools at the counter, booths that have probably been here for sixty years, and tables with mismatched chairs that almost seem to have been dropped off by patrons over the years.

Nothing matches and yet everything belongs.

"There's no escaping the law enforcement in a small town."

"Lucky me."

He grabs my notebook from under my hand, and I take it back. "Hey! No one said you could look at my notes. Ass."

"Please, you spent an hour talking to Sonya, and you walked out of there with nothing."

He only thinks that because I want him to. I don't need him or his stupid deputy following me around. Sure, I may not have gotten much, but I got enough to have an idea of where to go next.

"You know, I'm not sure I want to take investigative advice from you. Have you solved anything other than who stole someone's mail or took little Lance's bike?" I ask in my best mocking tone.

"Actually, last week, I was in charge of a hit and run."

"Ohhh, look at you, moving up in the world," I taunt. "Please, you can't find your way out of a paper bag, let alone track down anything or anyone." I goad him because the only time he seems to want to talk to me is when we're bickering. And right now, I'll take bickering.

Emmett looks out the large window and shrugs. "I guess those days are behind me."

"How? You're a cop."

"Of a town where nothing happens."

I raise one brow. "So far, you've had a murder, an attempted murder of your friend's sister, and the abduction of a mother and her son that ended with the perp committing suicide. I wouldn't exactly call that nothing."

"Maybe not nothing, but those are all solved and wrapped up."

I snort. "If that were the case, I wouldn't be here."

"Your reason for being here has little to nothing to do with any of those cases. You might have a paper-thin link to Bill, but like I said, all *my* cases are closed."

The waitress approaches, refilling my coffee mug and placing food in front of Emmett. I blink because he didn't order. "Why did she bring you that?"

"Because we all know each other, and I eat here every other day."

That sounds . . . horrible. "And she knew exactly what you wanted?"

It looks like a spinach, bacon, and cheese omelet with a side of home fries. I let out a laugh.

"What?"

"You," I say, feeling another giggle bubbling up. "I guess some things are still the same."

"Should I be different?"

"No," I say without thinking how it would sound. But it's the truth. "No, you shouldn't change. There's never been anything wrong with you. Well, other than the fact that you eat the same food every Wednesday."

"I don't . . ." He puts his fork down. "Jesus."

I smile. "Yeah. It's Wednesday."

When we were in the service, the team alternated cooking for each other. Monday was my day, and I always made homemade pizza. Tuesday was Hunt, who made the best macaroni and cheese. But Emmett had Wednesday, which was breakfast that always, *always* included omelets.

He shakes his head. "That's not why."

"Sure, it's not."

"It's not. I just like omelets."

"You do."

He grumbles while picking the fork back up. "Have something else to add?"

You're sexy. I'm sorry. Take me to bed?

Yeah, that is definitely not what I am going to say. "Just that you're an ass."

"That was never in question. What are you making notes about anyway? We didn't get anything."

"We got a lot from Sonya today."

"A lot?"

Okay, maybe not a lot, but we got something. "I have a starting point."

"Which is?"

"I'm sorry. I'm not at liberty to discuss the details of *my* ongoing investigation." I may sound like a petulant child, but he doesn't get to know what I've found after doubting me.

He shrugs. "I know you, Bennett. If you had something, you'd be dying to share."

"It's Mrs. Maxwell to you, darling."

"No."

"But we're married."

"Not for much longer," he warns.

"About that. I don't think the divorce is going to work out for me."

He puts the fork down again, pushing the plate away. "I've lost my appetite."

"Surely not over staying married to me."

"Why the fuck do you want to stay married?"

"Because I love . . . . annoying you."

"So, you want to make me miserable for the rest of my life?"

I shake my head. "No! Why would you think that?"

Emmett leans back, arms crossed over his broad chest. "Because the agreement we had doesn't work anymore."

"I don't want that agreement."

"Then sign the papers."

How do I explain to him that I don't want that agreement because I want a chance to figure this out? I am conflicted, lost, scared to love him, and scared to lose him.

"I don't want to lose you, Emmett. And I know it sounds crazy that I don't want a divorce when we haven't spoken in years, but it's so final. It's like we will never have a reason to talk again. You and I will move on, and it'll be as though it never happened. And we did happen."

"So, what do you want?" He moves to place his arms on the table. "You want to stay married just so you can keep me? I'm not a pet, Blakely."

"No, I just want some time. I want us to . . . try to be friends?" And maybe more. Maybe we can be everything we could've been.

"We don't have to stay married to be friends."

He's right. I know he is, and I'm too damn scared to admit why I really don't want to sign the papers. "I can't do it now. I don't have them with me. Besides, us divorcing doesn't get me out of here quicker. So, no rush, right?"

And I need time. Time to get myself together and figure out exactly what I want.

He seems to ponder this and then sits up straight. "Fine. We'll wager on it then."

"Wager on what?"

"The divorce. If I win, you sign the papers and head back across the country. If you win, I'll give us three months to rebuild the friendship you're claiming to want back. I'll stay here, you'll go back to DC, and at the end of those three months, you will agree to sign the papers anyway. It's a win-win. Otherwise, I'll get it contested, which I'm pretty sure neither of us has time for."

That isn't what I want at all. I want not to be a headcase with death fears, but instead, I put up steel walls reinforced with concrete around my heart. It's a fortress that cannot be breached, especially by Emmett.

It's not that I am afraid of falling in love and him dying because of it. I'm afraid of falling in love, losing him, and wanting to die myself. I'm terrified of sitting by another coffin and having to watch as the person I love is lowered into the ground.

Love is pain, and I have had enough of it.

I just really wish my head would get on board with this because, when I look at Emmett, I want to take a wrecking ball to that fortress.

"And what's the bet?"

"That this town is safe and you came all this way for nothing."

"Since you're not going to win, that works," I say, a little too smug.

"We'll see."

"Ahhh, Sheriff Maxwell, I thought that was you," a short, portly man says from the edge of the table. "And you must be his lovely wife who has blown into our little town."

Emmett rises, shaking the man's hand. "Mayor Stengel, this is Blakely Bennett. Blakely, this is our mayor."

I stand, extending my hand. "It's wonderful to meet you, Mayor."

"Please, call me Daniel."

"And you must call me Blake. All my friends do."

"And friends we are, indeed," Daniel says.

The mayor is the first person on my list who I wanted to talk to. Sonya mentioned him just once, but Bill had lunch with a few members of the town council a few weeks ago. She didn't know why, but it seemed odd that a man who wasn't linked to politics in any way would be meeting with the decision makers.

"Be careful, Mayor, this one has teeth and bites," Emmett warns him.

"Only those who need to be bit," I joke and glare at him.

Daniel laughs loudly. "Oh, it's good to see Emmett like his old self again. Usually, he's all business and never jokes."

"Really?" I ask.

"Definitely a sour puss if I've ever met one."

Still holding his hand, I place my other on top and do my best to make him feel comfortable with me. "Well, maybe we can have lunch and you can tell me all about our wonderful friend. I've missed a lot in the last few years."

"I would love that, Blake."

So would I.

"Great. It's a date."

"I look forward to it."

The mayor kisses the top of my hand and then shakes Emmett's.

"He is not involved," Emmett says as soon as he walks out the door.

"I never said he was."

"You were thinking it."

"I didn't know you were a mind reader."

Emmett inhales deeply through his nose. "I know you. I know the way your twisted mind works. These are good people in this town. They aren't involved in some strange underground ring of whatever you think they're running."

I raise my hands. "I never said a word, Emmett. All I have are the facts that led me here. If it turns out that there's nothing here, then I move on. I'm not trying to paint the town as somewhere filled with criminals. All I want is to know where my missing girl is. That's it."

And to be here with you.

"Fine. Do your digging, see for yourself that there's nothing to find in Rose Canyon, and then be on your way to ruin another man's life."

He grabs the fry off my plate, pops it into his mouth, and walks out, leaving me ready to kill him.

The town may be filled with good people, but none of them seem to be very talkative. No one has given me anything about Bill, and they say he was a quiet man who they never saw much of. Most were shocked by what he'd done.

"So, you know nothing about him, really?" I ask the woman behind the counter at RosieBeans.

"Nope. He didn't come in here much. But you know who does? Sheriff Maxwell. He's a wonderful man."

I fight back the groan. Every freaking person has told me that. I've heard all about how wonderful, handsome, and charming he is. The man's a woman's fantasy in real life. It's sickening really.

"That's great. He's a great guy, but about Bill Waugh . . ."

"I wish I could help you more, honey, but I told you all I know."

"And the shooting that was right in your parking lot, do you know anything about that?"

Her hand moves to her chest. "Isaac Davis was the best man I ever knew. I'm just broken over it. We all are."

Yes, I've heard that too.

"I'm so sorry for your loss. I know Emmett loved him like a brother."

"Oh," she says with wide eyes. "Isaac, Emmett, Spencer, and Holden were thick as thieves. Always seemed to understand each other without even saying a word. Those boys are all grieving him still. I see their pain."

I hate that he's hurting. Emmett has hurt enough, and I wish I could make it better.

"They say time helps. If you remember or think of anything about Bill, will you call me?" I extend my card.

"I will."

I smile, grab my donut, and walk out the door. There is nothing pointing to the fact that Keeley was ever here. I've shown everyone a photo, and it's hard to imagine that someone could be trafficking girls through here without anyone noticing. I have been here twenty-four hours, and it seems like everyone knows.

I take a step, and suddenly I'm wrenched backward. Strong arms wrap around my middle, preventing me from falling as a car flies past me.

My heart is pounding, and the person releases me. "That was close," he says, and I turn to see a very handsome man with light brown hair and dark brown eyes. "Are you okay?"

"Yes, thank you." He saved me from getting run over.

"Sorry to grab you like that."

"You saved me," I say with a laugh.

"I wouldn't go that far." His smile is easy and friendly. "Are you new here? I haven't seen you around before."

Wow, someone who doesn't know who I am. "Yes, I'm Blake."

"Ryan Wilkinson."

"Well, I really appreciate you making sure I wasn't killed. I'm usually the one in that position."

"Oh? Do you usually go around saving people?" he asks with a grin.

"I do. Well, I did. So, kind of."

"I'm intrigued now."

I laugh and try again. "I was a medic in the army for a long time. So, I guess that's what I meant about saving people."

"Really?" Ryan asks with a glint in his eyes. "I'm a paramedic, so I also go around saving people."

"We have that in common, it seems."

Ryan turns toward the entrance. "Would you . . . can I buy you a cup of coffee?"

"I'm pretty sure the *savee* should buy the *savior* the coffee," I correct.

"Maybe, but the man definitely should buy the beautiful woman the coffee."

Oh. Crap. I'm pretty sure he's flirting. "I wish I could, but my husband is probably at home wondering what's taking me so long."

The husband card comes in handy way more often than I'd ever admit.

"Of course. I'm sorry, I didn't see a ring."

"Occupational hazard," I say with a wide smile. "Anyway, thank you for saving my life just now and for the work you do on a daily basis."

He inclines his head. "Thank you as well."

"Hey, did you know Bill Waugh by any chance?"

"Bill? I knew of him. He died, right?"

"Yeah, he did."

"Why are you asking about Bill?"

"No reason. I just heard something and was curious. I should let you go, I'm sorry."

Ryan shakes his head. "Nothing to be sorry about. It was great to meet you, Blake. Be careful in parking lots."

"I'll do that."

Another strike on the Bill investigation, but I'm not ready to give up. I have a few more days to find something on him that will help me with Keeley. He was on that app and the last person to speak to her. I have no idea where they went, but I'm going to find out.

One way or another.

CHAPTER
Nine

EMMETT

A pot falls to the ground, and I wince. Anytime Blakely is in the kitchen, something is going to be broken or require a hospital visit. When she got home from her fact-finding mission yesterday, she seemed a little deflated. I shouldn't care since the sooner she admits there isn't anything to find, the sooner she's out of my life again, but I still feel bad.

I hate seeing her upset.

"Do you need help in there?" I ask.

"No! I'm fine."

"Okay . . ."

I have forty minutes before I need to head to Holden's for poker night, and I'm not skipping it just because she's here.

"I'm going to change," I let her know.

After a heartbeat she yells to me. "Change for what?"

"Poker."

"You're going out?"

"Yes."

Blakely's face falls. "But I was making dinner."

"Now you decide you want to be domesticated?"

She glares at me. "I was doing something nice for you."

"By what? Making dinner we won't be able to eat? I play poker with the guys every Thursday. It's our thing."

"And I am going to be kicked out of town in a few days. So, you can't skip? We could talk."

I laugh once. "There's nothing to talk about."

"I don't think that's true, Emmett. At least . . . I don't know. I have a lot to explain. Please don't go. Please stay."

Oh, that's rich. "I'm not the one who is known for leaving, sweetheart. You're the one who ran away."

"I didn't run away. I was deployed!"

This is the angle she wants to play, then fine. The thing is that it doesn't fucking matter what happened or why.

I fell for her.

We fucked.

She left.

I'm done.

"You're right. You did. Now, I have to go play poker."

She groans and stomps her foot. "Damn it, Emmett! I never lied to you! Not once in all the time we were together, married or otherwise. I never told you anything was different."

"I know."

She blinks. "Then what the hell are you mad about?"

"I'm not mad," I say, knowing that nothing will piss her off more than the fact that I don't care. She doesn't need to know I'm pretending that seeing her doesn't make my entire day brighter, that the goddamn perfume she wears doesn't make me hard, or that I didn't think of her as I jerked off in the shower today.

Am I mad? Damn right I am, but it's directed at me for wanting her.

"Sure you're not."

"I'm not mad at you, Blake."

"What the hell do you call it then? You and I—"

I cut her off. "Made a mistake. We were both in a shitty place, and we fucked up just like we fucked up years ago when we got married. We're pretty good at making mistakes."

"Our friendship was never a mistake," she says with what looks like tears in her eyes.

No, no, no. She can't cry. No way. I will never be able to watch her hurt.

"I don't regret that."

"And so that's it? We crossed a line one time and we lose everything?"

"We didn't lose anything because we never had anything."

I pull my shirt off and throw it onto the bed, and she inhales. I turn, giving her a full view, wanting to taunt her, make her see what she walked away from. I spent months honing every muscle, working myself to the bone to be better, bigger, and stronger even when they said I couldn't.

I'm not a vain guy, but I am proud of where I am now.

"You're staring," I say, watching for her reaction.

She doesn't disappoint. Blake shakes her head and then tucks her hair back. "You got a tattoo."

I've gotten several in the last few years. The one on my left pec is what she is staring at, and it's for my time as a Ranger. The tattoo is a skull with a Ranger's beret with a sword behind it and the words "Death before Dishonor" above it. Feathers connect the arc of words so the central image is encircled. It is something a few others in our unit had done when they got home.

"I wanted to remember the time I enjoyed when I was active."

"Which was?"

I could hurt her, make her feel like shit, but I won't. "When I was with my men. When we fought together . . . when I would've died before allowing someone I cared about to be hurt."

She can take that however she wants.

I start to unbuckle my pants, and her eyes widen. "What are you doing?"

"Changing."

"We're having a conversation."

I smirk. "No, you're staring at me while I get undressed. You can leave or stay and watch the show."

I've just challenged her, and if she's anything like the woman I loved, she will stand there come hell or high water.

"Well, that's not going to work."

I drop my pants and step out of them.

"Has anyone ever told you that you're a bit of a jerk lately?"

"I'm sure you have several times."

She grumbles under her breath. I'm enjoying this way too much. I could've already put new pants on and been close to being fully dressed by now, but I decide not to do that. I walk over to her, needing her to flinch, but she doesn't.

"Get dressed."

"Maybe you should get undressed so we're on an even playing field."

Why the fuck I just said that, I'll never know. I don't want to see her naked.

That's a lie.

I want to see her bare, open, and unguarded. Then I remember why that's a bad idea.

"Fine."

She tears her shirt off before throwing it where my pants are. Then she hooks her fingers in her shorts and slides them down before I can tell her to stop.

And then I wonder if I would've been able to get the words out anyway.

Blakely has always been stunning, and the years haven't changed that. Her deep brown hair flows around her shoulders, covering her breasts.

I want to grab a handful and tighten my fist in it, holding her where I want her.

She raises one perfectly arched brow and grins. "Now we're equal."

We are nowhere near equal. She has the upper hand—maybe she always has.

I take a step to her, as though my feet move of their own accord. Before I can think twice, my hands are in her hair, pulling her face to mine. Our mouths meet in anger and frustration.

My mind has clearly snapped. I hate her. No, that's a lie. I hate myself for not hating her. I want to look at her and not want her. I wish that I didn't think about her, wonder if she's happy or sad. Every fucking day for years I've thought of her in some way, and I want it to stop.

I need to get this divorce done so I can move on with my life.

But right now, all those wants and desires disappear. All I want is her.

She kisses me with the same ferocity as I go to her. I move my hands down the slim column of her neck, pushing her bra straps down as I move across her shoulders.

This may be a mistake, but I'll deal with it later.

I lift her, and she wraps her legs around my waist. Our lips don't part as I push her back against the wall, anchoring her on my good leg.

Our tongues slide against each other, her fingers sliding through my hair as I unhook her bra. As I toss it aside, she pulls back, baring herself to me.

Every image I have of her, of that night, was muted. Now I see her in color, and God, she's every hue that exists.

I kiss down her neck as she arches toward me. I lick around the nipple, and her gasp breaks the silence in the room.

I should stop this. I should put my damn clothes on and go to the poker game.

But the only way I'll be able to stop this is if she tells me to.

However, she doesn't do that. Instead, Blakely moves her hand down my body and frees my dick.

All that's between us now is her underwear.

As though she can read my thoughts, her eyes find mine, and she tilts her head as if to say—now what?

I move my lips to her ear. "Don't say a goddamn word. If you say anything, I'll stop. Do you understand? Anything. Doesn't matter what it is."

She nods.

This is her out, and she doesn't take it.

Whatever happens now doesn't change a fucking thing. I am

going to fuck her out of my system, and in a few days, she'll sign the damn papers and be gone.

I look into her brown eyes, seeing the woman I loved—or love, I don't know anymore—and tell myself it's never going to be more than this.

"Fuck it."

I pull her underwear to the side and before I can talk myself in or out of it, I push into her. Her heat envelops me, making me forget everything in the past. All that matters is this and us. Blakely's mouth opens, head back, dark brown hair falling around her face. This is how I will picture her.

I push deeper, her fingernails digging into my shoulders. I pump my hips, her head banging against the wall with every thrust. Blakely doesn't speak, but she does make soft noises of pleasure.

Gripping her jaw, I force her eyes on mine. I want to rage at her for making me weak or blame her for making me this way, but all I can do is remember why I loved her so damn much.

Blakely is like drinking water after being in the desert for too long. She's the sun on your face after a year of cloudy skies. No matter how much I wish it were different, she holds my heart and soul.

But this is it. This will never happen again, and I release her gaze, hoping she didn't see right through me just now.

I move my hand between us, rubbing her clit. She tightens around me, so I redouble my efforts, needing this to end before I lose my mind.

She opens her mouth to speak, but then she shuts it, eyes closing and lower lip trembling. I adjust my hips to give her a little more pressure.

That does it, and she screams out as her orgasm rushes through her. I'm right behind her, pulling out quickly and wrapping my hand around my cock, pumping as I come. At least I had enough sense to do that much since I didn't wear a damn condom.

"Emmett?" Blake says, breaking the spell.

I shake my head, grabbing a shirt off the floor to clean up.

"Emmett, we need to talk," she says.

I lift my hand. "There's nothing to talk about."

"Really?"

I grab my boxers and put them on before walking to the dresser and picking out a shirt and jeans. I need to get the fuck away from her. I have to leave her before she realizes the same thing I already have.

I pull my shirt on and face her. She at least put her shirt and underwear back on. "I don't have anything to say."

"You just fucked me against the wall, and you have nothing to say about it?"

"About it? Sure. I have things to say."

She crosses her arms. "I'm all ears."

"I want a divorce, and I have to go play poker now. I'm late."

Blakely's eyes flash with hurt and then anger. "You did not just say that to me, you asshole!"

Yeah. I am being a total asshole, but my head is a mess and talking is only going to complicate things. It's better if I leave.

"I didn't make promises, and I don't recall you suggesting we stop."

I walk out into the living room, angry at myself, at her, at the fact I just did that filling every empty space in the apartment.

When my hand is on the doorknob, she calls out to me. "Don't do this. Not like the past all over again."

I turn, all of that anger pulsing around me. "I didn't walk out when you went to sleep. I didn't lie to you."

"I thought . . ." She looks up at the ceiling. "I thought that maybe . . ."

"Maybe what? Maybe I'd stay and we could talk about our feelings since we made *another* mistake? Maybe you'd sneak off in the middle of the night again? Or that I would? I'm not sneaking. I'm leaving. The difference is that I'll be back in a few hours and not in two and a half years."

"Oh, that was a mistake, all right! Leave! Go! I don't care."

I nod. "So, it's okay for you to do it but not me? Got it. I told you I have plans, and what happened back there was the culmination of years of anger that just came to a breaking point. Nothing more."

"I guess you're right."

No, I'm not.

"I'll see you later."

"What else can make this better, Emmett?"

That's a loaded question if I've ever heard one. I could fall to my knees and give her every promise she could want, knowing that she would never take it. Or I can do what I didn't do two and a half years ago. I can keep some semblance of my pride and walk away.

I open the front door and stare out into the empty hallway. "Sign the fucking papers, Blake. It's time to move on." I exit, closing the door behind me, and lean against the wall. About two seconds later, there is a thud against the wood behind me.

Good. Let her be pissed, at least she's getting a tiny taste of what I've felt for the last two and a half years. Now she knows what it feels like to be left.

"Call," Holden says, tossing the chips in.

I have a full house, no way he beats me.

"I fold." Spencer huffs. "This game sucks."

"Because you're losing," I say with a smirk.

"Yeah, yeah."

"Want to borrow some money?" Holden taunts him.

Spencer flips him off.

"How's Brie settling into your place?" I ask, already knowing she's driving him crazy. When I went to drop off a package to Addison, Isaac's widow, she was getting ready to go shopping with Brie for the remodel at Spencer's.

Interesting, since he told me it was Brie's place that was having improvements done.

"She's gutting the kitchen."

Holden chuckles. "Good thing you held on to her place. You guys can live there during the renovations."

I lean back, staring at Spencer, waiting for him to dig out of this hole.

He shrugs. "I lied. There's not a renovation at her house."

"No shit?"

"Whatever. It was payback for all the hell you gave me. Besides, you and Blakely needed time to talk."

"How nice of you to force that."

"What happened here?" Holden asks.

I fill him in on the whole thing about Spencer lying about Brie's place and how they'd offered up his guest bedroom as a place for her to stay.

"Smooth." Holden laughs and extends his fist to Spencer.

"Right."

I could punch them both. "She's only here because she thinks Bill is somehow tied to a missing person's case she's looking into."

Spencer looks up. "She does? What makes her think that?"

"She has a photo of her missing girl with him, and Blakely saw the conversation they had on an app."

He taps his finger against the green felt. I can see his brain working just like hers does. "Not you too."

"What?"

"You think the same shit, don't you?"

Spencer shakes his head. "No, but Bill killing himself has left more questions than answers. I can't help but wonder who he meant when he said, 'They'll come for you next.' He also wasn't smart enough to orchestrate anything, but he was terrified of whoever he was working for. My gut says there could be something more here."

"And if you couldn't find it, you think Blake can?" I ask. Spencer Cross is one of the best investigative reporters in the world. He has uncovered things that people far smarter than Bill Waugh hid. You can't tell me he or Cole Security wouldn't be able to find it before my wife.

"We have no idea what information she has. I know Quinn was uneasy too, felt there was more to the story. Yeah, he was scared about losing his wife and kid, but Sonya told us about his paranoia that someone was coming. What if he was involved in something crazy? How many people are unmasked because of a stupid mistake? What about the serial killer who was pulled over for a broken taillight and that's how they found him? For all we know, she found a parking ticket that is what we need to place him," Spencer adds.

While all that sounds great, I'm not buying it. "So, who is it? Which mysterious person in this town could be linked to her missing girl?" I ask, arms crossed over my chest.

We know everyone who lives here, and I can't believe that someone in this town has ties to a missing girl.

Holden clears his throat. "We have all spent a lot of time away from here, so let's not pretend this town is the same as it was when we left. Let's also not forget that Bill Waugh grew up here too, and he was beating his wife and kid. Rose Canyon is filled with good, honest people, but they're still people."

Spencer nods. "Exactly. This town isn't perfect."

"I'm not saying it is," I clarify. "I'm just hard pressed to believe that there's someone who abducted a girl, which is what Blake is insinuating."

Spencer taps his thumb against the green felt. "I think I need to go over my notes again."

"We've been over your notes a million times."

"Not while we were looking for a link between Bill and a missing girl from DC. Maybe new eyes will see something I missed."

I groan. "You're going to go over it with Blake?"

He stops tapping. "Yup."

"Well, she has about five days left."

"You're really going to make her leave?" Spencer asks.

"Damn right I am!"

A man can only take so much. We had forty-eight hours

together before I fucked her against a wall. I can't imagine how I'm going to last a damn week as it is.

Holden laughs. "As if you want that."

"I do."

"Liar," they both say in unison.

I think about the hurt in her eyes when I left and wish I could rebuke them, but they're right, I want her to want to fight me on the divorce because she wants to be with me. I've always wanted a life with her. I just know better than to hope for it because she'll never give it to me.

CHAPTER

Ten

BLAKELY

~One and a Half Years Ago~

"Y ou've done an exceptional job, Captain," Colonel O'Brien says as he pins the Army Commendation Medal for bravery in combat onto my lapel.

Everyone here has family watching with tear-filled eyes—everyone except me.

"Thank you, sir."

He moves to the next person in line, and I focus on the window. I stare out at the blinding sun, hoping it will serve as an excuse as to why I am crying.

I may have been brave out there, but I am not when there aren't bullets flying.

I got back stateside three days ago to find the celebration in full swing. Hundreds of service members were hugging their husbands and wives. Children dressed in red, white, and blue were running around with their smiles so wide they could have broken their cheeks. Their mothers or fathers were finally home. Their world going back to right, and mine going back to hell.

When I was in the field, I could pretend I didn't miss or need Emmett. Walking away from him was what I needed to do. If I gave him more than a sliver of myself, I'd lose my heart without even knowing it.

But not here.

I'll be home in two days. The unit I was with was out of Florida, so I returned here, I have to debrief, and then I head to North Carolina. Where I'll have to face Emmett and figure out what is next, if he's even still there.

Finally, Colonel O'Brien steps back, still facing us, and salutes. We salute him back, and then everyone heads off to their families.

I stand here.

Lost. Alone. Pathetic.

"Last time we saw each other, you were quite desperate to find your husband," Colonel O'Brien says, causing me to look at him.

"Yes, sir."

"And he wasn't here to see you receive such a prestigious award?"

I look down at my shined shoes. "No, sir."

"I see. And why not?"

Because I'm an idiot. "We haven't spoken much since he returned to North Carolina."

Or at all. I've emailed sixteen times, and all of them went without response until yesterday. I told him about this award ceremony, not expecting an answer, and now I wish I'd never sent it.

It was one word.

Congrats.

Yeah. Congrats to me, I guess.

"He was busy. Umm, he had an appointment he couldn't miss."

He shakes his head. "You and I both know he wouldn't miss this. How is he doing since getting medically discharged?"

My breath catches, and he stares at me. "I-I didn't know it went through."

How could he not tell me? I didn't deserve even an email? My chest feels tight, and I want to scream. We were friends before we got married. He used to tell me everything, and it would seem that isn't the case any longer.

"About two weeks ago." Colonel O'Brien watches me. "I figured you would know."

He's not asking.

"We haven't spoken in months."

Understanding flashes in his eyes. "I see. When do you travel home?"

"The day after tomorrow."

"I'm going to overstep here, but I have known you for a long time, Captain. We've been through several of these evolutions together, and I'm going to pretend that you're my daughter for a moment." I brace myself. "I've been married three times, have four children, two of which no longer speak to me. I've been to dozens of awards ceremonies like this one and countless other joyous occasions, but I only remember the funerals. The phone calls where I apologize to a wife, husband, mother, or father are what haunt me at night. Like yourself, I was a medic, and I recall that feeling of wanting to save the world and being unable to do it. My first wife left after my second deployment when I changed, became distant and afraid of loss. I loved her. More than my second wife, that's for sure." He smiles, and I follow with one of my own. "I would've done anything to have her back. To love her the way I should've but was incapable of at that time. Don't make that mistake, Blakely. If you love him, fight for him."

CHAPTER
Eleven

BLAKELY

~Present~

T he fan above me spins slowly, the blades slicing through the air without any resistance. I close my eyes, seeing a very different scene than the white ceiling.

Dirt moves around me as we carry the stretcher and I apply pressure to the wound. "Captain, he's not going to make the flight!"

I glare at Watson. "He will! I'm going with him."

"You can't! What about the others?"

"Sergeant, I suggest you figure it out. This soldier needs me more." Blood is covering my uniform, but I don't care. I need to keep the pressure on his wound.

"Captain, we can't!"

I stare into his brown eyes that are full of fear. "We have to do our jobs. Save who you can, and I'll head back as soon as we get him to the hospital. One hour."

The flight there is fifteen minutes, we can do this.

We're loaded in, my fingers holding the artery closed. I explain the situation to the medic in the helicopter, and he nods before signaling to the pilot. Then we're up.

The soldier moans, and our eyes meet. "You and me. You keep fighting, and I'm going to keep holding on," I say. "Do you understand, Private?"

The tear trickles down his cheek, but he nods. He's maybe nineteen years old and has his whole life ahead of him. I need him to survive.

The sounds of the blades are loud, but we stay focused on each other. "Five minutes out," the pilot says into the headset.

"We have five more minutes, you and me. Five more minutes, do you understand?"

"Yes, ma'am."

Please, God, let him survive.

We start to make our approach, the horizon dropping as the landscape comes into view.

The other medic is signaling the alarm.

No, no, no, no. No. He can't.

"Private?" I call to him, but his eyes are closed. "Private!"

Still nothing.

"Start CPR!" I yell to the medic, who is already grabbing the bag. "Private, open your eyes! That's an order!"

I hold on to the artery, but I know. I know because the pulsing beneath my fingers isn't the same.

Moisture drops down between us, and I realize it's my tears. I fought so hard. I had this. I had him, and we were going to make it. He was supposed to make it.

They hoist us out, and I'm still straddling him, hand inside his chest, holding the damage closed.

The surgeon looks at him and checks his eyes. "He's gone," he says as though I didn't spend twenty minutes with my hand on his pulse.

I nod, tears falling soundlessly.

"I tried."

The surgeon doesn't spare us another glance as the next helicopter lands.

"Time of death, fourteen twenty-four," he says, handing a sheet of paper to the nurse beside him.

Her gaze finds mine. "Ma'am."

I need to get up. I have to let go, but I can't stop crying.

"Blakely." The medic shakes me. "Blakely, stop."

I can't.

"Blakely, open your eyes!"

It's Emmett's voice. Why is he here? That doesn't make sense because he's back stateside. He's at home, injured but healing, and safe. He is safe.

"Emmett!" I call out, unable to see him.

"Blakely, you're safe, wake up. Wake up!"

My eyes open, and I gasp, struggling for air. He pulls me to his chest, and I cling to him.

It was a dream. It was a dream. I'm okay.

Only I'm not. I'm covered in sweat, gripping Emmett as though he's my lifeline.

His hand is on the back of my head, smoothing my hair down. "You're safe, Blake."

I close my eyes, allowing myself the sliver of comfort he offers. Slowly, my breathing returns to normal and his hold loosens.

"Thank you."

He pulls back, gaze finding mine in the darkness. "What happened?"

"What always happens."

I don't have to explain, he already knows what it is. He's haunted in different ways by the same memories.

"Is it like this a lot?"

"No."

That's the worst part about it. If it were more frequent, I would expect it. I could plan for the emotional turmoil in some way. Instead, my mind lulls me into a false sense of security, keeping the nightmares at bay for a few weeks, only to come back in full force.

I shift, feeling uncomfortable like this. He isn't wearing a shirt, and his warm bare skin reminds me of earlier tonight.

Of when we touched, kissed, and loved before he walked away.

Just like I did to him years ago.

Emmett scoots back. "How often are the nightmares?"

I shrug. "Often enough."

"Scoot over," he says, and I stare at him.

"What?"

"You heard me. You're on my side."

"We slept like this last night."

"Well, we're not tonight." I scoff and he continues, "I didn't sleep the other night, and it was because you were on my side."

"Well"—I huff—"I like this side."

Emmett stands, pulls the covers back, and pushes me to the other side of the bed before climbing in.

"You're free to head to the couch," he says as he adjusts a pillow.

"I just had a nightmare."

"I know, and I'm here now. Lie down, Blake, and keep your hands to yourself. We can be adults."

I roll my eyes. "As if I wanted to touch you."

His deep chuckle echoes in the room. I could go to the couch, but that feels like defeat, so my only option is to feign indifference. I lie down, pull the covers up over my bare legs, and turn to face him.

Emmett clears his throat. "I was an asshole today. I never should have done that to you."

"No, you shouldn't have. To be fair, though, I didn't stop you during the sex, and I hurt you years ago."

He lets out a long sigh. "Doesn't make it right."

It doesn't, and I cried for a good hour after he left, but I'm sure that was a fraction of the pain that he felt when he woke up and found my note. I regret not saying something about how I truly felt before we had mind-blowing sex because we really should have talked first. He just looked so damn good, felt so amazing, and my libido outran my common sense.

"I appreciate the apology," I say and then ask, "Do you have nightmares?"

"Not anymore—or, at least, if I do, they don't wake me up."

"I see their faces."

"I do too, but not when I sleep. I see them on the street. I hear their voices calling for me when I'm in a store. I remember the funeral and the flag and the sound of the shots ringing out."

I release a long sigh, my heart aching for him. "I keep waiting for it to stop."

"I'm not."

I stare at him, blinking in surprise. "You want the memories?"

"I never want to forget them. Carrying their voices, their faces, and the memory of them is a way to honor them and what they gave up."

What he says makes sense to some extent, but it's horrible either way. "I wish I could carry them in a different way. I wish I remembered the laughter and the fun we had, even when we were in hell. I'm *haunted* by their deaths."

Emmett trails a finger down my cheek where a tear was falling. "You were the last person most of them saw, Blake. You watched the end, and I can't pretend to know what that was like for you."

Another tear falls. "For so long, I was so good at pretending that it wasn't devastating, but it was."

During the war, I never blinked. I shut it down, moved on, did my job so the casualties didn't rise.

"Pretending only lasts so long."

I don't think we're talking about the war anymore. This time, I reach for him, taking his fingers and lacing mine through them. "And what happens when reality isn't what we thought and we act out of fear and irrationality?"

"I don't know."

I yawn, and he brings our clasped hands between us, tucking them against his chest. "Close your eyes, Blakely. I'll chase away your demons for tonight."

When I wake, we aren't facing each other or holding hands. I'm draped over him, cheek on his chest, which has a small pool of my drool on it. He's also managed to hook his leg with mine.

I can't imagine what the hell I look like. I do my best to wipe off my face and his chest with the sheet, and I remove at least one of the tangles in my hair without waking him. Then, I puff my cheeks a few times so they aren't flattened and flip my hair so that I look like an angel when I take back my place on his chest.

"I was awake an hour ago," Emmett says, his sleep-roughened voice traveling down my spine.

Great.

"And you didn't think to disentangle yourself?"

"I'm very comfortable."

"You're actually like sleeping on a rock," I clarify.

"You didn't mind last night as you climbed on top of me as you slept."

I blow out a breath through my nose. "Climbed on top of you? Please. I was probably dreaming you were someone else."

"Sure you were."

I wasn't. I don't think I dreamed at all, actually. "Anyway." I push up, pulling my hair to one side and adjusting my shirt. "Thank you for last night."

"You'd do it for me."

I nod once. "I would." There's nothing I wouldn't do for him.

"I know."

The two of us look at each other, tension rising, and my chest is tight. God, I want to kiss him again. I want to throw myself into his arms, tell him I'm stupid and sorry, and beg him to love me while I find a way to heal, but I am so afraid of uttering the words.

I want to love him. I want nothing more than to allow myself a chance at happiness.

But if he says it's too late, that the damage between us is too extensive, it would finally be what does me in.

I wouldn't survive. I know that.

It would be a loss that would end my world.

I will never forget them pulling me off the line to tell me my husband had been shot.

The flight to Germany took a million years.

No matter who I asked for an update on his condition, they just told me that he was stable as far as they knew.

When I got to the hospital, I couldn't find him. They had moved him, the computer system hadn't been updated with his new room number, and I was frantic.

Then seeing him was like coming up for air. I could breathe again. It was life and happiness all rolled together in this beautiful cloud that I was floating on.

Making love to him was even better.

Emmett sits up, watching me as a storm rolls through his eyes. "We can't do this, you know that?"

"I know," I say, hating that it's the truth.

"There is no reason we can't be happy and move on."

For two and a half years, I have been trying to do exactly that. I have been working sixteen-hour days and spending at least an hour at the gym each day, and nothing helps. When I sit in the quiet, I see Emmett.

I shake my head. "And do you think once we're officially divorced that all of this will be better?"

His eyelids lower, and he releases a breath through his nose. "It sure as hell will be better than this. At least then I might not constantly wonder about you or have to lie over and over again about why I don't date or the fact I am married. It won't fix some of the shit we feel, but I'm tired of not feeling like I can move on. I hoped I could get this done without having to explain any of it to Holden and Spencer, but that ship sailed the day you strolled into town. If we can at least be adults and do what's right, then maybe you won't haunt me."

"So, you think of me?" I ask, wanting so badly to know he does.

"Not the way you hope."

I shrug. "It's still something, and I never meant to hurt you, Emmett. I hate that I did."

"The worst part is that I know that. You freaked out, and I get it, but we both deserve better than this sham."

He's right. I hurt him, and while my heart is breaking at the idea of losing what little thread I had left, I don't want to do that to him anymore. I want him to be free. I want him to have everything he wants.

"I can't sign them."

"Why not?"

"Because I burned them," I admit sheepishly.

"You burned the divorce papers?"

"In a bonfire-like blaze."

I was a little pissed off to say the least.

He laughs once. "Good thing I can get another copy printed. You know you're a fucking lunatic, right?"

I get out of the bed, smiling because this version of Emmett I can manage. "I may be that, husband, but more than anything, I'm your wife."

I walk into the bathroom with a huge grin, ready to start the day, find a kidnapper, and hopefully find a way to win him back.

CHAPTER
Twelve

EMMETT

Once my bathroom is free, I prepare myself for a very long, very cold shower. Not that the ice water is doing a damn thing for my erection.

I'm hard as steel, still able to smell her shampoo, feel her against my body, and hear those sweet sighs as she slept on top of me.

This woman is maddening.

I turn the water to hot and do the only thing I know will help. I take myself in hand and jerk off to the image of Blakely in my head.

Those eyes, staring at me as she walks toward me. Dark brown hair falling around her, covering her perfect tits so that just her nipples are peeking through her shiny locks. I see her incredible body, with curves in all the right places, where my hands fit and cup her.

I move faster, hearing her voice sighing my name. Once steam billows around me, I lean one hand against the wall.

I imagine her on her knees, my dick down her throat, and pretend the hot water is her mouth.

Two more pumps, and I spill all over the floor with my head back.

This has to stop.

She needs to leave so I can get control of my life back.

I finish up, get dressed, and head out to the living room in uniform.

Blakely is sitting on the couch, reading something written in a notebook. She looks up. "That was a long shower."

"When you're not worried about bullets flying at you, you tend to take your time," I reply.

"Touché."

"What are you reading?" I ask, noting the handwriting isn't hers.

"Oh, Spencer stopped by. I guess you mentioned that I was looking into Bill, so he brought me his notes and asked to see mine. We're going to meet tonight and see if anything intersects."

Of course he did. "You're not going to find anything."

"You keep saying that, and yet . . . you aren't helping prove that."

"I don't have to prove that there's nothing going on here because there is nothing showing me otherwise."

She crosses her arms. "You're so sure, and I don't get it. Your best friend was shot, and the man who did it killed himself. We have a photo, the texts on the app, all of which alludes to something happening here. I'll give you that there is nothing concrete *yet*, but there is a reason Keeley and Bill crossed paths, and I intend to find out what that is."

If only that were true.

I grab my gun belt, putting it on with a laugh. "I think you're here for something else."

"And what might that be?"

I have a few suspicions on what brought her here. She may be working a case, but she was all too happy to show up at that party. And kiss me. Not that I am any better, but why else would she burn the damn divorce papers if she didn't want us to reconcile? Blakely, even if she were pissed off, wouldn't do that unless she was also hurt.

"Me. You're here for me."

Blakely jerks her head up. "I'm sorry, what?"

"You're here for me," I repeat.

"I'm here for my case, which happens to be where you are. You . . . you . . . ugh."

I grin. I got her now. "If it were just about the case, why did you burn the divorce papers?"

"Because you pissed me off!" Blakely yells. "You . . . you just didn't care and sent me papers out of nowhere. I was mad, so I set it on fire. You hate me anyway."

"I don't hate you, darling, that's the issue."

"You don't?"

I holster my gun and reach for my hat, pretending that none of this matters and she doesn't affect me, which is bullshit. "Nope."

"Oh. What do you feel?"

I'm not giving this woman an inch until she gives me one first. "I'll answer that if you tell me why you really burned the papers."

"I just did," she replies.

"You were mad?"

"Yes."

"And hurt?" I ask.

"Yes."

"Because you love me?"

Blakely's mouth falls open. "I . . . what?"

"I've been thinking about it, and it's clear. You love me. You're afraid of that, because you think something bad is going to happen."

Her chest rises and falls, and then she looks down. "I'm always afraid that something bad is going to happen."

"I've yet to hear a denial on how you feel."

She shakes her head. "And what would it change? What if I said it? Would it even change anything?"

"I don't know, what do you think?" I put my hat on and wink at her, knowing that'll really set her off.

Sure enough, Blakely walks to me and flips my hat off. "Listen, you. All you've said is to sign the papers. Over and over. What if I tell you how I feel, and you still leave? What if you don't want me?

What if I don't want you, and I just think that's what I want because I'm scared of losing you?"

I don't doubt for one second she's afraid. But she's going to have to say the words if she wants me to consider giving her that honesty, which I'm not even sure I should. Still, I want her, and I am done lying to myself about that.

I lean in to her, noting every movement. The way her breathing grows shallow, her pulse in her neck moves quicker, and her pupils dilate. She's so full of shit. "You're going to have to be brave, Bennett."

"I'm not scared," she says breathily. Betraying herself.

"No?"

"No."

"So, you don't want me right now? You don't wish that I would lean in and press my lips to yours or strip away all the layers of pissed off that you cling to and make you scream like I did last night?"

Blakely's lips form into a thin line. "No."

"Liar." I pull her into my arms, knowing that it's going to piss her off. "If you want me to kiss you, wife, all you have to do is ask."

Her palms flatten against my chest, and I use every part of my training to keep my heart rate steady.

"Do you want to kiss me? Is that why you're asking?"

I want to kiss every fucking inch of her. I have always wanted that. She has always been something more to me, but I settled for what I could have.

However, she broke my fucking heart, and I am not going to let her have power in this situation. "Not really."

Her jaw falls. "Now who is the liar?"

I rest my nose against hers, brushing it up and down the smooth slope. "I wasn't the one climbing you like a tree last night. I wasn't the one who found an excuse to fly out here when I got divorce papers." My voice is low, and I feel her tremble slightly. "Tell me you want this, and I'll give it to you." I grin as I add, "Obey was part of your vows."

Her head snaps back, eyes blazing with heat and desire. "Go to hell."

I lean down so my lips are hovering over hers. "I've already been there, sweetheart. The Devil sent me back to you."

I release her, and she flops onto the couch with a humph. I grab my hat, tug it on, and keep a smile on my lips as I head to the door.

"Emmett?" I stop and then her hand is on my back. When I turn, she's right behind me, and then she has a hand on either side of my face as she pushes to her tiptoes. "I changed my mind."

"Oh?"

"Kiss me goodbye, husband."

I spin us so her back is against the door, and I have the control.

"Whatever you want, baby."

I bring my mouth to hers in a searing kiss, maintaining domination the entire time. I will not get lost in her. I will not give in to the sensation of her lips on mine, the taste of her, or the fact that for the last two and a half years I've felt like I'm drifting until this very fucking second. That when we are together, even if we're pissed at each other, I feel whole again.

She anchors me.

I step back suddenly enough that she staggers a bit, and I force myself to let out a laugh. "I knew you wanted me."

She sputters. "I-I do not . . . ugh!"

I kiss her cheek and open the door. "Happy researching. See you when I get home."

"Emmett!"

I lean back into the apartment. "Yes?"

"I hate you."

"Whatever you have to tell yourself."

Then I close the door and walk to the car with the biggest smile.

"Hello, Sheriff," Holden says as he sits across from me at the table in the diner.

"Good afternoon, Doctor."

"I have a joke for you."

"Is it not the fact that you moved back here?"

Holden snorts. "That's one word for it. But for real, I have a good one a patient told me."

"Can't wait."

"Why do chicken coops only have two doors?"

I blink, not sure where this is going. "I have no idea."

"Because if they had four, they'd be a chicken sedan." He laughs, and I roll my eyes. "It's so funny! A sedan, not a coop. My patients are hilarious."

"You are an idiot."

The bell above the door chimes, and everyone in the place freezes as Addison walks in. After Isaac was killed, she took some time and went to stay with friends back east, but she came back for Spencer and Brielle's party. Since then, she's barely left her house.

Holden and I stand as Addy looks around as if she's confused. "What? Do I have something on my face?"

Mayor Stengel coughs once. "Go on now, everyone back to your lunches and let our beautiful librarian go back to her life."

Holden and I approach her, and she hands Elodie, her one-year-old daughter, to Holden. "You came out around the town folk?"

"I did."

"I'm glad," I tell her.

"I can't keep hiding. It's not going to bring him back, you know?"

Holden settles Elodie in the highchair that the waitress brought over. "It's good that you're here. The town misses you."

She breathes heavily. "I miss it too, but I need to get back to Sugarloaf."

"For how long?" I ask.

"Just a few weeks. I want to pack up and give myself time to prepare to come back here."

I wish I could tell her how happy it makes me that she isn't selling her house and leaving for good. Addison is part of our patched-up family here. Elodie is what's left of Isaac, and Spencer, Holden, and I want to always be here for her.

"How long will you stay when you come back?"

Addy shrugs, looking around the room before meeting my gaze. "Hopefully permanently. This is my home, and I'm not going to keep away any longer. Unless something else happens and then I'm out."

"It won't. We want you back too much to let something happen."

Addy places both hands on the table. "Now, let's talk about you two idiots and the messes you've made."

Holden points at me. "He's the idiot with a mess. I'm the doctor with no mess."

"Fine." She turns to me first. "You're married?"

"You know this."

"Yes, and what a shock that was to find out. Want to explain why exactly none of us knew you had a ball and chain? If Isaac were alive, he'd kick your ass right now, Emmett. How could you keep this from all of us? We're a family."

"It was never supposed to be a marriage. It isn't now."

"That's a lie if I've ever heard one."

I really never thought I was this transparent. "And how do you figure?"

Addy smiles. "Because you didn't just vehemently deny it. Also, you can't keep your eyes off her. So, have you guys confessed your feelings?" Addy asks.

"He hasn't," Holden answers.

I glare at him. "How the hell do you know that?"

"You're grumpier than usual."

Addy giggles. "Do you *know* how you feel about her?"

"I'm divorcing her."

"That's avoiding the question if I've ever seen it."

Elodie yells and slaps her hands on the table.

I turn to her. "See, you don't like it when they gang up on

Uncle Emmett, do you?" She giggles, and I shift my attention back to Addy. "Did you and Isaac not have secrets?"

"Of course we did."

"Then I have mine too, and we can all assume Holden does as well. Did you know he has a stalker who doesn't understand geography?"

Her brows rise. "You do?"

"I don't know. I tried to file a police report, but our law enforcement isn't all that bright here."

"We knew that."

"You can't file a report for receiving a gift," I clarify.

"Fine, but if I end up getting abducted and ransomed, make sure you ask for proof of life."

Addy laughs. "Thank God we're not asking for proof of common sense."

The waitress, Diana, brings over drinks and places a BLT and fries in front of me. "I didn't order this," I explain.

She bites her lower lip. "I know, your wife did."

"My . . ." The waitress points, and I look over to Mayor Stengel's table to find Blakely giving me a little wave. "Send it back."

Diana smiles. "She said you'd say that, and I was to tell you that it's Friday, and on Fridays, you eat a BLT with fries. I don't know what that means, but . . ."

It's Friday, and we always ate BLTs with fries.

"How does she know you eat that on Fridays?" Addy asks.

"I don't."

"Yes, you do. You eat the same thing every weekday. I always thought it was weird, but you've always been a little off."

"Right?" Holden chimes in. "He's not normal."

"You should talk."

"You're right. We should."

Holden rises, and before I can say anything, he's walking toward Blakely and the mayor. They shake hands, Holden grabs the chair behind him, smirks at me, and sits with them. Addy giggles, and I decide that I'm in hell.

"Oh, don't be so worried. Holden's allegiance is always to you, he's just an ass who enjoys making you sweat."

"I know, but Blakely and I are complicated."

Addy smiles. "Aren't all marriages complicated?"

"We're not really married."

"Could've fooled me, Emmett Maxwell. I have been your friend since we were six years old, and you have only ever kept a secret when it meant the world to you."

I raise one brow. "How would you know if it was a secret?"

"I know you had a crush on me, and when you found out Isaac did, you pretended you didn't."

"That was friendship, not a secret."

She shrugs, grabbing a fry off my plate. "Maybe, but you never told me."

"You and Isaac were always meant for each other."

"We were, but then there was the time you didn't tell anyone that you kicked Michael Shapiro's ass because he almost assaulted me."

I grab a fry and point it at her. "That was your secret."

He's lucky I didn't kill him that day. He had cornered Addison, trying to get her to kiss him. I saw red, ripped him off her, and punched him in the face. Then I threatened him with everything I could think of, and he never bothered her again. I wanted to tell Isaac, Holden, and Spencer, but Addy begged me not to.

"Maybe, but it mattered to you. You've always been willing to sacrifice yourself for other people. It's probably what made you join the military and then become a police officer. You're a protector, and I'm going to guess that was one of the many reasons you married her."

Like she needed me. Losing Dylan almost killed her, and sure, part of my excuse was the financial gain, but I wanted to be there for her and would've done anything to have myself tied to her. I went in with both eyes open, knowing Blakely's desires for what we were, and I was fine with it. But our relationship changed, and she started to look at me differently. It made me want more.

"You're very perceptive this Friday afternoon."

"I'm always perceptive. I'm assuming you slept with her since she's been back and you were a jerk after?"

Okay, maybe perceptive is the wrong word. She's a goddamn mind reader. "Why do you say that?"

"Because I can see the guilt all over you."

I could tell Addison anything. She's like a sister to all of us and has never judged the dumb shit we did, but admitting this to her is impossible.

She places her hand on mine. "You don't have to tell me if you don't want to, but I will always listen."

I place my other hand atop hers. "You're a good friend, Addison Davis."

"I know." She pauses a moment, then asks, "Emmett, do you want to divorce her, truly?"

I glance over at Blake and then back to Addy. "I don't know. I haven't handled things well with her. I think that's part of the issue, we never have. We were best friends, and when we slept together, it destroyed everything we were. But I care about her. I always have, and I don't think that'll ever change. I want her, but I need her to be brave enough to finally admit she wants me too."

"Well, talk to her. She's here, Emmett. That's saying something. You can either keep saying and doing dumb things or be an adult and communicate, which I know is a foreign concept to men."

The laugh comes from deep in my chest. "I hear you, and you're probably right."

"I am right. I'm always right. Didn't Isaac ever tell you that?"

"He did."

Addy sighs before she glances over at Blakely. "You should probably save her from Holden."

"He would never." And he wouldn't. That is a line he would never cross.

"No, but it gives you a chance to be the hero and open the door to all that communication you need to be having."

I'm no hero. I have the names of the men I lost to prove it.

"Addy?"

"Yeah?"

I want to ask her about when she and Isaac broke up. I remember him talking about second chances being better than the first if you're smart, but think better of bringing him up.

"Thank you," I say instead.

As I stand, she grabs my forearm. "That's not what you wanted to say. I'm going to assume it's about Isaac."

I sigh and nod. "About when you guys went through that rough patch in college."

"Did you know it was me that suggested the breakup?"

"Yes."

All we heard about for weeks was how he didn't understand why she would do that to him when he loved her so damn much.

So, I ask her what Isaac didn't. "Why?"

"Because sometimes you need to walk away to remember why you want to stay."

CHAPTER
Thirteen

BLAKELY

M y day was filled with interviews and my nosey husband. He crashed my meeting with the mayor, and I ended up having to come to the mayor's office so we can talk.

Spencer's notes left me with a lot more questions regarding the town's beloved mayor. He's a part of this. I can feel it in my bones.

The office is exactly what I envisioned. It's on the top floor of the municipal building in the center of the town. The building is old, with wood paneling, wood floors, and a drop ceiling. Just outside his door, there is a relatively small desk where his assistant sits. She's a sweet-looking older woman with warm, green eyes and a kind smile.

Inside his actual office is much of the same, only the paneling stops midway and the top half is painted a warm white, bookcases frame the back wall, and two large camel leather chairs are in the center.

Of course, his desk takes up most of the space along the windows, and behind it is a winged-back chair.

"Your town is truly beautiful," I say, looking at the bookcase, which is filled with photos, trophies, and memorabilia. One of the photos is of the mayor, a beautiful woman with long blonde hair, and a boy who couldn't be more than seven or eight. Another is a ribbon cutting ceremony. Then there's a photo of Emmett, Holden, Spencer, and who I assume is Isaac at a football game. "You knew this quad well?" I ask, pointing to it.

"Everyone knew them well. They're all great men. Losing Isaac Davis was a tragedy to this town, one none of us will get over."

Here's the door I needed to open. "I can imagine, especially at the hands of another person in this town."

Mayor Stengel nods. "Yes, that was definitely another blow. Then to have it go down the way it did and have Brielle injured too. I was beside myself over it all."

I pick up a photo of his family, looking at the faces.

"Did you know Bill well?"

He shrugs, taking the photo from me and placing it back on the shelf. "As well as anyone did, I guess. He wasn't a friendly person, but he wasn't around much."

"Oh? Did he travel a lot?"

"As much as any salesman does."

This is the first I'm hearing of his occupation. Even Sonya didn't seem to know what he did, just that he was changing jobs a lot and he didn't give her any information.

Knowing that I need to tread carefully, I move the conversation back to Emmett and his friends. "I know Emmett missed Rose Canyon when we were deployed together. He always spoke highly of it and the people who lived here."

"We are a close group. A lot of the citizens have lived here for generations. My great-grandfather was the mayor and so was his father and so on. It's a town founded on traditions. I had hoped my own boy would take up the mantle of leadership, but that hasn't been his path so far."

"Oh? What does your son do?"

He shakes his head. "He works for the fire department as of now. He's also training to be a paramedic."

"Is his name Ryan?" I ask.

"Ryan?"

I never would've guessed they were related, especially since they have different last names. "It may not be who I'm thinking of, but I met a Ryan Wilkinson. He actually saved me from being run over in a parking lot."

Mayor Stengel smiles widely. "Oh, that's not my son. Ryan is a good guy, though, and does a lot of volunteer work. I thought you were talking about my wife's first son for a second, his name is Paul Ryan. We all call him Ryan. *My* son's name is Stephen."

That must be a very happy home for Paul. Being named as the other child and not claimed by his stepfather. When I was young, my best friend, Cara, also came from a broken home. We were in this strange club of fathers who left. It was definitely not one I wanted a membership card to, but there we were. In some ways, maybe my father disappearing was the best option because Cara had her own struggles. Her father remarried right after the divorce and had kids with his new wife. She was always . . . the other child.

I remember her crying about how she hated having a distinction that separated her from the rest of her family. She just wanted to be Cara, but it didn't matter to her stepmother or father.

I can only imagine for Paul Ryan that it felt the same.

"Well, I hope to meet them both someday."

The mayor takes a seat, extending his hand for me to do the same. "And how long do you plan to be here, Mrs. Maxwell?"

"It's actually Bennett. I never took Emmett's name."

"How very unconventional of you."

I force a smile. "We are a very unconventional couple."

"My apologies, Ms. Bennett. Are you planning to stay long?"

"I'm not sure. It really depends on several things," I say, keeping my tone light.

"I see. What brought you here to begin with?"

I tilt my head as though that question is mindboggling, which it is. "I came to see if I could save my marriage, why else would I be here?"

The mayor smiles, but there's something underneath it that's almost predatory. "This is a very small town, Ms. Bennett. Let's not pretend you weren't seen sneaking around outside of Bill and Sonya's home."

I laugh a little. "Yes, I was, but that was a misunderstanding."

"What was?"

"The whole thing."

"Yes, but why were you at Sonya Waugh's home?"

I shrug. "Because my husband worked on that case and I wanted to offer support."

He taps his fingers on the desk. "Why don't we dispense with the lies? You are the wife of my sheriff, a wonderful man who this town respects. I am many things, but a fool is not one of them. I know that you're looking into Bill Waugh's death and that you were also a member of the FBI for a period of time. I, too, have friends in the agency."

I lean back, keeping my face impassive. "You've learned a lot about me in the few days I've been here."

"I've done what homework I can. As you can imagine, my goal is to protect this town. So, why are you investigating Bill?"

There's not a chance in hell I'm going to relay anything until he tells me why he wants to know. One of the tactics I learned is to always be the last one to say yes and never show your hand first.

Mayor Stengel already did that by telling me he has a contact who gave information about me, but I have no idea if what he's told me is all he knows. Also, I no longer work for the FBI, so there's nothing they could have told him specifically about why I'm here, aside from that I asked them to place a flag on Bill's name.

"What did the FBI contact tell you?"

"Just that you were interested in Mr. Waugh, but I can't imagine why."

"Does a murderer typically deserve your concern?"

He leans back in his chair, steepling his fingers in front of him. "He was more than just a murderer. He was a husband and a father. Do you not have empathy?"

"Not for men who gun down people, beat their wife and child, and then run, no. I don't typically hold them in high regard."

"I never said high regard."

No, you just have concern for him when there should be nothing but contempt. There is no reason the mayor should be concerned with this unless he doesn't want something uncovered.

"Well, while I don't like you bothering my constituents, I want to make it clear that you're to leave Sonya and Myles alone. They've been through hell these last few months. The children of that youth center have been through enough as well and don't need the reminder of someone being murdered and trying to kill Brielle as well."

I find it odd that he brings up the youth center. Almost as if he's nervous of anyone poking around there. The mayor approved the budget to fund it, and from what I have learned from others in the town, they weren't on board in the beginning, and it almost cost him his job. So why did he agree to use the town funds against the town's wishes?

Maybe he really is a good man and wanted to provide a safe environment for the children here. I've learned that most politicians don't act out of the kindness of their hearts so much as the benefit of lining their pockets. So, what could the mayor possibly get out of having a youth center in his town?

I need to dig into him more. I also have to approach this cautiously, or I'll find myself hitting walls if he starts rumors about me.

"I apologize if I'm coming off defensive. It's just that I have a very hard time with casualties. As you know, my entire job was to save lives, and seeing any family suffer is hard for me."

He nods slowly. "Of course. I owe you an apology myself. You haven't done anything to warrant my suspicion. Protecting the people of Rose Canyon is something I don't play around with."

Time for flattery. "Which you do an exceptional job at. This is a town worth protecting."

Mayor Stengel smiles. "Yes, I agree." He rises, and I follow suit. "Please let me know if I can be of any assistance."

I incline my head. "Thank you, that's extremely kind."

And won't be necessary because the mayor just became a person of interest.

❊

Emmett enters the apartment, tosses his keys into the bowl by the entryway, and sighs when he sees me on the couch.

I made dinner for us, well, I ordered pizza and then plopped myself on the couch with a book.

My brain is on overload, and I need to allow everything to marinate.

"Hi, honey, how was work?" I ask, moving my eyes back to the page.

"It was fine."

"Pizza is in the kitchen."

"Thanks . . ."

"I had an interesting day," I tell him as he enters the kitchen.

"How is that?"

"Well, after you ruined my lunch, I went to the mayor's office and had a nice chat with him."

Emmett exits with a few slices of pizza on a plate. "Nice touch with the BLT today."

"I thought you'd appreciate that."

He rolls his eyes. "You know, I can eat other things."

"That's not the point—"

"I think it is the point, Blakely. We aren't the same people, and just because I eat on a schedule, doesn't mean you know me."

I put the book down and look at him. "Are we finally going to have a meaningful conversation about us?"

It's been days of tiptoeing, and I'm done.

I can't keep pretending that I don't feel anything for this man when I feel everything.

"No. We're not because there is no damn point."

"This could've been our life if we weren't so stupid, you know?

You coming home from work with me here, waiting with dinner. We could've had nights where I wake up drooling on your chest and days where we spent it together like we used to."

He stops moving. "I didn't run away from it, you did."

Finally. Finally, he brought it up. "Yes, I ran. I ran, and do you know why?"

"Because you're a fucking coward."

I blink, and my jaw drops a bit.

Emmett steps toward me. "You're a coward when it comes to feelings or attachment. You are the bravest, most breathtaking woman when you aren't worried about your own safety. I watched you run into the fray like a goddamn warrior if you thought it would help another." He advances with each sentence. "I died a thousand deaths every time you did that, and you never once considered that I would be the one standing over your grave if something happened. You didn't worry or care about that because you were too afraid of it being me who you'd lose."

"Emmett—"

"No, when I got shot, I was terrified. Not just because I'd been shot, but also because I knew I was going to lose you. I was going to watch you drift away because you couldn't handle the idea of loss again. I understood that. I was fucking prepared for it, Blake."

I move to him this time, my heart aching at his words. "I didn't know."

He scoffs. "Of course you didn't. I didn't want you to. But then you showed up at the hospital, and you weren't cold or distant. You were strong and ready to do whatever it took to help. I thought, fuck, this is it. She finally sees that it's not about the possibility of loss anymore. It's about living and losing that person because we didn't try."

"I wanted to try!"

"You ran away in the middle of the fucking night, leaving me on the floor. Don't tell me you wanted to try."

"I did!" The tears fall as the years of hurt surface. "I wanted it. I wanted you! I wanted you and me, but that was fucking terrifying! The last person I loved died in my arms, and then you were shot.

You and I had . . . that night was perfect. Even in all the chaos, we were perfect. I thought that you were the same as me."

He shakes his head. "How the hell was that the same?"

"Because you didn't love me. You and I had a deal, damn it, and you broke it. We promised each other we would never fall in love. We promised we would always be just friends, and then you went and got shot, and I was scared. I realized that you were more! You were more, and I didn't want more!" I step closer, slamming my hand on his chest. "I didn't want more because it was more to lose."

Emmett pulls me against him, and then his mouth crushes mine. My arms are trapped between us, so no matter how much I may want to pull him closer, I can't. The kiss this morning was punishment, but this one is for pleasure.

His hand snakes up my back, fingers tangling in my hair, and then he moans. That sound destroys me. I push against his chest, and he releases me. I give him two seconds to steady his footing and then launch myself into his arms, just like the other night. Emmett catches me, my legs wrap around him, my mouth fuses to his, and I hold on because I know what letting go feels like.

There's no walking out this time.

He kisses me back, pouring the last two and a half years' worth of hell into it. It's not gentle or soft. This is frantic and hostile.

I pull back, holding his face between my palms. "Not again. Not like the other night. Not like a million nights ago. Talk to me and let's stop punishing each other."

"I had no plans on leaving you after that night, and I never should've the other night," he says after a few seconds of us staring at each other.

I close my eyes for a moment. "I wanted to be strong that night and stay. I wished so hard I could stop myself."

"And now? What about now?"

"What about now?" I ask, confused as to what he's asking.

"Are you going to walk out again?"

No. I'll stay, but only if you want me to.

Those words die in my chest. I can't say them.

"Do you want me to stay?"

Emmett steps back, my legs dropping to the ground and my heart following. "That's not what I asked, and until you can answer that, I won't say anything. You wanted to talk, and yet, you can't. Let me know when you decide what you really want, Blake. I'm willing to give you love, but you have to be willing to take it."

And then he walks out the front door.

CHAPTER
Fourteen

BLAKELY

~Four years and ten months ago~

"I'm freezing," I say, rubbing my hands up and down my arms. My teeth are already chattering and the temperature continues to drop. All day long, I've been roasting as we walk through towns in the sandbox, but at night, it's like the air turns to ice around us.

Emmett pulls a blanket from his pack. "Come here."

I attempt to ignore the request and shake my head, but the shivering won't stop, and I no longer care about looking weak. I move beside him, and he wraps the blanket around us before pulling me tight against his side.

The warmth of his body, the fire, and the blanket at least stop the rattling of my teeth. "Th-thanks."

"I can't let you die of hypothermia. Who would save our asses when we're shot?"

I sigh and shake my head. "Maybe you should all try to get shot less then."

"Fair point."

This is our fifth month together out here. I thought all my

training prepared me, but I was a naïve idiot. Nothing could have prepared me for this.

I am starting to think I'm an idiot and picked the wrong job.

It could just be the cold talking, though.

"I'm glad tonight seems quiet," he muses, looking at the sky. "It feels like a gift."

He's right, and I could almost pretend we're not at war and on a date.

"I'm sure since you got saddled with me as your watch companion, it was not a good gift."

He laughs quietly. "You at least talk. McDavis doesn't say two words other than bomb and run."

"Both are good advice considering where we are."

"Yes, but a little conversation wouldn't hurt."

He's not wrong. We are out here, always thinking and watching out for each other and ourselves. There's no real downtime other than nights like this.

We have to stay hunkered down for three more days, keeping our footprints invisible as we wait for further orders. Two teams scout during the day, and at night, we hide in these caves, only allowing a low fire for certain hours before extinguishing it.

"Okay, tell me more about you, Emmett Maxwell."

His chuckle echoes in the cave. "Not much to tell. I'm from a small town in Oregon, where literally nothing happens. I joined the army because I needed to help support my dad, who started having some medical issues, and it seemed like fun."

"Are you having fun?" I ask with a brow raised.

"Aren't you?"

"Not exactly."

Emmett grins. "Then you're looking at this the wrong way."

"Please enlighten me."

"I'm happy to." Emmett leans back against the rock behind him, hands behind his head. "First, we're camping, who doesn't love camping?"

"This isn't camping."

"It is. We're in a cave, we have a fire, and we have sleeping bags."

If that's the case, then this is the worst camping trip I've ever been on. But I guess if he wants to look at it that way, I'm not going to pee in his Cheerios.

"Too bad we don't have marshmallows."

"Then it would be a party. The army doesn't allow parties."

"So, how else is this fun?" I ask.

He shifts, ducking his head to peer just out of the cave. "Look there."

I have to contort myself into the most awkward position to see what he's pointing at. "Umm, what are you looking at?"

"The sky."

"Oh, the joy of that . . ."

He nudges me. "You are seriously missing it."

"It's a sky. We have one at home too."

"And that's the fun. Imagine that, right now, someone else is gazing at the same star."

I sigh and tamper down my giggle. "Okay, Fievel."

"Shut up."

My body starts to shake again. "Can I snuggle again?" I ask. Emmett opens his arm, and I tuck back in. "You're like an electric blanket."

"You are so lucky you're not on watch with Jameston."

I shudder. "I would freeze to death before I cuddled with him."

"So, you like me?" Emmett's teasing tone keeps me from denying it.

As a woman in the service, I always feel like I have to be extra cautious. I have to be nice, but not too nice. I have to make the boys feel comfortable, but never flirt, and I have to have the ability to do everything they can do, but not hurt their fragile male egos.

It's a balancing act that is exhausting.

With a few guys here, I don't have to walk that tightrope as carefully. Emmett being one of those guys.

He never makes me feel small or stupid. He doesn't hit on me, which I'm not sure if I like or not because he's crazy hot. When we're on watch or in the field, he is protective, but not overbearingly so.

I like being deployed with him and his unit.

"I think you're a good guy."

"You like me."

I huff. "I like being on this team with you."

"Because you know I am amazing, just say it, Blake."

"You're so not."

"You're a bad liar," he tosses back.

"When I go to the next team in a few weeks, you're going to hate that I am gone."

Emmett stiffens. "What do you mean a few weeks?"

"I was told that I am probably going to move to a regular unit. That your commanders don't like a female being out here."

"That's not happening."

I glance up at him, finding his strong jawline is tight, and his teeth are clenched. "What's not?"

"You're not leaving."

"That's great you think that . . ."

"I'll make a call about this."

I want to smile and cry at the same time. I have tried so hard to be invaluable out here and prove my worth. There's nothing I won't do to help one of these men when they need me, and it's nice to have verification that one of them is willing to do the same for me.

"You don't have to do that, even though I appreciate it. It's part of this job, isn't it? Being transferred around."

"This team has been together a long time. We don't welcome just anyone into the fold. There's trust, and that comes from us staying as a unit. You're a part of that now, and taking you away would be like cutting off an appendage. I know the other officers feel the same about you, Bennett. We all trust you, and I hope you know that."

I'm momentarily stunned. "Thank you."

"I mean it, and I'm going to fix it."

"Well, you can't fix it that I never leave you. That's impossible."

"Not completely impossible," he says with a laugh and pulls me back against him.

"How so?"

"I could marry you."

I laugh and then cover my mouth to keep the sound from echoing. "Oh, yeah, that's totally a good plan." There is no lack of sarcasm in that reply.

"You asked."

"I didn't think you were completely unhinged."

His laugh moves his chest, but there's no sound. "I would do it to keep you from leaving."

"And imagine all the money we'd make."

"See, our marriage is already looking more appealing. We'd both get a jump in pay and stay together, so our friendship would be sealed for life."

I listen to the beat of his heart as I allow this insane conversation to continue. "We'd have one major issue."

"And what is that?"

"I could never love you."

"I didn't say a thing about love."

I snort. "You'd fall in love with me. Most people do. I am truly wonderful."

"Okay, so rule number one of our marriage is no falling in love."

I sit up, pulling the blanket with me. "And no sex."

"What?"

"We can't have sex." It's really about self-preservation. "Sex leads to feelings, and that would break rule number one."

"I feel like there's a story there."

"Daddy issues." There's nothing really to say. My father left. I have trust issues, and I can't love a man in the military since I'm pretty sure he'll leave. Or cheat . . . or die. All three of those are a no thank you from me.

"I have Mommy issues, so we're a perfect match."

"If this is a proposal, you're doing amazing. I'm totally impressed."

Emmett grins. "No need to impress you since we're not having sex."

"Men. You're all the same. You only give the romance when you're getting something else."

"It goes both ways, sweetheart."

I shake my head. "Okay, so we have friendship, no sex, no love, no romance, extra money, and we will be stationed together?"

"I'm waiting for the downside," he says.

"Well, as much as I hate to bring it up, what about the fact that you'll be married. Like, married. You can't sleep with other women . . ."

Emmett's eyes narrow and he turns his head a bit. "Excuse me? Why the fuck not?"

"Because you'll be a homewrecker if you do that."

"We won't have a home."

"We'll be married."

"On paper."

How do I explain this fictional situation in a way he'll understand? "Well, if either of us had sex with someone else, we'd be in trouble with the command."

He scoffs. "Half the chain of command cheats. Next."

I wish he were lying. "Well, still, what we're talking about here is ten levels of illegal to the military. We would need to keep up appearances."

He rubs his chin. "Okay, you'll have to feign being in love with me. Shouldn't be hard."

I deadpan.

"And you'll be able to fake being in love with me?"

Emmett shrugs. "I'll manage."

"Gee, thanks. That brings us back to the sex."

"I'm waiting for a reason that makes sense."

I bite my lower lip. "I . . . I don't know. Just that it seems wrong."

"Unless we're the ones having sex."

I snort. "That breaks our other rules."

Emmett sighs heavily and rests back on the rock. "Well, there's only one thing to do then."

"What's that?"

"Get married and agree to only sleep with each other, or come to some kind of arrangement that works for both of us."

I burst out laughing. "Fine. We can argue later."

CHAPTER

Fifteen

EMMETT

~Present~

"**G**ood morning, Sheriff," Mrs. James says as she stands in line at RosieBeans.

"Good morning to you as well. It's good to see you."

Holden's aunt is the sweetest woman. When his parents divorced during his senior year in high school and decided they'd rather both leave town, she stepped in and took him in. Thank God because I never thought a divorce could get as ugly as theirs did.

They hated each other after his sister died and used Holden as a pawn. Mrs. James is why he made it out without being completely fucked up. I also like her because she made us cookies and sent me care packages.

"I have been waiting for you to bring that wife of yours around to meet me. Holden tells me she's very sweet."

"Holden has never been the best judge of character."

She scoffs. "Oh, stop it. I'm sure she's lovely if she's married to you."

"You know, I'm thinking of leaving her for someone more worldly."

Her smile lights up the room. "You were always a flirt."

I shrug. It's the only way to get out of a conversation with some of the women in the town—flirt. "I speak the truth."

"Now that's a lie, but I'll let it slide. How is your mama?"

Each time I see her, she asks, and I have the same response each time. "I haven't had a chance to check on her."

My mother decided that, at sixty-two, she no longer wanted to be married. She served my father with papers, packed her shit, and that was the last time I talked to her. About three years ago, she called, but I really wasn't interested in listening. The only person she's kept in touch with is Mama James. Mainly because Mama James is the only person who is too kind to cut her off.

"I'm sure you'll do that soon." She pats my arm.

"Yes, ma'am."

"And your daddy?"

"Good. I'm going to visit him soon."

Like clockwork, I go to the nursing home every Sunday. Maybe I really am predictable.

"You let him know I asked about him."

"I will."

Even though we both know he won't remember it. My father is in the late stages of early onset dementia. He was in his early sixties when he was diagnosed, which was two months after my mother ran off. I watched, day by day, as my father became someone I didn't know. He'd forget me, my sister, or where he lived, but he never forgot my mother.

He still talks about her each time I go, asking if she's okay and if she remembered to do something.

It's heartbreaking to watch.

My father lived with Hannah in our childhood home here. About five years ago, she moved to Pennsylvania and took my father with her. He was miserable, and his dementia seemed to worsen. Once I found out I was being discharged, we decided to move him back to Oregon and put him in a facility that could handle his care. Since being back, he's been doing much better.

"Is Hannah coming back to visit soon?"

I snort. "We both know that's not happening."

She loathes this town and the memories here. "Never count out the power of love, Emmett Maxwell."

"I won't."

"Did you read in the paper about that missing girl in Portland?" I shake my head, and she continues, "Oh, it's a shame. She is the fourth one in the last three months. I'm surprised it hasn't crossed your desk since we're not that far. But it's making headlines now."

Yes, and it's also why Blakely is here, a missing girl.

"What did the article say?"

"Just that they were all runaways, but it was alarming because it's as though they just vanish. One of the missing girls is from California, and her father is kicking up a lot of dust about it. Said his daughter called, saying she met someone online, and he was concerned."

My mind starts to spin. That's what Blake said happened, that the girl she's searching for met Bill on an app and then no one ever saw her again.

"Thank you, Mrs. James. I'm going to make some phone calls and see what I can do to help."

She pats my hand. "You're a wonderful man. I have always loved you as if you were my own."

I laugh. "You called us all hellions."

"And you were. The four of you together were a tornado inside of a hurricane, but separately, you were all beautiful fluffy clouds that I loved."

I lean in and kiss her cheek. "You were always our favorite too."

"Emmett, your order is up," Sommer calls.

"Thanks again. I'll let my father know you asked about him."

"Be safe."

"I always am."

I walk up to the counter, and Sommer hands me my coffee and a danish with her signature smile. "My number is on the bag, if you need it."

I lift my coffee cup. "Thanks for the danish."

"I'm serious."

I don't know how many times I have to turn her down before she takes the hint. "I appreciate it, but I'm married."

"Not for long," she says quietly, but I hear it.

"Bye, Mrs. James. Don't get into trouble down at the church today. I don't want to hear that you ladies got too rowdy."

She laughs. "I'll do my best, but we are a lively bunch."

The six elderly women of the town meet at the church every week to knit blankets and caps for the newborns. They drink coffee, have cake, and talk more shit than anyone else could do in a week. If anyone wants to keep something sacred, they avoid the Six Who Knit.

I'm sure my nuptials will be the main topic of conversation this week. I've seen three of the six this week, and all have asked about Blakely.

I push the door open and slam right into someone, spilling my coffee all over myself and the person I ran into.

"Oh shit!"

"I'm so—"

I look into Blakely's dark brown eyes as she swipes at the coffee on her shirt. "I didn't see you."

"I didn't think you'd run into coffee," I say as I hand her a napkin. "Well, maybe you would."

She laughs once. "No, but I was coming to find you."

I was tired of staring at the ceiling in my bedroom, so I went into work early—very early. I wasn't avoiding her so much as I really didn't want to see her, which is the same thing, but it feels better saying it the other way.

Sommer comes running around the counter. "Emmett! Oh! Are you okay?" She thrusts a rag at me.

"I'm fine." I hand the rag to Blake, asking, "Are you okay?"

She is arching back, trying to keep her shirt off her chest, wiping as she looks up. "I'm good. I've had worse. Thank God it was iced coffee."

I smile. "Very true."

Sommer places her hand on my arm. "Can I get you another?"

"Why don't we worry about my wife first?"

Her eyes bulge, and she pulls her hand away. Maybe having Blakely around isn't such a bad thing.

"Now you want me to be your wife?"

"It's what you are."

"Yes, it is." She throws the rag at me, and I catch it before it hits my face. "Oops."

I could wring her neck. "You're mad because I called you what you are?"

Jesus, she's fucking infuriating.

"No, I'm mad because you left before we could talk! I needed to think. You know that I have to let things percolate before I can make decisions."

"Give me a break! You've had how long to think. You know what you want and what you don't."

She glares at me. "Yeah, and for some dumb reason *you're* what I want!"

CHAPTER

Sixteen

BLAKELY

There. I said it.

His blue eyes widen, and his Adam's apple bobs as he stares at me.

Yeah, I'm pretty stunned too, but it's the truth.

I want him.

Yes, I'm scared to lose him, but we're not in the army anymore. We have safer jobs, and while he's in law enforcement, his risk is low. I can keep running from the truth—and love—or I can grab on with both hands and pray we can make it. I'm choosing him, and if he chooses otherwise, well, I can't control that.

"Emmett?" I say, feeling a whole lot of embarrassment as people start to stop and stare at us.

"You want what?" His voice is measured.

"You."

"Me?"

"I mean, I've said it twice now."

Not sure where the confusion is coming from.

He grabs my wrist and pulls me out of the coffee shop. He really does this a lot. "Where are we going?"

"Outside where no one will listen."

Fat chance of that. I'd bet my right arm these people will have their ears pressed to the glass as soon as we step outside.

When we get to our cars, he stops to face me. God, he's good looking when he's mystified.

"Explain, Blake, because I haven't slept in what feels like a week now, and . . ."

"I want you. I want us. I don't know how much clearer I need to be."

He shakes his head. "You are about as clear as molasses. You move that fast too. Better question, why?"

I push aside the snide comment after I just told him what I want and remember that we are working through a host of trust issues, so I shouldn't be too surprised. "Because I know what life without you in it is like, and I don't want that. Since coming here, I have been happier, more content, and felt safer than I have since the day I walked out your door." I step toward him. "I want to try because giving up hasn't been working well."

His hand lifts, cupping my cheek. "All I've wanted was to make you happy and keep you safe. When you left, I knew chasing you would only make you run farther."

He's right. If he had pursued me, I would've kept him at arm's length. I wasn't ready, and I would've fucked it up even worse because it terrifies me.

"I won't lie, Emmett. I'm scared."

"What is it you're afraid of?"

I stare up at him, studying the planes of his face, the line of his jaw, and those deep blue eyes that know me well. "Losing you. Losing you in a way that I could never get you back. I can't have another flag on my mantle, Emmett. I can't watch another person I love be taken."

His other hand cradles my face, forcing me to keep my gaze on him. "I can't make promises, Blakely. You know that. We don't make promises we can't keep, but I can tell you that I will do everything I can to make sure you never worry about that."

"You're a cop. I'm always going to worry."

"But you've pointed out that I live in a town where nothing

happens. You and I have to trust each other like we did before. We were both in far more danger then, not that I don't think your job now is dangerous, because I do. How can you think I don't worry about you?"

My lips part, and I suck in a soft breath. I honestly never did. I was a combat medic with a team of lunatics, of course I thrived on the thrill and danger, but that was who we were. Now, I do nothing even remotely dangerous. "I'm not in danger."

"You have no idea what you're stepping into. You're searching for a missing girl who may be tied to someone who murdered my best friend, right?"

"Yes."

"And that's the equivalent of an accountant?"

I smile at that. "Hey, they deal with the IRS, who knows what's going on in their heads."

"My point is that we have no guarantees. Hell, Isaac was a high school teacher and coach, and he was gunned down in this parking lot. No one is safe from everything, but if we never try, what's the point in living?"

I lift up on my toes, pressing my lips to his. "I don't want to be afraid anymore."

"Then let me love you."

Our heads stay touching. "I won't leave you this time."

He kisses me then, slowly and sweetly, until we hear a few hoots and hollers from the café, breaking the moment.

Once I change my shirt, I head to visit with Sonya again to see if she's had a chance to go through Bill's things to see if anything stuck out as strange.

My phone rings as I get in the car. I smile widely when I see it's Emmett. Jesus, not even thirty minutes after agreeing to date as a married couple and I'm a lovesick puppy. I am not going to like this part of myself.

"Hey. Miss me already?"

He laughs once. "I wish it was for that. Where are you now?"

"I'm just getting in the car to head to Sonya's. Why?"

"I'm going to send George to pick you up in the squad car."

"For what?"

Emmett releases a heavy sigh. "Blake, just get in the damn car. You'll want to come see this."

I roll my eyes. "Fine. I'll see you soon."

He hangs up, and I get out of my rental car and lean against the hood to wait for my chariot to escort me to wherever I am needed.

As I stand here, a couple exits the apartment building. The woman waves, and the guy grabs her arm. "Blakely?" he calls to me, but the sun is bright, and I have to shield my eyes so I can see who it is.

"Hey, Ryan!"

"Don't step too far in the street, you may get hit."

"Funny," I say with a laugh.

"This is Tessa, she lives here . . . wait, is this where you live?"

"I'm just staying here, kind of visiting. I live in DC —technically."

"Who are you visiting?" Tessa asks. "Sorry, I'm a little nosey, but I know everyone here. My husband is the super, well, he sort of is. He has another job too."

My eyes pop open because Ryan totally hit on me, and now I find out he's married. "You're the super here?" I ask, moving the question back to him.

"I'm not her husband," he says quickly. "Nick is."

"Oh, I'm sorry, I totally thought—"

Tessa laughs. "No way! Nick, Stephen, and Ryan are best friends. They grew up together and are totally connected at the hip. Marry one, you marry them all is what everyone said. He's here because I needed someone to check my blood pressure. I was getting high readings, and sometimes I get nervous because I'm just a few weeks pregnant. I was so scared that something was wrong, so Nick called Ryan and he came, but we're going to take a walk and calm myself."

"Congratulations on the baby," I say, still unpacking all she said.

"Thank you. I'm not crazy, I swear. I'm a nurse, so you'd think I would be able to do this myself, but I lost a baby six months ago, and . . . I'm a little terrified."

The look in her eyes and the pain in her voice are enough to cause a pang in my black heart. "I'm so sorry. I'm glad that Ryan was able to help you out. You're all very lucky to have each other."

Tessa nods. "I think so. But I just totally unloaded on you! Can we blame the hormones? I promise it was them."

I smile. "It's always the hormones."

Ryan snorts. "She's always this way. She rambles nonstop."

Tessa shrugs. "Whatever. You never said, though, who are you visiting?" Tessa asks.

"Oh, Emmett Maxwell."

"The sheriff! How wonderful! We love Emmett, and it's been such a comfort having him in the building. I didn't know he had someone staying with him."

"Well, to be fair," I say with a smile, "I was supposed to stay in Brielle's apartment, but they sort of forced the two of us into his place."

Ryan's eyes narrow just slightly. "I thought you were married."

"I am. To Emmett."

Tessa's mouth opens into a large O. She stares at me and then squeals. "You're the wife! This is what I was telling you about earlier, Ryan. Emmett was rumored to be married to someone very beautiful, and here you are! Stunning—and his wife. Wow, what an amazing story you two must have. I heard you were in the war with him?"

Lord this girl can talk. Maybe I should've befriended Tessa in the beginning. I would bet she knows everything that goes on here. "Yes, we served together."

"But he was an Army Ranger, right?"

"He was. I was attached to them as a combat medic."

"Wow! That's incredible. And how did you get married? Was it one of those amazing love stories where you locked eyes across the battlefield and just knew? I always thought that would make a romantic story."

Ryan laughs, placing both hands on her shoulders. "Okay, crazy lady, let's get you into the shade."

She slaps his stomach. "Shut up."

"You're rambling on about shit that isn't your business. How about you let her talk while you come up for air?" Ryan chides.

"It's fine. Honestly, we got married for . . . well, it doesn't matter. It wasn't glamorous or romantic, but it's sort of us."

None of that is a lie. We weren't planned, and we sure as hell aren't conventional, but I wouldn't trade it for anything.

"But you're here now!" Tessa says with her voice rising a bit. "That's exciting, and you are staying with him. I'm a romantic, and I am going to hope for the best."

"I'll take whatever sunshine and good vibes you are willing to share." The police cruiser pulls up, and Deputy Holman hits the horn twice. "That's my ride. It was great meeting you, Tessa, and good to see you again, Ryan."

I open the door and smile at my old friend. "Hello, George."

He sighs through his nose. "Do you have any weapons I should be aware of?"

I fight back the urge to laugh. "I do not, but if I wanted to cause you harm, I wouldn't admit to having a weapon. Not to mention there's not much more damaging than my hands. I could probably kill you with them."

George rears back. "Maybe you should get in the back behind the glass."

Now I can't help it. "But where would the adventure be in that for our super fun car ride?"

I get in the front seat before he can place me back there. I doubt Emmett would be happy with him if that happened anyway.

We drive in silence, but the radio randomly goes off as whoever the other deputy is handles a traffic stop.

"Busy day?" I ask after fifteen minutes.

I like the silence, but this is painful.

"Yup."

"How did you get stuck with this job?"

He shrugs. "I'm just lucky, I guess."

We can go with that. It's better than a one-word answer. "Speaking of luck, I never heard, are you married?"

"Nope."

"Could be your lack of communication skills," I say under my breath. "Is there anyone you have your eye on?"

George looks over at me, eyeing me curiously. "Maybe."

I can work with maybe. "Oh?"

"She's a doctor."

That could be a challenge setting his sights high, but who knows. Maybe George Holman is a genius under all that . . . well, not smart exterior. "Have you asked her out yet?"

"No."

Okay, I can't do this. He's on his own with this. "Where are we heading? Should I let someone know my location?"

"We're heading to the hospital."

"Is Emmett hurt?" I ask, worry filling me.

"No. Why would he be?"

"Because he called and told me you were coming to get me and no other information."

George shrugs. "He asked me to come pick you up for him and bring you to the hospital. That's all I know."

"Okay."

Still means nothing. He could be hurt and didn't want to let me know until I got there, or maybe he didn't tell George for a host of reasons. I am going to be a damn wreck for the rest of this trip.

"How long before we're there?" I ask.

He points over to a building. "Two minutes."

Two minutes I can do.

George grabs his radio and calls to Emmett, informing him of his location.

Emmett's deep voice echoes in the squad car. "I'll be out front waiting."

We pull into the circular entrance, and sure enough, Emmett is there, and I let out a deep breath. He's fine and not in a wheelchair. Not sure why he has me here, but if it's not because he's hurt, then I'm fine with whatever it is.

He opens my door and helps me out. "How sweet."

"Don't act so surprised."

I grin. "You owe me for that car ride. So, why am I at the hospital?"

"After I left the coffee shop, I called the police chief in Portland. He grew up in Rose Canyon, and with the increase of chatter about several missing girls in his town, I wanted to talk to him about it and see what I could find out. He mentioned they had three Jane Does right now. I wanted to have you look at them and see if any were your missing person or anyone you recognized from the case with the agency."

I really hope none of them are Keeley. I want to find her and bring her home so she can heal in whatever way she can.

I nod.

We walk down to the morgue and find Holden with the medical examiner.

"We are on a video call with the ME in Portland," Holden explains. "We'll show you three photos, and you just have to let us know if you recognize any."

"I understand."

The first girl pops up, and while I have seen more dead bodies than I care to admit, this one causes me to gasp. It's not Keeley, but the girl is no more than thirteen with blonde hair and a future that was stolen.

I look to Emmett and shake my head. "That's not her."

"I'll show you the next image." The ME there flashes a new photo up.

This one could be Keeley, but I don't think it is. She's thin and has dark hair, but her face doesn't have the same contours. It's hard when you're looking at a photo, and the pictures I have of Keeley are at least a year old. "Does she have a scar behind her right ear?" I ask.

"She does not."

"What about a tattoo on her ankle? Her best friend said they both got them a month before she went missing."

The ME pauses. "She does. She has a butterfly."

I breathe a sigh of relief. "It's not her."

"Okay, here's the last photo."

I wait, my body growing tight, praying it's not her. I don't want to have to give that news to her family. I don't want for her life to be gone and this case to end this way.

She pulls it up on the screen, and I could weep. I have to hold back the tears. It's her. The contour of her nose is the same as Keeley's, and the birth mark under her right eye is the same. Before I can ask, the ME clears her throat. "She has a tattoo of a—"

"Broken heart."

The medical examiner nods with her eyes downcast.

That's what I thought. "It's her. Her name was Keeley McLain, and her parents are Daniel and Meredith McLain."

A hand rests on my shoulder, and I turn into Emmett's chest. I don't know why it's hitting me so hard, but my lungs are tight and a tear falls. Emmett's strong arms wrap around me, holding me together as I feel like falling apart.

This isn't my daughter or friend, but she mattered. Her family loved her enough to hire me when the police wrote their daughter off as a runaway.

I look up. "I have to tell her family."

"I know."

I never had to make the notification before, but I always called to offer any additional information to the family that I could. I was often the last person they saw.

"Sheriff," the medical examiner in Portland says. "I'm going to send over the official autopsy report, but I want you all to be aware that the cause of death was an overdose. There are puncture marks along her arms and legs. It's unclear whether she was doing it or someone else was injecting her, but her toxicology reports will also be in there. I'm happy to answer anything for the family as well."

"Thank you," I reply to her.

The screen goes blank and my heart sinks. Emmett's hand moves to my neck, his thumb brushing back and forth. "I'm sorry, baby."

Me too. I am so sorry this is the ending of Keeley's story. "Who would do this?" I ask, almost absently.

"I don't know, but we're going to find out."

CHAPTER
Seventeen

EMMETT

I find Spencer in his office, reading over something on his computer screen. "Are you back to writing?" I ask.

He looks up, slightly startled. "You could announce yourself before you make it back here."

"Where's the fun in letting you know I'm here? Besides, you clearly need your senses sharpened if I was able to get the drop on you."

He flips me off. "My senses are plenty sharp."

"Did you hear about the missing girls?" I ask, cutting to the reason why I'm here.

"I did."

"And?"

"And what?"

Of all the things Spencer is, stupid isn't one. He's sharp and his mind is always five steps ahead of everyone else's. It's like a puzzle in his brain that no one else can see until it's done, and then it makes sense. He has thoughts on this, I know he does.

"Dude."

His smile grows. "Fine. I think that someone is taking runaways. I think that Bill's message at the end was about that.

There was something in Brie's notes about Myles that I never thought much about, but I wonder . . ."

"Wonder what?"

He rummages through the file and then points. "Myles told Brie that his dad was going to see a friend in Maryland and would be gone a few days. Maryland had no bearing on Brielle's memory, but depending on where he was, it could've been the DC area. If he met with Keeley and someone else there, it would be a connection to these missing girls."

"It's a great theory, but we have no idea who that other person he met with is. Plus, meeting people isn't a crime. What about the money?" I question.

"He traveled a lot, but he worked for the water plant, which isn't exactly lucrative and doesn't require their contractors to travel unless there is a natural disaster or something like that."

"That's true, but wasn't he part of the clean-up crew, though?" I vaguely remember him saying that. "Maybe he went into the field more often."

"That's true."

"I wish his phone had been retrieved. Sonya said he smashed it and threw it out the window when they left town. That would answer so much. I've asked for a subpoena, but you know it takes weeks to get anything back."

Spencer nods. "Not to mention how long it'll take that company to reply. If we had the phone, we could send it to Mark and have their tech guys scrub it."

"Maybe I can send George to look for any remnants, with any luck, we can find the SIM card or something salvageable."

It's been months, so there's no telling if anything remains or can be used, but it's worth a try. Keeley is dead, and if this ties to Bill, I'll try anything.

He rises, goes to the corkboard, and flips it over to reveal hundreds of different bits of information that he dug up when he was trying to help Brielle retrace years of her life. "If you tell Brielle about this, I'll fucking kill you."

"You kept this up?"

"I never felt certain I wouldn't need this information again," he explains. "I covered it so she'd never see it, but I wasn't going to just let this all go. Not when he basically told us it wasn't over."

Makes sense. "Anything there worth looking at?"

I walk over, tracing the lines he drew that connected Isaac, Brie, Bill Waugh, her co-workers, and others in the town. "You have the mayor's son on here?"

"I hate that kid," Spencer says. "I have him down because he's an adult spending far too much time at the youth center. When her office was trashed, it made sense to mark him as a possible suspect, I guess."

"Well, one of the girls who worked there filed a police report claiming he assaulted her, but she dropped the charges a day later."

Spencer's brows lift. "His father stepped in?"

"What do you think?" I counter.

"Yeah, his father is always bailing him out."

"But not his brother." Paul is never afforded the same perks. He's not seen as the mayor's son.

"Very true. Maybe we should put Paul on here."

"Doesn't hurt to keep our options open."

Spencer writes Paul's name and then turns to me. "How did it go with the ME? Anything new there?"

"One of the girls from Portland was Blakely's case."

His eyes widen. "Interesting."

"That's a word."

"Sorry, I mean, it's horrific, but that leads me to wonder how a runaway got from Virginia to Oregon? Blakely mentioned Keeley and Bill having contact through a dating app, but is there anything else linking her to him?"

"Not that I know of, but I've put in a call to the Chief in Portland so I can get a copy of the police report from the night she was found. Maybe there was something at the scene, or a witness saw something."

"And what does all that mean for you?" Spencer asks.

"That I'm going to start an off-the-books investigation to see if anyone in our town knows more about Bill than we thought or is involved and we missed something bigger."

Not sure what the fuck else he thinks I would do.

"Well, tomorrow will be the perfect time."

"Don't remind me."

"Please, the town festival is everyone's favorite thing. Not to mention, everyone lets their guard down at things like that. If there's a bunch of us watching, we may notice something."

It's possible, but I don't think the person involved is dumb enough to do something at the festival.

"I guess, that's if people manage to drag their focus from Blakely long enough to talk to each other."

He laughs. "They're like sharks, they smell blood in the water."

"Well, it's not like she doesn't deserve a little of this."

Spencer flips the board back over. "They drive us crazy and yet we love them."

"True."

"So, what's your plan?"

"I already told you." Does he even listen? "We'll observe."

"You're an idiot. I mean with your wife who you don't want. Is she going home? Staying here? Did you guys finally kiss and make up?"

My friends are goddamn idiots. "None of your business."

Also, I have no idea. I love her, but I am not moving to Virginia, and I don't know if she wants to come here. There is a lot of shit to work out, and right now might not be the time to talk about any of it.

However, I can't forget the way she melted against me as though she knew I wouldn't let any harm come to her, even if I had to go to hell to battle the devil himself.

"So, you have no plan regarding Blake?"

"I have nothing to say to you."

"Look," Spencer says as he blows out a long breath, "I spent a lot of time tiptoeing around my feelings for Brie. I knew I loved her, and I was so sure I was going to fuck it up, that I didn't shout it from the rooftops like I should have. Don't do that. If you want her, tell her and do whatever you need to so you don't lose her."

"Is that your Ted Talk?"

"Yup."

"It sucked," I lie.

"Well, I think Isaac would've told you the same thing. He wasn't afraid of love. He was afraid of losing the people he loved, so he let us all know. I think that's where the rest of us are getting it wrong."

I shake my head, wondering who in the hell this dude is. "When did you become like this?"

"When I lost Brielle. You share that burden, Emmett. You know what losing someone you love is like, and why you would even entertain allowing it again, I have no idea."

"I don't plan to lose her."

"Good. Now, go to your wife and fix your life."

"And what about this information?"

Spencer smiles. "We dig."

I open the door to my apartment and the scent of pizza is in the air. I smile because this was our thing. Pizza and beer after a long day.

"Blake?"

"Hey! I'm in the kitchen!"

"Making pizza?" I ask.

"No! I ordered. But I made something else . . ."

Now I'm intrigued. "I'll be there in a minute. I'm going to change."

"K!"

I walk back into my room, which is a damn disaster. I forgot what a mess this woman is. There are clothes thrown all over, her bag is open with things hanging out of the side, and I almost don't want to look in the bathroom since she's been home for hours and I'm sure it's a disaster.

I toss my uniform in the hamper, grateful I have two days off, and lock my gun. Then I pull on shorts and a sleeveless sweatshirt I've had since college.

When I make my way into the kitchen, she's standing there with a cake and a grin and . . . nothing else.

I blink, my mouth extremely dry as I take in every curve and angle of her body. She's even more beautiful than I remembered, and I've done a lot of remembering over the years. I thought I knew her body better than my own, but seeing her naked in my kitchen proves how much of a disservice that fantasy was.

"What are you doing?" I manage to get the words out.

"See, I feel like we did things wrong, you know? We didn't have a real wedding, a cake, a honeymoon, or any of that. Our version of dating was talking in a cave after a firefight."

I smile. "I thought it was romantic."

"It was our version of it, but maybe that's where we screwed up. Maybe we needed the roses, dates, and cake. Maybe we needed the nights without gunfire?"

I move toward her, wanting to have my cake and eat her too. She stays put, watching me with lust swimming in those brown eyes.

My finger slides across the icing, and I bring it to her lips, running it along the seam of her lips. "There's a lot we could do with cake and roses and champagne."

Her brows lift in question. "Oh?"

I take the cake from her and set it on the counter before swiping another fingerful of icing. "A lot more," I say low and rough. Then I slide my finger down her neck, stopping right before the swell of her breast.

I really want to put some there and spend hours licking it off.

"I didn't know you were so inventive with food."

My thumb rubs against her sugary lips, and I nod. "I think I'm more inventive with you, sweetheart."

"What plans do you have, husband?"

That word sends a pulse down my body, stopping at my cock. God, I want to take her right here, remind her that I am, in fact, her damn husband, and she's my wife. She's mine, and I am never going to let her forget it again.

This time, I want to make it special. I don't want desperation or fear because I'd just been shot. I don't want anger after she showed up in my life uninvited. I want her, vulnerable to me.

"First, I think you have some food on you, I should make sure it doesn't get sticky." I bring my mouth to her neck first, running my tongue down her smooth skin, licking up the icing.

"Did you get it all?"

"Not even close."

"I have some on my lips."

"Does it taste good?" I ask.

Her tongue darts out, not removing it all, and she moans. "Very, but I think it needs something else."

"What's that?" I really fucking hope her answer is my cock.

The grin on her lips tells me it is exactly that. Blake pushes my chest just a little, and then, keeping her eyes on me, she sinks to her knees.

"Blake . . ."

"Let me, Emmett. Let me, please."

I close my eyes, releasing a breath through my nose. She slides the shorts off with ease and runs her fingernails lightly down my thighs. "You're going to be the death of me," I manage to get out before her hand wraps around my cock.

"Then I hope you go after I'm done."

She takes me deep into her throat. My knees buckle, and I catch myself on the counter, holding on tight. Blake's head bobs in perfect rhythm, moving between shallow and deep as she feels the change in my body.

I have dreamed of her mouth around my cock so many times, and it was nothing compared to this.

Nothing.

Her hand moves along with her mouth for a while, then she releases me, kissing down my shaft before licking my balls.

"Fuck, Blake, I can't take more."

"Oh, but you must."

I shake my head, fingers so tight on the counter my knuckles are white. "Remember you're next, love. I am going to cover you with icing," I say, but she moans as she sucks me deep again and then stops.

"Talk if you want me to suck. If not, I'll assume you're not enjoying it."

I look to the ceiling, hating and loving every moment of this. Focusing on anything but her is impossible, but this is the game we play. We both love this part of who we are, the way we push each other.

"Once you're dirty, it'll be my job to clean you." My voice cracks as she runs her tongue around the head. "I'm going to lick every fucking inch of your skin. I'm going to make you come on my tongue and then on my cock. I'm going to take you over and over again, make your body forget everything but me and how you feel when I'm inside you."

Her movements grow a bit frantic, and I make the mistake of glancing down at her.

She's a fucking goddess before me. I push off the counter, demanding my legs keep me upright so I can watch her better. She squirms a little, and I know she needs relief.

"Touch yourself, Blake," I command. I rub my thumb against her cheek. "Show me how you wish I was there, between your legs. Show me how you'd want me to touch you if I could right now."

Her hand sinks down on a long moan.

"That's it, gorgeous. Touch your clit for me, imagine my hand there. Would it feel good?"

Her eyes close, and I take that as a yes.

"I would put pressure there, right where you want it, rubbing until you were shaking." I see her struggling to catch her breath.

"I'm going to move because your mouth is heaven." She opens her jaw a bit, and I flex my hips. My hand is on her head now, making sure I keep the angle. "I'm so close, but I am not going to come like this. I am going to hold off because I want to be inside you when I finish. I want to do all the things I couldn't the last time." I pump again, holding on to my self-control. "Put a finger inside, Blake, feel how wet you are for me?"

She groans, and I am done.

I can't keep going.

I pull back, and she gasps. Then I'm on the ground, pushing her against the cold tile floor and settling myself between her open thighs.

"Emmett . . ."

"You need me, don't you?"

She looks up, brown eyes fixated on me. "Yes."

"Good."

I could toy with her, but I don't. I am far too anxious for it too. I lick her pussy, long and slow, tasting her and knowing there will never be enough of this. I want to have her every damn day.

Blake tries to move, but I hold her where I want her, listening to her quickening breaths and what almost sounds like sobs. I flick her clit, over and over until she tries to squeeze my head with her legs.

"Fuck! Emmett! I can't . . ." She sits up, hands in my hair. "Now!"

I didn't need her to tell me, I can feel her body tighten and am already giving her more. I make every second count, loving her with my mouth until she falls slack against the floor.

I lift my head slowly and then slink up her body.

She is struggling for breath as her eyelids flutter open. My heart is in my hand, ready for her to take it. Her fingers touch my cheek. "I have regretted leaving every day since it happened. I thought of you, wanted to make it right, but I didn't know how. I am sorry I broke us, Emmett. Please don't break my heart after tonight. Don't leave me."

I lean down, pressing my forehead to hers. "The only way I'll leave you is if I'm dead, and even then, I think I'd find a way back to you."

She laughs a little, but I feel the warm tear that falls between us. "I want you to make love to me."

I smile at that. "I plan to."

And then I slide into her and give her everything I have.

CHAPTER
Eighteen
EMMETT

I roll over, expecting to find Blakely beside me, but there's nothing but cold sheets. Immediately, I sit up, wondering if she fucking left again.

Hastily, I slip on my shorts and head to look, anger starting to build. This woman needs shackles or a jail cell to keep her from making rash decisions.

When I get to the end of the hallway, I find her sitting on the couch. She didn't leave.

Relief floods me, but it takes a second for my heart to calm.

Her legs are tucked under her, and her hair is in a loose braid that hangs over her shoulder. She's sipping tea and flipping through the notebook Spencer gave her the other day.

"Are you planning to sleep at all?" I ask.

She looks up with a smile. "No. Someone had my blood pressure up."

"Who might that be?"

"You."

I walk over to her, feeling rather proud of myself. "I thought you were supposed to be exhausted after that many orgasms." I flop down beside her, leaning on one elbow to be closer to her.

She shakes her head. "I was, but you were snoring, and I'd forgotten how freaking loud you are."

"If I recall correctly, you snore just as badly."

"I do not!"

Yes, she does. "It's fine. I love you regardless."

Blakely grins and then shifts to kiss my nose. "I love you regardless too."

I refuse to say anything about the fact that she admitted her feelings. Lord knows she may rush out the front door with her running tendencies.

"So, are you not going to sleep?" I ask, keeping my tone even.

"Nope. What about you?"

"No," I say, not having any intentions of sleeping but having every intention of getting her back into bed.

She returns to the notebook, scanning the page as I lie down and rest my head on her lap. "What are your thoughts on the mayor's son?"

Now I'm awake again. "Which one?"

"Stephen. I find it interesting that, a few years ago, he was being threatened with jail time for an alleged assault on a woman, and now he's an upstanding member of the community?"

This is the second person in the last six hours to mention him.

I sit up, pulling her legs across mine. "I wouldn't say upstanding, but he was never charged with anything. The girl dropped the claim, so I don't think it's fair we just assume he's involved. Plus, assault and abducting girls isn't the same."

"I'm not saying that, but he is one of the few people Spencer references as having ties to Bill."

"They worked together, but they weren't tied together."

Blake puts the notebook down. "Forget about Stephen and Bill. Let's talk about the connections between the girls." She bounces to the next topic. "I don't think it's a coincidence that all the girls were runaways. They would've been easy targets to abduct."

"I don't think so either, but the fact is, we don't have anything substantial that ties Bill, Stephen, the mayor, or anyone for that matter to abducting and drugging girls. All we have is a photo of

Bill and Keeley that was taken shortly before she was reported as missing. There is also the fact that she ended up in Portland, which could be Bill's doing but could also be a million other people as well. Portland has two other Jane Does, neither of whom have any obvious tie to Bill or Rose Canyon."

"Yet!"

"Yet. But everything else is a lot of guessing and leaps. Until you have something concrete . . ."

"That's what investigating is, Emmett. It's theories and gut feelings. It's looking at the angles, making guesses and seeing if there's evidence to support them. You know that."

I nod. She's right. We have to examine anything and everything. Between all of us, we'll find something, and then we'll know which direction to run. Sometimes you have to trust your gut and pray you find what's there. What I do know is that three girls are dead and one was last seen with Bill. If there's more to it, then I'm going to find it.

I sigh heavily. "We're not going to solve it tonight, sweetheart. Let's go to bed and worry about it in the morning."

"I can't sleep," she admits. "After having to tell Keeley's parents and answer what questions I could for them, it's just . . . I don't know."

"I can help you forget."

Blake grins. "I bet you could."

"Do you want that, love?" I ask, running my hand up her leg.

"I could go with a little forgetting . . ."

And I help her do just that.

We spend the day together—mostly naked, which works for me. And then my phone is blowing up with messages about the festival, where and when we should meet, can they park here since we're closer, blah, blah, blah.

The phone pings again, and Blake looks over. "Do you have a girlfriend who is upset your wife is back in town?"

I snort. "I don't have the emotional capacity for another woman in my life. You're like fifteen versions of crazy all balled in one."

She glares at me. "You'll pay for that."

"I assumed I would."

"So, why is your phone suddenly going crazy? Is it work?"

I shake my head. "It's about the festival. Holden is coming here, we'll meet Spencer and Brie there, and the entire town is awaiting your arrival."

Blakely's jaw drops. "I'm sorry, what?"

"Did you not see the signs everywhere?"

"I did, but I wasn't planning to go."

"For a private investigator, you kind of suck."

With her arms crossed, she purses her lips. God she's cute when she's pissed off. "I wouldn't talk about that if I were you."

"Listen, we had almost years' worth of video footage to sort through to find out the parent that Brielle argued with. It was a grainy image, so no one was even sure it was her at one point. Let's not act like I had anything to go off. I had a crazy mayor, devastated friends, and I was a little off my game."

"You had a missing kid who would've led you right to the killer."

"A child who had no connection to Isaac, a thin connection to Brielle, and who was never reported as missing because it was the summer and his mother and father were with him. Yes, a total clue there."

Believe me, I'm not proud of the fact we didn't catch the killer right away. We have limited resources, untrained officers, and there was almost no evidence at the scene. I did the best I could with what I had. Thankfully, Spencer was able to get someone to digitally enhance that image.

"I wasn't there and you're right, the evidence and resources you had put you at a disadvantage."

I release a heavy breath. "I tried, but I was also devastated . . . the whole town was. We've spent a lot of energy moving on. It may sound strange, but losing Isaac was like losing a member of your family. Everyone hurt. Everyone struggled. We canceled everything, and this festival is the first big event since his death."

We had the MOTY awards, but even that was scaled down. Usually there is a huge event after, but I didn't want that. So we had the dinner and that was it.

"I'm glad you're having it then. So what should I expect at this festival?"

"First, it's a small-town festival, so there will be a lot of nothing. Don't get too excited about that. Second, *everyone* goes. Doesn't matter what you're doing, you show your face. So, that means you'll be exposed to everyone in the town."

Blake nods. "That's okay. I can people watch."

"*However*, you won't have a chance to observe people because I promise, you won't have a free minute to think. You're going to be the center of the show."

"What makes them think I'll be there?"

"You're my wife," I say as though it should be obvious.

She stares blankly. "I'm waiting for further explanation."

"You're the wife of a small-town cop. You have to go."

"Does it matter that I married you before you were the sheriff?"

"Nope."

I don't invent the rules, I just enforce them . . . with all the skills of a butcher with a dull knife based on the look she's giving me.

"That's ridiculous."

"Maybe so, but it works for all our benefits. You'll see everyone, we'll watch them, and you'll also get a chance to talk to people you probably wouldn't approach."

The only issue is Blakely doesn't really love talking to people. Or people really.

"This is my future, isn't it?"

I take her hand in mine. "What do you want our future to be?"

Blakely's eyes move to the rug, and I wait. One of the mistakes I've made is not letting her process. She doesn't make any decision quickly, not ones that truly matter to her at least. She has to think, work through it, and allow herself time to consider each avenue before she decides which path she wants to walk down.

"I know I want us. Do you?"

"Yes. I have always wanted us."

Her brown eyes shimmer with emotion. "I don't know how we do this. Where do we live? How do we date being married?"

"Do you like DC?"

"I don't know."

"Do you want to stay there?"

I want her with me in this small town, a place we can build a life together. As much as I wish it would be easy to just pick up and go, it's not. I have to think about my father and his well-being too.

"It's not about where we'll live so much. It's that we're married, but we have never allowed our feelings to be real. Now, it's like I have all the feelings."

I smile, dropping the moving talk and attempting to keep it light. "Good ones?"

"And scary ones. You're my husband—legally, but are we really a couple? You know? The sex is fantastic, so you're winning on that score. I know you love me, another smart decision. All of this is good, but I worry about the bad. When we fight."

"We make up."

She lifts her finger to my lips. "Shh. I'm talking a real fight. We don't really fight, we just have hurt the other, you know . . . not speaking, divorce papers—"

"I called the lawyer yesterday."

"I'm sorry, what?"

"I called my lawyer and told him to revoke the divorce filing or whatever he has to do. I canceled it—essentially."

It takes her a second to compose herself before speaking again. "You canceled it? Like an insurance plan you no longer need."

"Basically. I have to fill out a new form, sign some papers, but yeah . . ."

"Huh." She sits back, dropping my hand from hers.

This isn't going as planned. "I thought you'd be happy about this."

"I am," she says quickly. "I just didn't expect you to do it so fast. Like, we've been together a few days, and you already decided."

Here we go. It's like fight or flight constantly with her. "Blake, look at me." She does. "The scary is there for me too. I'm just not afraid of trying. I'm not worried about when we fight because we've been fighting since the day we met—for covers, warmth, friendship, and trust. I know who you are when you don't know yourself. You and I, though, we're *worth* fighting for. There is no one else I want to be pissed off at."

A tear falls down her cheek. "That was sweet."

"It was true." I lean in and kiss her. "I didn't want to divorce you because I didn't want you. I wanted to divorce you because I loved you and couldn't make it stop. Each time someone talked about their wife, it made me hate where we were. I watched Spencer fall in love with Brielle, and it killed me. My best friend, who was never going to get married, fell so hard. Isaac and Addy, they had the love of a lifetime, and she lost him. In that tragedy, I saw how love could hurt and also save. I need the damn hurt to stop."

"And has it?" Her sweet voice asks softly.

"Only since you came back."

"Then let's make sure it never hurts again, for either of us."

That's a plan I can live with.

CHAPTER
Nineteen
BLAKELY

Deep breath in. Deep breath out.

   I can do this.

I have walked through firefights and IED minefields. I am Blakely fucking Bennett-Maxwell.

Oh God, here it comes again.

No, no way. I am fine. I am the sheriff's wife, and I am a badass. Who cares that there is an entire town full of people who want to meet me and interrogate me? I am cool as a cucumber.

"Blake?" I jump at the sound of my name but turn to find Brielle walking toward me. "Sorry! I didn't mean to scare you."

I force a smile and exhale. "I'm just a little nervous."

"Don't be, Addy and I will be with you the whole time." She glances back. "Where the hell is she?"

Addison comes around the corner with her daughter in the stroller. "Sorry! Elodie dropped her favorite football, and I had to run back to find it. You look great, Blake."

I glance down at the dress I'm wearing and shift. "Thanks . . . I appreciate you letting me borrow it," I say to Brie.

I didn't come with a full wardrobe, and thankfully, we are about the same size.

"It looks much better on you than it did on me."

"I doubt that, but I appreciate it."

Brie winks and turns to Addison. "She's nervous."

"Of course she is. It's not easy being an outsider here."

I nod. "You can say that."

"Everyone is really nice. They'll ask their dumb questions, and Brie and I will do our best to intervene. The worst will be the Six Who Knit."

I blink at that. "I'm sorry, the what?"

Brielle laughs. "It's six old women who literally knit at the church and talk more shit than you could ever imagine. They know everything and love nothing more than gossip."

"Wow, a knitting gang."

Addison rests her hand on my shoulder. "You'll be fine. I promise. Where's Emmett?"

"He was supposed to be off but ended up needing to be on duty. George requested his help, and it's a good thing he did because there was an issue at one of the tents, something about encroaching and an unauthorized bench. He instructed me to wait here for you guys and Spencer and Holden."

"They should be here soon," Brie explains. "They had to go deface the MOTY parking spot."

"The what?" I ask.

She rolls her eyes. "MOTY is Man of the Year, who happens to be Emmett this year. Spencer and Holden are asshats and put a caution tape and a tarp over it last night. Then the idiots went and pulled Mr. Scanlon's tent over to encroach on Mr. Pennington's space—who hate each other—and are finishing their painting in Emmett's honor."

Oh, he's going to love that. "It's safe to assume it's not a nice painting?"

Addy snorts. "Not even a slim chance of that. When Isaac was nominated, Spencer and Emmett painted a life-size photo of him wearing a Speedo in his driveway."

"So, this is a thing with them?"

Brielle sighs. "They'll do anything to embarrass the other."

Sounds like the military.

"Well, I hope it's something good they did to Emmett then."
I'm all for a good prank.

"I'm sure it is. I wanted no part in it," Brie says, glancing behind her. "Well, I don't know where they are, but the sooner we get in there, the sooner this'll be over."

"Then let's go and make the best of it."

We walk into the festival, and I am blown away. The streets are lined with vendor tents all the way down, all of the stores have flags hanging off them, and at the far end there is a Ferris wheel as well as some other rides. As we walk a little farther, the smell of fresh cookies hits me, making my mouth water.

Several people stop me, talking, explaining who they are. I'm turned left and then right and then left. Where the hell is the group?

Another man introduces himself, tells me all about his daughter who wants to join the army. I nod, not remembering anyone's name and trying to focus.

When I get a short reprieve, I look around for Brielle, Holden, Addy, or Spencer and see none.

Then I hear someone shout. "Look out!" A kid runs through the crowd with a little girl chasing him.

I move quickly, as a woman grips my arm. "Careful."

My head whips around. "I'm so sorry."

"Don't be, I just didn't want someone running you over," she says with a smile. "I'm Debra and you, oh, you must be Blakely!"

Here we go. "Yes, I'm Blake. It's lovely to meet you."

"Oh, the pleasure is all mine. I have known your husband since he was a little boy. I was his first-grade teacher."

"And she's one of the biggest gossips in this town," Addison says with a huge grin on her face. "It's good to see you, Mrs. H."

"My lovely girl, I have missed you." Debra takes Addison's face in her hands. "Don't you stay away anymore."

"I'm here now, and that's something."

"What's something?" Holden asks as he walks up. "That I am the most eligible bachelor in Rose Canyon?"

Brielle laughs. "You're the only one left! Hi, Mrs. H."

"Hello, darling. If I didn't know better, I would think you're trying to keep me from talking to Blakely."

That's exactly what they're doing, and it's been working wonderfully.

"Never," Holden says, clutching his chest. "You wound me."

"Debra, you're needed at the pies table." A lovely older woman says as she walks toward us.

"Oh, posh! My grandsons haven't a brain cell left between the two of them." Debra walks off, waving her hand as she makes her way through the crowd.

The other woman turns to me. "Aren't you just the prettiest woman I've ever seen." She takes my hand. I have yet to meet anyone unkind or devious. In what seemed like a matter of five minutes, I have met everyone who lives here.

"Thank you."

"Holden"—she looks to him—"be a nice boy, please."

"Oh, of course." He steps forward. "Blakely, this is my beautiful, wonderful, fabulous, most-kindhearted aunt, Mama James."

The elderly woman comes closer, taking my other hand. "I am all of these children's surrogate mother, and now I'm yours since you're married to our Emmett, well, if you'll have me."

I try not to let that simple sentence pierce my heart, but it does. I lost my mother. She died of a broken heart after Dylan. I've been an orphan, lost without a parent to talk to or ask for advice. It's been so hard, and this woman just offered me something that she didn't have to.

She releases one hand, resting it on the side of my cheek. "Don't cry, sweet girl. I promise I'm nice."

I laugh. "I lost my mother a few years ago, and you just . . . you made me feel like I wasn't alone."

Her smile could warm the coldest of places. She loops her arm in mine and starts to walk. "You're not alone. You have Emmett, which means you have an entire community of nosey neighbors who will pester you about babies and when you're going to do something you have no intention of doing."

"It sounds . . . frightening."

"Oh, it is. Don't give anyone an inch here, other than me."

Holden scoffs. "Especially not to her. She's the head of the committee of old women who pester."

"Is that an official committee?" I ask. "I like pestering, and while I'm not old, I'm happy to insert myself."

Her light laughter is almost musical. "I think we're going to be best friends, Blakely Maxwell."

For the first time ever, I don't have the urge to correct someone when they assume I took Emmett's last name. So, I let Mama James say it without protest.

As soon as Mama James and I start talking, the town backs off, which is as strange as it is amusing. It's as though they're either afraid of her, which seems completely unlikely, or they just respect her enough not to intrude, which is far more likely.

Holden leans his head between ours. "She's like a repellant. It's why I keep her so healthy. If something happens to her, the vultures will descend."

"Hush your mouth, Holden James. I will start letting the town know you're interested in a wife. Then we'll see what kind of repellant I am."

I love her. It's official. She's my favorite person—other than Emmett—in this town. "You could always do it just for fun."

"If he keeps it up, I just might."

Someone waves to Mama James, and she pats my arm. "I need to say hello to someone. Your husband is just a few feet away, staring at you like a blind man seeing the sun for the first time."

I glance over to Emmett, who is leaning against a street lamp, arms crossed over his broad chest, wearing his very unflattering brown uniform, but he wears it to perfection. I smile. He smiles back and then crooks his finger at me.

I swear, we're having a total *Dirty Dancing* moment, and I am here for it. Well, minus the dirty dancing itself or carrying a watermelon.

A few people try to approach me, but Emmett makes his way toward me, and they back off. "Hi."

"Hi," I reply.

"You look stunning."

I shrug. Brielle had me wear a light green dress that has a very low back and sweetheart neckline. It's soft, demure, and still a little edgy. The only other time Emmett has seen me in a dress was when he came with me to the back-to-back funerals of Dylan and my mother.

Not even our wedding day.

We both wore our uniforms.

"I'm totally out of my element."

"We both are."

"You're at least in a uniform," I remind him. "I'm not sure how that is out of your element."

"More in the way that I have to trust other people to keep you safe."

I shake my head. "Silly Emmett, I am perfectly capable of doing that myself."

"Maybe so, but I will always jump in front of a bullet for you."

"Let's hope it never comes to that."

However, that's the sweetest thing, and considering our backgrounds, it really does mean a lot.

"Have you noticed anyone here that isn't normally?" I ask, glancing around.

"I haven't been focusing."

My shoulders drop, and I have to restrain myself from yelling at him. "What do you mean you haven't been focusing?" I say through my teeth as I smile at someone who waves.

"I've been too busy watching . . . other things."

"Like what? There's a crazy person in your town."

"I'm aware of that. She's a lunatic, that's for sure."

I glare at him, catching the meaning. "So, what has stolen your attention so thoroughly that you haven't been doing what you were supposed to be doing?"

"You."

"What?"

"You. You are what's keeping me distracted. Your long legs, lean body, and perfect breasts that are just peaking up enough for me to see. I can't keep my eyes off you."

My ire is gone now. "Sheriff, you are making me blush."

He laughs. "Now, I know that's not true."

"Fine. I don't blush. Still, that's sweet." I look behind me and spot George with Dr. Dehring. She's holding his arm as he guides her through the crowd. "Wow, that's something."

Emmett looks over my shoulder. "He's had a thing for her since she moved here."

I smile. "That's so cute. I didn't know it was her."

"She replaced Dr. Girardo, who is friends with Holden, right after Brielle's memory returned. Brie really likes her, said she's really kind and patient."

I don't know why, but it makes me happy. "George could definitely do worse than that. She keeps smiling at him."

"I'm jealous." Emmett turns my chin his way. "I wish I could walk around with you and let the world see how happy I am that we're together. I would parade you around, let everyone stare and envy that I somehow got the girl."

I lean in, my hand resting on his chest. "You are very sweet, Sheriff. I would like that too, but you're working and we cannot."

"No, we cannot."

"But . . ." I give him a saucy smile. "You *could* kiss me. Right here. Right in front of the town. You could—"

He doesn't waste another second before his arms are around me and his lips are on mine. People clap and catcall as he dips me, kissing me with so much emotion that I might never be the same again.

CHAPTER

Twenty

EMMETT

After the crowd dies down, I put her to rights and grin.

"Proud of yourself, huh?" she asks.

"I am, rather."

Blakely shakes her head with a laugh. "You're an idiot. Now that you've proven your point, why don't we go back to people watching?"

We should, it's just that I keep finding her in the crowd. It's as if she's walking the streets alone, and I can't look away.

"I know. I hate that I have to work tonight and can't take you around."

"It's okay. It's giving me a chance to see what living here will be like, after all, you won't be with me all the time after I move here. That would be weird."

A slow smile tugs on my lips because, while we'd kind of discussed it, we hadn't actually come to any decision.

"You're serious about really moving here?"

"Of course I am."

"Because?"

"Because I love you, Emmett. I have spent years denying it, trying to will it to be different, but here I am—completely and utterly in love with your stupid ass."

Fuck this woman owns me. "You said it before."

"I know, but you didn't seem to react."

"You have a habit of running when you get up in your feelings," I remind her. "I was allowing you a chance to decide if it was a slipup."

"It wasn't. I love you."

"Good."

"You think so, huh?"

"Considering we're married, I'd say it's a really good step in the right direction."

Blakely laughs. "I agree."

I take a second to look around, watching for anyone watching us or trying not to watch us, but everyone is talking, eating our famous Bang-Bang Scallops, and enjoying the festival.

All except for one person.

Stephen Stengel is at the picnic table, but he's sitting sideways, seemingly watching the crowd, but he *never* scans my way.

"What do you see?" Blakely asks, not turning her head.

I smile down at her. "Someone is watching us."

"That seems to be the whole theme of tonight."

"Yeah, but he is the only one making it a point to look like they aren't staring," I explain.

"Who is it?"

"Grab your phone and text the group, but don't look away from me."

Blakely nods. "What am I saying?"

"Tell them to look at the picnic table to the left of where I'm facing. We're going to walk to see if anyone follows."

I want to see if Stephen stays put or if I'm imagining it. It could be that Blakely seems fixated on him and that has spilled over onto me, but there's just something weird about the way he's looking around.

She sends the text and then puts her phone into her purse. "Okay, let's walk, and you can tell me who I am not looking at."

"Stephen Stengel, but he's done nothing wrong. I just want to see if he tracks us."

"And if he does?"

I push back the hair that fell in her eyes. "Then he goes to the top of our list."

"And you'll tell me I'm right and you're wrong."

Of course that's what she cares most about. "How about I love you, and I plan to spend the rest of my life letting you be right even when you're wrong?"

Blakely laughs softly. "Perfect, but I'm always right."

I shift, and she opens her eyes a little. "What time is it?"

"I have no idea, but the sun is out."

She groans. "Sleep. Need it."

I chuckle and lean back to grab my phone. It's eleven in the morning, and after getting home and having amazing sex, we must have passed out on the couch. Not that I mind at all, but I also forgot to set my alarm, which means I have about an hour before I'd usually leave to visit my father in the nursing home.

Blakely knew some of what I've dealt with regarding my father, but a lot has happened in the last two and a half years.

"I want to take you somewhere," I say, not sure if this is a good idea, but if he's having a good day, then I want him to meet her.

"Does it involve dead people?"

She's insane. "No, but it involves someone I love very much."

Blakely's eyes pop open, and she freezes. "What?"

"My father."

Instantly she relaxes. "Oh. I'm sorry. Of course—wait, I thought your dad was living with your sister?"

"He moved here about three months after I got here. I visit with him every Sunday, and I'd really like if you'd come with me."

Her soft smile does something to my heart. "I'd love that. What are we going to tell him?"

"That we're married."

"We are that. I would love to meet him."

I kiss her quickly. "Good. Get ready, and we'll head out."

We get dressed, head to the car, and start the drive out to see my dad. It only takes about thirty minutes, but the closer we get, the more worried I become.

He could be completely out of it today and not know who I am or where he is. I tap my fingers on the dash, trying to figure out how I'll handle it if that's the case. Blakely's hand moves to my thigh.

"Talk to me."

I glance at her and release a deep breath. It's Blakely, and before she walked out on me, there wasn't anything I wouldn't have told her. Even though she says she wants this, a part of me worries she'll change her mind. I'm not sure how much of myself I'm willing to risk.

As though she can see into my mind, she squeezes my leg. "I know I've failed you, Em. I've let you down, but . . . I'm here and I'm not going anywhere."

I entwine our fingers. "It's partially that, the other part is that I don't really know where to start. My father's condition has deteriorated quickly. It's impossible to know what we're walking into, and I can't prepare you for that."

"I am a medic."

"I'm aware of that, but this is still difficult to explain."

She squeezes my hand slightly. "Try."

I sigh, making a right onto the highway that'll take us out to the home. "There are some days he's the man I remember. He smiles when I get there, knows my name, and can have some semblance of a conversation. However, no matter how cognizant he is, he's never fully himself. He always believes he and my mother are together still."

"Have you seen her since she left?" Blake asks hesitantly.

"No, and I have no plans to."

"Has your sister?"

I look over. "No."

"Okay."

That woman walked out and gave zero fucks about any of us, I have no desire to see or talk to her.

"No matter what kind of day your father is having, I am just glad you're sharing this with me. It means a lot, and I am excited to meet him. It's a sort of normal thing we're doing."

"There's nothing normal about us, babe."

"That's true, but we're at least trying."

She's right. We're trying, and that's more than I ever thought we'd do.

CHAPTER
Twenty~One
BLAKELY

Emmett and I walk through the residence hand in hand. It's a beautiful place that sits near a cliff with spectacular views and an outdoor area that offers something for everyone. The inside is immaculate, and every person we pass is smiling.

"Good afternoon, Emmett."

"Nita, this is my wife, Blakely."

Her dark brown eyes widen. "Wife? I didn't know you were married."

I laugh. "I'm his dirty secret. It's nice to meet you, Nita."

She extends her hand to me. "It's wonderful to meet you. I am just a little shocked, that's all. When did you two meet?"

"We were in the army together," I explain. "We've been married a few years."

Her jaw drops. "Wow. Okay. Well, it's a good day for Mr. Maxwell today. He's in good spirits and asked when his son would be arriving."

It's as though I can feel the tension drain from Emmett's body. He smiles widely and squeezes my hand a little. "Great. Is he outside or in his room?"

"He should be in the recreation room."

"Thank you, Nita."

"Any time, Emmett."

As we walk down the hall, I glance up at him. "Does he know anything about me?"

Emmett stops for a second. "I tell my father everything about me and my sister's lives. He may not remember, but I told him about you every week."

My heart pounds, and I suck in a breath. "What?"

"Every time I came, I talked about you, Blake. It wasn't always good, but I mentioned your name to him so many times, I wouldn't doubt he knows. My father is the only person in this town who knew we were married because I knew he'd never remember."

"Why would you tell him?"

For some reason, his answer to this question matters. If it was because he hated me, then I understand, but if it was more . . . it matters.

"Because I think that someday I wanted this to be our reality. I wanted to walk you in here as my wife, and if that day came, I needed him to know your name or at least have heard it before."

My fingertips brush the stubble on his cheek. "I don't deserve you, Emmett."

"I think you're wrong. I think we are exactly what the other deserves. Come on, I want you to meet my father."

Everything inside me is falling apart. The truths I held, relied on, and needed so that I could live are fracturing around me. I wanted to protect myself from love because it was the only way I could survive. If I gave in to it, I would drown.

It's not drowning, though.

It's breathing.

I am so afraid because I never want to go back to the way it was.

We enter the room, and immediately I feel a sense of calm. The room is a warm white with sheer curtains billowing in the light wind, giving the room an open and clean feeling. The salty air is warm and welcoming. The sunlight comes in through the floor-to-ceiling windows, and you can't help but want to smile.

If I were living here, this is a room that I would never want to leave, and it's clear why so many people are here. At the large table on the right, a woman is doing a puzzle, rocking back and forth as she tries to fit the pieces. A man with light gray hair sits by the window, just watching the waves crash against the rocks below. Over in the corner, there's a BINGO game going on, and residents are calling out numbers and laughing.

He shakes my arm lightly, and I look over to the other corner where a man with salt-and-pepper hair is in a rocking chair with a book in his hand. His glasses are set upon the bridge of his nose, and even though I've never met Emmett's father, I would know him instantly.

I smile at Emmett. "We know what you're going to look like as you age."

"Let's hope it's only in looks."

"I would take care of you no matter what," I promise, and then regret saying it. His mother didn't stay or come back once she found out Hank was sick, and I don't like the parallel.

"I hope so."

"Let's go say hi."

The apprehension fills his eyes, but he walks, and I follow. "Hi, Dad."

The man looks up, pulling the glasses off, revealing the same blue eyes that I love. "Emmett. You're late today. I was just doing some reading to avoid checking my watch."

Emmett grins. "Sorry about that. I should've asked Nita to adjust your alarm." His father grumbles about not needing an alarm, and Emmett clears his throat. "I'd like you to meet someone."

He looks to me as though he just realized I was here, and his eyes widen. "Well, hello there."

"Hi, Mr. Maxwell."

"And who might you be?"

"I'm Blakely Bennett. I . . ."

"You were in the war with Emmett," his father says, and I nod. "I was."

He looks to Emmett. "Did you marry her, son?"

Emmett laughs. "I did."

"Good. A girl this pretty wouldn't last long in my day. If she's smart too, you would have had no chance if you waited."

I love him. He is now my new favorite Maxwell. "I'd say Emmett is pretty smart because he listened to you."

His father puffs out his chest a little. "I know women, my girl. You're all elusive creatures who drive men to the edge, but we can't help but want to jump if it'll make you happy."

"And what of the men who force us to the edge?"

The warm smile paints his lips. "That's our only defense."

Emmett snorts, but I ignore him. "May I sit with you?"

He grabs the chair next to his, pulling it close. "Emmett, go get some lemonade and stale cookies while I spend some time with my new daughter."

"I'm not leaving you two alone, you're both trouble."

His dad waves his hand. "Oh, please. I'll forget what we talked about tomorrow, let me regale her with the stories of your misspent youth while they're here." He taps his head and then shoos him away.

Emmett sighs heavily but leans in to kiss my cheek. "Behave, I know all my tricks thanks to him."

I smile, looking up at a younger version of the man beside me. "It's a good thing we're married then."

He kisses my lips. "Very good thing."

When he's gone, my father-in-law pats my hand. "I prayed for you, young lady."

"Me?"

"I don't remember everything, but Emmett has spoken of you. He told me he had a wife who he loved but didn't think it would work."

"That was my fault," I say. "I ran from him."

"We all run from love. It's terrifying. It's why my wife left."

I swallow a sound of surprise because Emmett said his father always speaks of his wife as though they're still together. I don't want to cause him any distress, so I do my best to allow the conversation to flow as though he has no issues with his memory. "When did she leave?"

He looks out the window. "I'm not sure, but I know my heart has hurt for a while."

"I'm sorry, Mr. Maxwell."

He rears back a little, scrunching his nose. "None of that. You call me Hank or Dad."

I smile. "I didn't have a dad."

"You do now, even if I might not remember, it will be true in my heart."

"And it will be in mine."

He takes my hand. "Tell me about how you came back, I need a happy story."

I do as he asks and give him the PG version of how I came back to Emmett and how I have no plans on leaving.

"Where are we going?" I ask, hating that he won't tell me.

"God you're horrible when you're left in the dark."

I roll my eyes. "No shit."

"It's fun watching you be annoyed."

I flick his ear, and he winces. "Ouch! Shit, that hurt."

"Big baby."

"I'm the baby? You just flicked me."

I shrug. "Your dad said I should keep you in line, I'm following orders."

Emmett laughs. "He would say that."

I lean back in the seat, turning my head to watch him. "Are days like today few and far between?"

"Days like today are unicorns pooping marshmallows. My father has never been like that. I don't know if it's the new medication he got approved for or what."

"He knows a lot more than you think. He spoke of your mom . . ."

Emmett pulls into a parking lot and parks the car but doesn't release the wheel. His hands are gripped tight as he clears his throat. "What did he say?"

"That he knows she's gone. He was relating it to us."

His head snaps toward me, eyes blazing with rage. "You are nothing like her. Nothing! She's a selfish bitch who left my father when he needed her more than anything. He was falling apart, dealing with his memory gaps, and she was a constant for him."

As much as I wish I could argue that I am nothing like that, I pretty much am exactly like her. "Please let me know where exactly you see the difference. I left you right after you had surgery to repair a bullet wound. You know, when you needed me. Oh, after we had sex for the first time. You were already broken, and I slinked off to go back to war."

"You went back to work, Blake. I knew you were leaving. I knew you were on two-week emergency family leave and had to return. No one cares about the spouse in the military."

Why I feel the need to vilify myself when he's not, I'll never understand, but I need all of this to come out. I think we both do. "And what if she left for the same reasons?"

"Last I checked, she wasn't a combat medic."

"No, but I didn't leave because I was. I left because I was terrified. I was so afraid of losing you, of having to bury you and go on in a world without you, that I created a safer version where my heart was safe from the pain. I'm not excusing it or saying that's why she did, but I can imagine it for just a second."

"Don't," Emmett warns, his knuckles going white. "Don't try to excuse it."

"I'm not. I'm just giving you a flip side. You said that your mother loved your father, that they got married out of high school, right?"

His jaw ticks. "Yes."

"So, here is your mom, in love with your dad, and she's

watching the man she loves leave. Each day he remembers less and less . . ."

Emmett turns to me. "Blakely, if that were us, and you were leaving me a little each day, I would fucking hate it. I would be . . . I don't even know how to describe it. It would kill me to watch you deteriorate, but I would rather have every minute that was good, every smile when you recognized me, every kiss and hug than walk away because I was terrified of the bad. She's not a martyr. She's not the victim. While I understand what you're saying, you didn't walk out on me that way. We didn't have fifty years behind us, kids, grandkids, and a home. You left because you were scared, and you came back. She never has."

I take his hands in mine. "I am not making her any of those things. I just wonder if she was afraid."

"Maybe she was, but she didn't care enough to let any of us know."

My chest is tight, and I want so badly to cry for her, for Hank, for Emmett and everyone in that family. I don't know her, so I could be totally off with her intentions, but I just can't help but wonder if she wanted to lose him on her terms.

I could never make that choice now. Not the way I feel about Emmett now. It almost killed me when I did it before. Even though it would hurt me, I would stay by his side and be the fixed point in his sea of uncertainty.

"I love you, Emmett. I love you, and I am so sorry that the people you trusted most in the world have walked away."

"You and I were two broken people that night who needed each other. You walked away because I terrified the part of you that deemed us something different. And again, the big thing is that you're here now . . . and you're not afraid."

I push myself close, our noses just touching. "I'm terrified of losing you now that I know how much I love you."

"You're not going to lose me, Blake. Not now. Not ever."

CHAPTER

Twenty-Two

EMMETT

We pull onto a very long driveway that leads to a house tucked back in the woods.

"Great, you're totally planning to kill me and leave me here!" Blake says.

"Yup. Part two of our date is death and burial."

"You're such a romantic."

I snort. "Just shut up and be prepared for a surprise."

"So far, you're really sucking at remembering who you married."

"Oh, I remember, all right," I say with a grin.

Blake huffs and crosses her arms. "How much longer do you think, darling?"

The house comes into view a moment later. "Now." I put the car in park and exit the vehicle.

"Do you own this property?"

I shake my head. "Nope."

"Do you know someone who does, or are we trespassing?"

"The owners are Christine and Paige, they're a lovely couple who I have known for a very long time."

Blake nods slowly. "Okay, are they good friends?"

"Christine used to be the sheriff. When she retired, I was appointed."

We are here for several reasons, but I want to leave the second one a secret for a bit, which Christine agreed to help me with.

"So, we're here for investigative purposes?"

I nod. "Yes, for one."

Blakely's face lights up. "Now this is a date!"

Only my wife would think investigating murders and talking to someone who may have information is a date.

"Sure, we'll call it that."

Christine and Paige exit the house with warm smiles. "Hey there, Sheriff Maxwell. Fancy seeing you around these woods."

"Chris, it's lovely to see you, as always. Paige, you look beautiful."

"Note he didn't say that I looked beautiful," Christine says with a huff.

"Oh, he knows who to flatter," Paige says, walking toward us. "And you must be his bride."

Blake comes to stand beside me. "I'm Blakely, but Blake is fine."

Christine follows behind her wife. "It's an absolute pleasure to meet you, Blake. I'm Chris, and this is Paige. We've known Emmett since he was a know-it-all teenager who should've been in the back of my cruiser more often than not."

Blake grins. "Well, Emmett almost had me arrested, and I think that's a crime, so we should repay him with the same treatment," she explains, giving me a disapproving look.

"He's a fool."

"We can all agree on that," I say to them all. "However, we are here to find out what you can tell us about the mayor and what you might know regarding the missing girls."

Chris rubs the back of her head. "I don't know much. I've been out of the loop for a year now."

Paige rolls her eyes. "Liar."

"I'm not lying, woman. I don't *know* anything."

"But you have suspicions," I hedge. I know she does because

when I called her, she told me this was a conversation left to the woods.

So, here we are, in the woods.

Blakely moves to her, her voice soft as she says, "I was working the case of a missing girl. She was sixteen, dark brown hair, green eyes, and a smile that would light up a room. The last known person to have contact with her was from Rose Canyon."

Christine looks to me. "Who?"

"Bill Waugh."

"He moved away after high school."

I nod. "And he moved back not too long ago with a wife and kid."

"Yes, I heard. Like I said, I've been out here in the woods for a while now. I try to keep away from Rose Canyon."

"Someone mentioned that you had unofficially talked to Sonya about leaving Bill and encouraged her to file a restraining order," Blake mentions.

She turns to Blake. "What does that have to do with the price of eggs?"

Blakely's eyes squint. "What?"

Paige laughs. "Why do you think that means something bigger?"

"Because three girls turned up dead in Portland, and when Bill killed himself, he warned Spencer that someone was coming. I think that Bill was afraid of whoever he was working for. I think there's someone in a position of power that terrified him enough to kill himself to avoid their wrath. There are a few people who I looked into," she says, glancing at me. "First was Emmett."

Well, that's interesting. "Excuse me?"

"Sorry, baby, but you're in a position of power. I had to rule you out before I even got on the plane."

"So glad I passed the test."

She shrugs. "Second was Councilman Colgan."

At that, Christine bursts out laughing. "He couldn't find directions on a one-way street. Colgan is a lot of things, but smart ain't one. He's only the councilman because he and Stengel go way back."

"Yes, which is why I considered him," Blake explains. "I think the third is the most plausible. The mayor or his son."

Paige and Christine share a look. "Stephen is . . ." Christine shakes her head. "Well, he's someone I don't understand. I was always wary of him. He has crazy eyes, if you know what I mean. I don't know, I could never explain it. There have been a few complaints about him over the years, but nothing was substantiated."

"Like what?" I ask.

When I asked Christine if we could come out and talk, she was reluctant at first but eventually agreed. Her expression suggests that she very much wishes she had never picked up my call.

"I know you want to keep out of this, but I could really use your help."

Christine sighs. "See, I was fair to everyone no matter their race, gender, who they loved, or what they wore. I didn't care if you came from the town or migrated in. I just wanted the people to be safe. I'd heard rumblings once that the mayor was paying people to do something illegal."

"What was it?" Blake asks before I can.

"I found out that he was moving drugs through his son. Stephen started working for the rescue squad and would put the drugs in the ambulance and run them around town on fake calls." Christine meets my gaze and doesn't break it. "So, I looked into the claim, watching both of them as best as I could. I knew the date they were going to move those drugs, and I waited, watched him go out with his lights going, and I followed him. Emmett, I searched that damn ambulance. I spent hours combing over every inch. I was sure that I was going to find it. No one knew I was going. No one had a clue what I was looking for. I did it four times, and never once was there anything." She focuses back on Blakely. "But I have never forgotten how terrified he looked. If you have a gut feeling, I wouldn't walk away from it."

"Thank you, Chris."

She nods once. "Now, you both didn't hear a goddamn thing from me, got it?"

"Of course."

Paige takes Christine's hand and squeezes. "Now, are you ready for part two of this visit?"

Blakely's eyes shift around. "What is part two?"

Paige's grin grows.

"Honey, you have an amazing husband, that's all I am going to say about that."

CHAPTER
Twenty-Three
BLAKELY

"A puppy! You're giving me a puppy!" I hold the little fluffball in my arms as she wiggles in excitement, licking my face when she gets close enough.

"Pick whichever one you want."

I want them all. Every last little baby that's here because they're all so freaking cute. The one I had jumps off my lap, and two more take her place.

"Emmett! We can't get a puppy."

"Why not?"

I snuggle the next one, kissing its head, and giggle as another tries to climb up my back. "Because, we don't get to have a dog, remember?"

He crouches, picking up the one that was on my back and tucking it against his chest. "We may not have before, but this is a new us, and we are getting a puppy and whatever else we want."

I smile, fighting back the urge to cry. We are a new version of us, and . . . well, hell, we *can* have a dog. Neither of us are living a military life anymore, we're both adults, married, and I am staying here. There is no reason we can't get a dog.

I put down the puppy that was in my lap and just watch this incredibly sexy man, all muscles and power, holding this mini

Labradoodle puppy as if it's the most precious thing. She's going to be around twenty-five pounds and is a chocolate color with a little white stripe up her nose. Her coat is wavy and soft as silk.

If I didn't love him before, I sure as hell would now.

Who can resist a hot guy with a puppy? No one. It's like the universe's version of catnip for women.

"I think we should get this one," I say, patting her head while she lays content in Emmett's arms.

"You think?"

I nod. "She likes you."

"Like all women do."

Christine snorts. "Not all, sweetcheeks."

I laugh and then cover it with a cough.

Emmett chuckles. "Well, I stand corrected."

"This one does, don't you?" I pet her little head again, her lids lowering as she finds safety in his arms.

Yeah, you're safe with him, sweet girl.

"Do you want this one?" Emmett asks.

"Yeah, she's perfect."

Paige walks over and removes the collar from around her neck. "I've always said that most people come here to pick a puppy, but the puppy often chooses them. It's truly a special moment between you all."

Emmett grins. "Do you have all the stuff for her?"

"Yes, we grabbed everything."

"What do you mean?" I ask.

"I figured we'd be walking out of here with a puppy, so I asked Chris and Paige to grab all the supplies we'd need."

Christine calls back from the other room. "At a premium."

"Yes, it's damn near extortion."

"I think it's worth every penny," I say, kissing her nose. "What should we name her?"

"I have no idea," Emmett says.

I think about it for a second and dismiss anything military related. Neither of us need that reminder. Besides, this little fluffy love isn't something I want associated with war.

No, I want her name to make me smile. To be about us and what we've endured as a couple.

"We got married in May," I note.

"You want to name her May?"

"No, I'm just thinking."

Paige brings in the travel crate and places it down. "It's Sunday, right?"

"Yes."

"I got here a week ago on Sunday," I say aloud, my mind working.

"You left me on a Sunday too."

"Thanks for that reminder. We got married on a Sunday," I remind him of a happier thing.

"We did."

"All the important things, and picking her up, happen on a Sunday. I think that's what we should name her."

His smile is wide and there is so much warmth in his eyes. "Sunday."

"Sundays are good days."

He leans close to me and kisses me softly. "Every day we're together will be a good day, Blake. Not just Sunday."

The one thing neither of us really considered was that we don't actually know how to take care of a dog.

So, we spent two hours with Paige and Chris, listening closely as they gave us their best tips, and then the hour ride home researching anything else.

We are going to screw up, but it's okay because we have a dog that we love.

Emmett had to go clean up the vandalized parking spot that his two best friends left after the third complaint about the penis painting in the center of town, so it's just me and Sunday for a bit.

I have a very clear schedule written out, and I am ready to kick ass at being a dog mom.

"Come on, Sunday, go potty," I urge her as we stand outside the apartment. Last night, our little baby slept beside us in the bed. She spent most of the time on Emmett's chest, but at one point, I woke up and found her nose-to-nose with me. I love her so much already.

This morning, she scarfed down her breakfast, we played, snuggled, and then she passed out for about an hour. She's only had one accident, but that's probably because Emmett and I have been taking her out every two hours like clockwork.

Sunday walks around the grass, sniffing everything before finally dropping down to pee. "Yes! Good girl, Sunday! Yes!"

She looks up at me like I'm a crazy person, which is reasonable since I am yelling about her using the bathroom, and then I give her a treat once she comes back to me. "Good girl, yes, you go potty outside."

"I wish I got a treat each time I did that," a deep voice says from behind me.

I jump a little, and then I turn to face the man. He seems familiar, but I have no idea why. "I'm sorry, have we met?"

He's tall, stocky, and has a goatee that doesn't quite connect at the sides. I can't place what about him seems like we know each other.

"I don't think I've had the pleasure. I'm Stephen Stengel, and you must be the sheriff's wife."

And there it is. The mayor's son. I let a wide smile tug at my lips and relax my stance into something casual and unassuming before saying, "Oh! Hey! It's so nice to meet you."

"Likewise."

"Do you live here too? Emmett never mentioned who all the tenants were."

He shakes his head. "No, I'm here to see Tessa and Nick."

"Tessa is so sweet. I met her the other day."

"She's the best. Why she's with Nick, I'll never understand."

I smile. "Isn't that how it always is? One person in the couple is undeserving of the other, but somehow, fate allows it."

Stephen grins. "You're a romantic."

I am not, but I shrug. "I blame it on my foolish heart."

"Is that what brought you to Rose Canyon?"

"Partially."

Sunday starts to bounce around at my feet, demanding attention, and Stephen crouches. "Hello, little one. You're adorable."

"This is Sunday, she's my new baby."

"I love dogs. I lost mine about two years ago," he explains.

"I'm sorry."

I pick her up, tucking her into my arm, and he rises. "He lived a good life, that's what matters. So, are you planning to stay long here?"

"I'm staying as long as I can."

Stephen looks up at the second floor and then back. "Good. I'm sure we'll run into each other again. My father said you were in his office a few days ago, and that you're a very smart woman. That's high praise from him."

Interesting that his dad would bring me up. "Are you and your dad close?"

He scoffs. "No. We have dinner every week because my mother demands it. I'm not exactly a politician, and that grates his nerves."

I need to get on some kind of level with him. I decide the father angle might be the best.

"The sins of our fathers, right?"

"You and your father don't get along?"

I shake my head. "My father was an admiral in the navy. He left my mother shortly after my brother was born. We never really saw each other after that."

"I can empathize, my father has had a mistress for almost twenty years."

My eyes widen at that. "I . . . wow."

Stephen chuckles. "The town."

"Duh. Sorry, I should have guessed that." Although, I wouldn't doubt if there was more to that. "If you aren't following in his foot-steps, what is it that you do?" I ask, already knowing the answer as we start to walk toward the entrance of the building.

"I'm a fireman and EMT."

"Very admirable and also sort of like your dad."

His brows lower. "How so?"

"Still in public service."

Stephen grins. "Yes, but I actually help people where he lies for a living."

I'm not so sure I believe that, but I incline my head. "There's that."

He opens the door for me, and I smile. "Thank you."

"Of course."

Tessa lives on the floor below Emmett's, so Stephen follows me to the steps. "So, did you grow up with Tessa and Nick?"

"Yeah. Nick, Ryan, and I have been friends since forever."

I can't help but wonder if they are all connected then. If they've been that close of friends, they all must know that Stephen and Bill spent time together.

I force a smile. "That's amazing. Sort of like Emmett, Holden, Isaac, and Spencer were. You guys all seem to love it here."

He chuckles. "More like this town holds the residents hostage."

"It's like the Hotel California?" I ask, and he pulls his head back in confusion. Jesus, now I've aged myself. "You know, the Eagles? You can visit anytime you like, but you can never leave?" His confusion doesn't clear, so I add, "It's a song."

He shakes his head. "Never heard of it."

"It's a classic. Please, pull it up on your phone and listen. My mother loved it, and we would listen to it constantly."

"I'll do that." We reach the first landing and pause because he needs to go right, and I need to go up the stairs. "It was truly a pleasure talking to you."

He smiles. "You too, and thank you for letting me meet Sunday."

"She's sort of perfect, huh?"

"She is." Stephen rubs her head as she naps in my arms. "Well,

Blakely Bennett, I should let you go back to your day. I'm sure I'll see you around."

"You sure will. Have a great day."

I turn and walk up the stairs, feeling as though he's watching me the entire way. When I get to the apartment, I put Sunday in her kennel and go back through the notes I have on Stephen.

CHAPTER

Twenty-Four

EMMETT

"Another girl?" I ask Holden as he sits in his office. "It's the same as the other girls. Same age, no identification, official cause of death is listed as overdose. She was young, pretty, and reported as a runaway. Thankfully, they were able to find her family, but the other two still haven't been identified. It's following a pattern, and we either have a serial killer, which I don't think, or these girls are being drugged into compliance and then having their bodies dumped if they OD."

I scratch my head and sigh. "Did we miss it before? Has this been going on in our backyard and none of us noticed?"

"I'm sure it happens more than any of us want to consider, but something may have changed."

"Yeah, Bill killed himself. That's the change. Let's just assume for one minute that Blake and Spencer's theories are right, and Bill was trafficking girls. If his job was to get the girls here, the easiest way to do that would be to drug them into compliance. With him gone, there's a kink in the chain, so maybe his replacement is careless."

Holden glances out the window. "But Keeley's friend said that she was already doing drugs."

"We have no idea which ones. It makes sense they keep them

drugged so they're unaware of where they are. If Bill was supplying, injecting, or just monitoring them while they were in his care, now that's gone."

"It's a solid theory, but it doesn't help us figure out who the new guy is or even if there is a new guy." Holden leans back, tapping his fingers on his legs, which is his tell for when he's contemplating. "Okay, let's break down what we know about Bill. He left town right after high school?"

"Yeah. He went out to Wyoming for a time, worked for a water company out there and met Sonya."

"And then what?"

"He came back to Rose Canyon with Sonya and their son. He wasn't very social, at least not in a way that I remember. We know he worked for the water plant for at least two years, but after that, I can't find work history. Sonya said he was always changing jobs, and he'd told her he was traveling for training."

"He was close with Nick in school. He was seen with Stephen. It's not a far leap to think they may have talked occasionally."

Nick and Tessa live in my building, but I wasn't living in the apartment before Isaac's murder, so I can't say if Bill ever visited them. I can say, though, that I never saw Bill and Nick hanging out together in town. Nick is a great guy, and Tessa is probably the nicest person on this earth, so I have a hard time believing they are involved at all. Also, for all we know, their friendship fell to shit.

"Still, he was mostly a loner, which makes sense if he was involved in whatever crazy shit is going on here. The more people he hung around with, the higher the chances were that someone would start asking questions he wouldn't want to answer."

"Do you feel like we're living in some fucked-up movie right now? Because this is Rose Canyon, where nothing happens, and all of a sudden, someone in town is linked to at least two deaths— possibly more that we don't know about yet. I'm just saying, this is all a bit crazy, and I may pack my shit, grab Mama James, and go back to Cali where apparently, shit is normal."

I roll my eyes. "Yeah, so normal. Also, your aunt will kick your ass before you drag her out of this town."

"True, but my point is that there's something weird going on, and I don't like it."

"Spencer isn't going to either."

Holden laughs. "No shit, he's going to have the National Guard protecting Brielle when we tell him this."

"Exactly. I'm glad Addy won't be back for a while too. Maybe I can convince her to stay a little longer in Pennsylvania. You know I'm not usually an alarmist, but I wonder if we should consider calling his friends back into town."

When Brielle's safety was in jeopardy, Spencer had a team of elite ex-SEALs come. I spent a lot of time with them, helping to make sure Brie was safe. They're excellent at protection, and Quinn Miller was instrumental in helping Spencer when Brie was an idiot and thought she was a SEAL herself.

As an ex-Ranger, I liked having them in the town as a second layer.

"You want to call the Cole Security guys here?"

"I doubt we can afford their rates, but maybe they'll do us a solid since they're friends of Spencer's. Blakely is demanding justice for Keeley, and she's not going to let up until she knows what happened to her. She's about as subtle as a bullet when she feels passionate about something. Her safety means nothing if she believes it's the best course of action."

"And you think you can get her on board with having a protective detail?"

Not a chance in hell. "No, but I can get her on board with working with them as an investigative team."

Holden shakes his head. "Good luck, my friend."

I'm going to need it.

On my way back to the station, my phone rings. "Sheriff Maxwell," I answer.

"Sheriff, this is Detective Scott in Portland, how are you?"

"I'm doing well, yourself?"

"Same." He pauses. "I would be better if I were calling with good news, but I'm afraid I'm not. I am reaching out because I could use your help."

"Of course, what can I do?"

Detective Scott sighs heavily. "I know you're aware of the Jane Does who arrived in our ME's office around the same time as Keeley McLain did."

"Yes, I am."

"One of the girls has been identified, and after we notified her parents, they gave us permission to go through her belongings for any clues. There wasn't anything physical there, but her family granted us permission to scrub her laptop. It appears she was using an app to talk to someone that was located in Rose Canyon."

My heart stops for a second. "To whom?"

I hear pages moving. "Dut dut duh duuuh, oh, here it is, a Bill Waugh. However, when I ran his name in our database, it shows he's deceased. I contacted the webmaster for the site, who demanded a warrant before he'd pull the records for the account, but he did say that the account in question has been active several times in the past few weeks. The last chat was two days ago."

Yes, Bill is dead, and now this confirms some of my suspicions. I explain the situation surrounding Bill's death, Blakely's case, and a few of our theories. Detective Scott listens, asking some questions, and then we both fall silent.

It's a lot to take in, and there are a lot more questions than answers.

"If your hunch is right, this is going to require a joint investigation as well as requesting the FBI. I'm going to talk to my lieutenant, and pending his approval, I'd like to come to Rose Canyon and go over this later in the week so we have as much information as we can."

"Absolutely. My wife is the private investigator who uncovered the connection of Keeley and Bill Waugh, so it might be beneficial to allow her to sit in on the meeting."

"I wouldn't be opposed to it so long as she remembers she's a civilian and can adhere to the chain of command on this one." Good luck trying to get that to happen. Blakely is as likely to call off her search as I am to sprout wings.

"Sounds good," I say and then disconnect the call.

My mind reels with the information he gave me. Everything Blakely has been saying might actually be true. If the line went dead two days ago, which was right after the festival, then they may be laying low because they know we're onto them.

I pull into the station and immediately dial a number I hoped I wouldn't need unless it was to invite the person to grab a beer with me.

"Emmett Maxwell, how are things in small-town USA?" Mark Dixon asks, and I imagine him smirking.

"There have been a string of missing girls popping up in the area. One of them brought someone I love into the mix."

"What the fuck is going on up there?" His voice is no longer light. "Are Brielle and Spencer in danger?"

"I think, to some extent, we all are. My wife was investigating one of the missing girls, and she found a link between the girl and Bill Waugh that suggested he was one of the last people to have contact with her before she went missing. I have no idea if or what we're going to uncover, and I'd like to make sure there's another set of eyes up here if I can."

"Wait, you said wife."

"We got married before our last deployment."

Mark chuckles. "Ahh, one of those marriages. So glad I never did that shit."

"Well, I did, and I love her, and she's here."

"And you want us to come out there?" he asks.

I park the car but don't move to get out. "We're a three-person station, and I think there are people higher than me involved. I know it's a big ask. I know you're all incredibly busy and expensive, but I'm concerned about the people in this town, my wife, and my friends, and I could use people I trust."

The line is silent for a minute. "I'm not sure how long I can float it, but I think we could spare some guys. I know Quinn will want to come out because it's bugged him since we left that he felt something was off. I'll probably send Liam, who's new to the team but who I would trust to guard my own daughter. Maybe Jackson can send one of his guys up from California. It won't be a perfect detail, but they're who I would want by my side. It's who I would go to war with."

"Thanks, Mark, because that's exactly what this feels like . . . a battle of some kind."

I go inside the station to pull whatever reports I have as well as run a search for missing girls that match the descriptions of the Jane Does. I look for girls between the ages of sixteen and twenty-one, runaways, average height, and cause of death being overdose.

When the results populate, I feel sick. There are so many it's overwhelming. I adjust the search parameters to the last three years and in the Portland area.

That is when my heart stops. There are at least two dozen girls, all of them similar in appearance, but the dates they were reported as missing are spaced out enough that you'd have to actively be looking for a connection to see it. Add in that it is happening in a large city with an undermanned police department, and you'll find a shadow for criminals to operate in.

If something like this were to happen in Rose Canyon, it would never go unnoticed.

Out here, life is supposed to be easier.

Still, there's a chance someone here is or was involved.

I walk over to the old filing cabinet, which is full of files we have yet to input into the system, and start flipping through files and reports.

"I want you to stop looking into these missing girls," the mayor says without coming fully into my office.

"I'm sorry, what?"

"Don't play dumb with me, son. I got a call from the mayor in Portland. He wanted to know what Rose Canyon's interest was with these cases. You can imagine my surprise since I didn't know we *had* an interest."

I close the filing cabinet drawer and lean against it. "I didn't realize the mayor was going to have issues with me helping investigate missing teenagers."

It seems crazy that an hour ago I was speaking to the detective, and the possibility of us sharing information has reached both our mayors.

"Is that what you're doing? Helping Portland detectives, or are you using the town's resources to help your girlfriend?"

"Wife," I correct, injecting steel in my voice. "And no, that is not what I'm doing. For a man who seems to have the drop on information, I would think you would have already known that Blakely closed her case. What I'm doing is what any good sheriff would do in this situation, and that is to cooperate with other precincts in an effort to protect civilians."

Mayor Stengel steps forward. "You have obligations to this town. What about the issues we're having?"

"What issues?"

The fact that he's questioning my loyalty to the people here grates, but I am going to do my best to stay cool.

"Exactly, Emmett. You don't even know what's going on. What about Mrs. Murphy, who had her car broken into? You had Holman work that case, and we all know how adept he is. Then I got a complaint of destruction of property at RosieBeans. Again, Holman was the officer handling it. Since your *wife* showed up, you haven't responded to a single incident. Yet, you somehow have time to handle missing persons cases almost two hours away? Absolutely not. I will not allow you to neglect the great people of this town."

"And why are you invested in this?"

He loses it. "Because this is my town! I am the mayor! I am the one who has to ensure that everyone here is doing their job. That's why. Why are you questioning *me*?"

Because he's sounding extremely suspicious.

However, I maintain my air of calm. Being that the town doesn't have its own police force, I know that the mayor could have me moved. I'm contracted by the county, mostly because I'm from here and was requested. The mayor and the town council hold the power over if I stay or another sheriff comes in.

"I apologize," I say, and he shifts back.

"What?" I watch the anger deflate from him in one second.

"I apologize for making you feel as if I'm neglecting this town, but I assure you that my first priority has always been and will always be to protect the people of Rose Canyon. So, while my intentions were never to derelict that duty, if I have, I am grateful you've informed me of it."

The mayor's stance changes to one of almost joy. He thinks he has me, and I inwardly smile. Good.

"I thought you were going to fight me on this."

I sigh, turning away to appear as though I'm hiding my shame. "No, you're probably right. I have been distracted by Blakely being here." I turn quickly. "But I love her, you know? I just want this to work."

There are two things this mayor loves—this town and his wife. He's been with Polly since he was twenty-two. He champions marriage above all else. His family values are what got him elected.

"I understand that. I applaud you for taking your vows seriously. It's not every day you see a man out there fighting for his marriage. Too often, people just give up, so it's admirable you're giving her what she needs." The mayor's smile seems genuine, and then he shakes his head. "That is why I'm telling you to let Portland handle their own cases. Focus on this town so you can give her a safe place to live where she won't be in danger. Understand?"

Oh, I understand that you don't want me digging around and just made a thinly veiled threat to get me to stop.

I look down and nod. "I understand."

And I am going to do the opposite of what he asked, but I'm just going to make sure I hide it a hell of a lot better and protect my wife in another way.

Blakely pounces on me the second I walk in the door.

"Did you know that Nick and Tessa are friends with Stephen?"

"Hello to you too."

She rolls her eyes and picks up Sunday. "Hi. Listen, I was outside with Sunday earlier, and Stephen came over to me."

"Stephen Stengel?"

"Yes. He was visiting Nick."

I shrug. "They're friends."

"Yes, but he's our lead."

"No, you don't have a lead." I take the dog from her arms and kiss the top of her head. "Did you miss Daddy? Did you? Because I'm sure your mommy has been going nonstop since she's a crazy person and doesn't know how to let things go," I say to my sweet puppy.

She licks my nose, and I grin. I turn to Blake. "Do I not get a kiss from you?"

The groan that comes from her chest does nothing for my ego. "Fine." She gives me a peck on the lips. "Now, can we talk about Stephen?"

"No."

"Emmett!"

"Blakely . . ."

"I swear to God! You are so annoying. Emmett, listen, Stephen was here. He was here, and he talked about his dad and sins of the father. Well, I guess I said that, but he agreed. Then I watched out the window for hours."

"You did what?" I ask, keeping my tone level, but already the emotions are starting to form. She needs to stay away from Stephen, the mayor, the town council, everyone. God, maybe I can ship her ass back to DC for a bit.

That idea has some merit.

"I watched. Obviously. Do you know he drives a Mercedes? How does a fireman and EMT have that kind of money?"

I huff. "His father is the mayor, Blake. Let's not pretend that he doesn't come from money."

"Fair point, but still. It was a nice one."

"You're reaching," I warn.

"Maybe I am, but don't you want to know about what happened to those girls? How are you just going on with your life like it didn't happen?"

I shake my head, put Sunday down, and release a measured breath. "If you think I don't care, then you don't know me at all."

"I didn't mean it that way."

"You said it. I care, but they weren't killed in my town. We have nothing tying anyone to this town other than a connection to Bill Waugh, who is dead. I can't go running around looking into the mayor's son because he once worked with Bill." I walk to her, taking her hands in mine. "Can we focus on us? Can we maybe, just this once, have some of what we need?"

"You know I want that too," she says quickly. "I want to make up for all the time we've lost, but I also need to do my job."

"You did your job when you found Keeley. No, it wasn't the outcome any of us hoped for, but you solved your case."

She looks down, and I know this is weighing on her. If she knew that Portland had another Jane Doe that matched the profile, it would make her relentless. The mayor in Portland is doing what he can to bury the story until we know more, but news and social media will get wind of it eventually.

I need her to go back home for a week or two tops.

"I feel like I failed."

Tilting her chin up, I look into those brown eyes filled with sadness. "You didn't fail, baby. You did everything you could, and you gave Keeley's parents closure. Look, maybe you should go to DC for the week, pack your stuff, and go see her family. You want to stay here, let's make it so you're not paying rent in a place you're not going to live in."

"You want me to move in? Like, give up my place?"

"You want shared custody of Sunday?"

She shakes her head. "No, but . . . I just don't want to move too fast."

I laugh. "Then we never should have gotten married."

"That was different."

"I know, but I love you, Blake. I want our life together, and I don't want to do long distance, do you?"

"No, of course not. I know I want to stay here. I just wasn't sure you were ready for me to move across the country."

I lift my hand to her face. "I don't want bits and pieces. I don't want you there and me here. I would go, fuck, I would move anywhere for you if that's what you wanted."

"No. No, you need to be here with your dad."

I am glad I don't have to explain that to her. My father couldn't handle moving facilities again, and I really don't want to leave him.

"Then go back to DC and pack what you can. Find someone to sublet your place or whatever, and then I'll fly out there and help you move."

Blakely bites her lower lip. "I did only bring enough clothes for a few days. I'm wearing my day-one outfit for the second time."

I rub my thumb against her cheekbone as I try to hide the relief crashing through me like a wave. "Just a week and then we can have forever."

Her arms wrap around me as I rest my chin on her head. It took her showing back up here to turn my world upside down, and I have never been happier about that. Now, I have a week to set it to right and pray she doesn't get caught in the middle.

CHAPTER
Twenty-Five
BLAKELY

The flight back home sucked. I cried when I said goodbye to Sunday, who is going to spend time with Brielle when Emmett has to work. And, of course, I was sad about leaving Emmett.

It's crazy that this is where my life is now. Just a few weeks ago, I was contemplating how to talk to him again. Now, we're happy and together. We want this marriage to work, and we want it for all the right reasons.

It's funny how things work out.

My driver takes us the scenic route into DC, down Constitution and past good ole Abe, the reflection pond, and the WWII memorial. The Washington Monument is after that and then all the museums.

"Have you ever seen the Capitol?" he asks, his New York accent thick.

"I'm from here."

He looks a little deflated. "Oh. I didn't know."

"It's fine. I'm moving to the West Coast soon and think we take these monuments for granted living here anyway. It was nice to get to see them."

"It is very true. I'm from New York, and I never once went to the Statue of Liberty or the Empire State building. I regret that. I did go to the World Trade Center, though. My pops worked there."

I nod. "I imagine it was hard for you on September 11th?"

The sound he makes is sort of a laugh, but I know there's no humor there. "That's an understatement. I left three years after it. I couldn't be there, you know? I would see the skyline, and I couldn't handle it. Lost four of my friends and some neighbors that day, and I don't know . . . it broke my spirit."

"I'm sorry. It changed a lot of people's lives in ways we don't always think about." It changed mine. It's why I joined the military. I needed to serve my country because I remembered it all. The fear, the patriotism, and the way the world ached. I wanted to be part of helping everyone heal. So, after I finished nursing school, I enlisted.

Little did I know that single choice would alter everything, and I would never use those skills after getting out.

"Ehh, it is what it is, right? I mean, we make our choices and move on. I came down here and made a good life for myself, so I can't complain. Other than the bagels. I can complain about the bagels. Also, would it kill someone to put a decent deli or Italian restaurant somewhere down here?"

I laugh a little. "I was in New York for a few weeks during a training exercise, and I can attest to the bagels."

He turns in his seat while we're stopped at a red light. "I'm Tony. It's nice to meet you."

"Blakely, nice to meet you too."

"You're all right if you know something about bagels. Most locals think the chain crap you get is great. It's shit. I actually have my cousin mail me bagels from Brooklyn."

The way his accent forms around the words takes me back to when I was there, and I smile. "That's a great idea."

"Well, I'm not eating the cardboard here. Where are you from originally?"

"My mother was from New Orleans and my dad was from

Nebraska. He was military, so we moved a lot when I was a kid, but we settled down in Norfolk. He got stationed there, and when my parents divorced, my mother stayed there since it was easier."

"Must've been tough . . ."

It really wasn't. Dad left when I was six, so I don't really remember the moving part, but I do remember the constant revolving door of kids in my school as families moved in or moved away. I would make a friend, and a year or two later, she'd be gone. That part sucked. I was a military brat without the relocation.

"It was, and it wasn't. I loved where we lived, and my mother did her best."

He makes a right onto my street. "We're just about there."

I look up at the tall buildings, finding my apartment, which is the upper floor of a row home that is nestled between two government buildings. It seems so out of place in the heart of the city.

We pull up, and I take a look at everything, nothing looks different, light is still on in the back of the house, so it wasn't always pitch black.

"Thanks, Tony," I say as I climb out of the car and add a nice tip to my app.

"Be safe out there, Blakely."

"You too."

I grab my bag, walk up the steps, and slip my key into the lock before I glance back over my shoulder. Right now, everything seems good and nothing is niggling in my gut, so I go inside.

My neighbor on the first floor has been collecting my mail, so I stop there to pick up the large bundle of bills and bullshit.

Then I head up to my apartment on the next floor, ready to be inside so I can video chat Emmett and see Sunday. The mail gets tossed onto the table, my bag gets dropped on the couch, and just as I'm kicking off my shoes, a hand wraps around me from behind, covering my mouth.

CHAPTER

Twenty-Six

EMMETT

"Y ou with a dog is a sight to be seen," Holden muses as I chase Sunday around the living room, trying to get her to give me back the sock she has in her mouth.

"Shut up."

Spencer laughs. "Dude, stop chasing her. She thinks it's a game. You have to at least *attempt* to be smarter than the dog."

I grab the sock as she moves past and then scoop her up. "Ha!" I yell in triumph. "Since Blake left this morning, she's been a maniac."

"They say that dogs take after their owners, so it's only fitting she's more like you now that the sensible one is gone," Holden says with a chuckle.

I hate my friends some days. "The fact that you think Blakely is sensible shows you know nothing about her."

"How is Blake?" Spencer asks.

"I haven't heard from her yet. She should've landed about an hour ago. She said she'd call once she's settled." I shrug, place Sunday in her pen area, and sit at the table.

This is my best attempt at acting. The truth is that I'm not apathetic about any of this. I have had this pit in my stomach since she left. I feel like a fucking asshole for lying to get her out of town, and I miss her. It's only been six hours, and I feel like my heart is missing.

I don't know how I was able to go on with my life the last time she left. I know she'll be back this time, but it's still driving me crazy.

"She'll call," Holden tries to reassure me. "Women have always loved you for some odd reason."

"It's the muscles," Spencer informs him. "Chicks dig muscles."

"You think? I always thought it was his height."

Spencer and Holden look at me. "Now it'll be the dog. No woman can resist a man with a puppy or a baby."

Holden nods. "For real. I am thinking of getting me one."

"A baby or a puppy?" I ask.

"Both. Maybe then I'll be a chick magnet like Emmett." His sarcasm is dripping on every syllable. I open my mouth, but he lifts his hand. "If you say a fucking word about my ex-wife, I'll kill you."

"You could try," I taunt him.

Holden could probably kill me without leaving evidence behind, but that doesn't mean I couldn't do the same to him, just in other more violent ways.

"Anyway. While we could end up in a two-hour long discussion about who could kill who easier, let's go over the information we have so far and figure out what the next play is," Spencer says, laying out all the paperwork Cole Security gave him on Stephen and the mayor.

For the next hour, we sift through it, showing one another a document that seems relevant. We work as a team, each seeing things from different angles and discussing it at length before sorting it into one of three stacks—useless, possibly useless, and valuable.

I grab a photo of Bill and Stephen that was taken outside of the youth center about three months before Isaac's murder. "Well, here's proof that Stephen and Bill knew each other, but we don't have anything linking him to missing girls, other than a rumor about him running drugs that was investigated and turned up nothing. It isn't even enough for me to open a case file on him, let alone bring him in for questioning." I drop the photo and then push the last paper to the side. "I need something that is irrefutable."

"We aren't going to get that, Emmett. We have limited resources, and we're working outside of any actual case. Keeley's death is Portland's case, and I'm still waiting on the ME's reports they promised to send over. You could always call the detective and have them sent before your meeting, if he's willing to share it," Holden suggests.

"I already did. I'm waiting on those."

Spencer leans back. "Are we even sure Stephen is involved?"

"Blake is—or, at least, she thinks there's enough to suspect him. I am more inclined to believe the mayor is the one running the show, and he got his son involved. Especially after his threatening visit."

They sit there with their jaws hanging as I fill them in on his demand that I stop looking into Portland cases.

Spencer rubs his chin. "Yeah, I don't have words for that bullshit. What does Chris say?"

"I didn't call her. She's given me what she felt comfortable with, and I don't want to push."

"I feel like she's saying more by not saying anything, to be honest," Spencer notes.

I would agree with him.

I glance over at the clock and then at my phone. I put in her flight number and see it landed two hours ago. Why the hell didn't she call me?

"What is it?" Holden asks.

"I haven't heard from Blake yet, and her flight landed hours ago."

"Do you think she fell asleep or something?"

Sure, that's possible, but it seems out of character for her not to at least drop me a text to let me know she landed safely. "I'm going to call her."

They nod, and I walk to the other side of the room. Her phone rings several times before going to voice mail.

"Blake, it's me. I haven't heard from you and wanted to check in, give me a call when you get this or just shoot me a text. I love you."

I hang up and go back to where my friends are, a pit forming in my stomach.

"Did she answer?"

I shake my head.

Spencer places his hand on my shoulder. "She'll call."

"If it were Brie, would you be so okay with it?" I ask.

"No."

"Right. I can't explain it, but it's not sitting well."

Holden looks to Spencer. "Do you know anyone in DC?"

Spencer already has his phone out, making a call. "Hey, Charlie, it's Spencer." He pauses, and his lips twitch up at the corners. "Yeah, I heard that some of your buddies are coming out." He laughs. "I wish that were the case, but you know, crazy shit happens in small towns because no one thinks it will." Whatever she says causes him to snort. "Listen, do you have anyone in DC who can check on a friend? She's kind of tangled up in some stuff going on out here, but she just flew into the city, and we haven't been able to reach her." He nods at me. "Perfect. I didn't know you were there." Another pause. "It's actually Emmett's wife."

I can hear her yell through the phone.

Spencer laughs and hands me the phone. Oh, goodie.

"Hey, Charlie."

"You're married?" she all but yells.

"Yes, I got married a few years ago. Military thing."

She chuckles under her breath. "Apparently, you have feelings."

"I do."

"That's sweet. Is that why you called Mark to have them come out? He said something about safety of the people you all love."

"Yup," I reply.

"Okay, listen, I'm near the National Mall, but I can get to her fairly quickly. Just text me the address, and I'll stop in and have her call you."

"Thank you."

"No problem."

I hand the phone back to Spencer and then text her from my phone.

Spencer pats my back. "I'm sure she's fine. She's a smart woman who went through the same training you did."

"I know. I just . . . wish she'd called, that's all."

"Charlie is going to check on her, so why don't we get back to figuring this all out? Once we do, she can come back and all will be well."

I force a smile. He's right. "I'm going to take Sunday out so she doesn't piss in the house."

"Uhh," Holden says, moving the chair across from him. "You might be too late on that one."

"Shit." I grab the puppy and her leash and head toward the door. "Clean that up for me, I'm going to take her downstairs."

Holden starts to mutter a protest, but I'm already walking out the door. Once I get downstairs, I check my phone for anything from Charlie or Blakely, but it's been fewer than two minutes, so Charlie probably hasn't even left the parking lot yet.

Sunday walks around the grassy area, sniffing everything she can reach.

"Hey, Emmett!"

I turn to see Tessa walking toward the building. "Hey, how are you?"

"Good. I heard you got a new puppy! That's so exciting. I met Blakely, and she is just adorable. I love her. With Brielle gone, it's nice having a girl our age living in the building," she says quickly without dropping her huge smile. "I am so happy for her and Spencer. And now you! It's so great seeing people happy and married."

Tessa is one of those people who can have an entire conversation without anyone else needing to be there. She rambles on, and the best way to get through it is to let her tire herself out.

"You're happily married, any tips?"

She clasps her hands in front of her. "Gosh! I would have to think on that. Nick would probably be able to give you a better answer since he's learned how to deal with me. We all know I am quite the handful."

"I wouldn't say that." It's more like a mouthful.

"That's sweet. Nick is out of town on a boys' weekend with Stephen and Ryan, so I'll let him know you need advice when he gets back."

"Oh, where did they go?"

"They went to Arizona, I think . . . or maybe it was Virginia. One of those states with an 'a' on the end. I swear, they talk and I just zone out. They've been taking a lot more trips lately, always around a ballgame. Nick has a dream to visit all the stadiums in the US, and so they catch games when they can."

I have to work incredibly hard not to freak out that she said Virginia. If Stephen is there—I can't even let myself go there.

"What game did they say they were going to?"

"A few. They sort of road trip it for three days each time. I think it was Virginia! They were going to DC and then to Baltimore to see a game. I'm pretty sure they said something about sightseeing too."

My heart is in my throat, all the ease I was trying to feel with Charlie going has drained away.

"Tessa, can I—"

The words die out when I see Holden and Spencer rushing out of the building.

"Is she dead?" I ask, looking at the worry in their eyes.

Holden shakes his head. "No, but she's gone, and there were signs of a struggle."

CHAPTER
Twenty~Seven
BLAKELY

"**D**o you always have to be so fucking dramatic?" I ask Chase, my contact in the FBI. "You couldn't just call and be like, 'Hey, I have some news'?"

He shrugs. "If I could risk contact with you, I would."

"Well, you owe me a new lamp." Before I realized it was him, I grabbed it off the side table and threw it at him. He had enough sense to move before it hit him. A shame, that. I would've liked to cause him injury after he scared the shit out of me.

We're walking the National Mall where there is very little chance of anyone noticing us. It's dark, but there are still tourists milling about at each monument.

"It's you who's going to owe me, sunshine."

"And why is that?"

"Because I found something connecting Bill to someone else."

"I'm assuming it's rather important, considering you didn't want to give me this information over the phone?"

He nods, looking around. "I've been working with a joint task force charged with looking into the increase in missing teenagers. Now, it's not normally something people take note of, it's almost as if the public couldn't care less unless they're grabbed from their homes. But the Portland FBI office got a request to look over a report to see if it was a case we were going to adopt."

"Then I'm glad I sent the report to you."

Chase asked that I share anything I found, so I did. Even if he weren't a friend, I would have since not sharing information like that only gets more people killed. We all know this is bigger than any one person or team can track alone, and I don't have the resources the FBI does.

"Wait, you said four."

"Yeah, the one that was just found a day or so ago. I got notified by the Portland FBI office."

"When did they step in?"

Chase shrugs. "I'm not sure it's official yet. They don't have enough evidence to make it a federal case since most of these girls are assumed runaways, and there is no law preventing a minor from crossing state lines by themselves."

I loathe red tape. "So, what is the consensus?"

"Your theory about Bill Waugh being in contact has been true for Keeley and now two other girls," Chase says, placing his hand on my back to lead me up the winding trail to the Washington Monument. "We don't have a warrant yet, but the webmaster states they are unable to provide transcripts from the app remotely, which is bullshit. In the meantime, I did some more digging into the mayor, but nothing stands out, and he doesn't seem to be gaining anything financially. He's not poor, but he's mortgaged to the hilt."

"What about his son?"

Chase shakes his head. "I couldn't find a link there either, but listen, all this aside, you should know that I was alerted that Stephen also flew into DC today."

I jerk my head in shock. "Are you sure?"

"His flight landed six hours before yours."

My jaw falls open. "And you think I'm in danger?"

"I think you kicked a hornet's nest when you went out there, and someone is pissed off."

A woman behind us chuckles. "If your husband isn't the hornet who is going to sting you first."

I turn quickly to find a tall woman with jet-black hair framing her face like an inky river smiling. Her hands are raised as she pulls to a stop. "I come in peace. My name is Charisma Dixon, you can call me Charlie. I'm a friend of your husband, Emmett."

"How do you know he's my husband?"

"He was worried when you didn't call, so he asked me to go to your apartment and check on you. When I found the broken lamp"—I turn to glare at Chase—"I did what I do and found you."

"How did you track us?" Chase asks.

"Please, the FBI aren't known for their ability to be stealthy." Charisma turns to me. "And it didn't take me long, considering my agency is always watching."

That's . . . scary.

"You're slightly terrifying," Chase notes, echoing my thoughts.

"You have no idea. I'm going to reach into my pocket and grab my phone."

My eyes narrow a little. "Why are you telling me that?"

"I have no idea if either of you is armed. I'm just being cautious. I have no desire to be shot again."

Again? Who the hell is this girl?

She extracts her phone before extending it to me. "Call Emmett. His number is the last one dialed, so just hit send again. He's probably out of his mind by now."

Emmett and I had a code when we deployed. A way of letting the other know that we were okay and the other person should carry on.

I shake my head at her offer. "You call him."

"Me? Trust me, he wants to talk to you," Charlie says, phone still extended.

"Call him and ask him one question."

She grins as though she knows why I'm asking this. "What's the question?"

"Does he want to build a snowman?"

Charlie laughs and then places the call before putting it on speaker. "Charlie? Did you find her? Is she safe? I'm driving to the airport, losing my fucking mind!" Emmett's voice is filled with concern.

She raises one perfectly arched brow at me. "I have her here. She's perfectly safe."

"Blake?" he calls out to me, but I shake my head and notch up my chin.

Charlie rolls her eyes, but her smile is wide. "She is worried this is a trick, Emmett. So, do you want—"

"I hate the snow. I hate the cold," he responds so quickly that she has to purse her lips to keep from laughing.

"Emmett!" I say, grabbing the phone and taking the call off speaker. "I'm fine. It was a very overeager friend who was concerned."

"Jesus Christ," he says, his voice shaking. "I was so worried. You didn't call."

"I got in the Uber and ended up talking to the driver. My phone was on 1%, and I needed it to get into my apartment. I figured I would plug it in and call you, but . . . anyway. I'm fine."

He sighs heavily. "Listen, you need to come back."

"Because Stephen is here?" I ask.

"How the hell did you know that?"

"My overeager friend is watching my back."

"Yes. That's why. I can't get to you until tomorrow. The flights—"

I stop him there. "Why would you come out here? I'm sorry I didn't call, but I'm okay, I promise."

"Blake," he says, relaying his displeasure in that single syllable.

"Listen, I can handle myself, and clearly, you have scary friends out here." I look at Charlie, who shrugs.

"If Stephen is involved, and something happens . . ."

That first word is what gives me pause.

If.

Whoever is involved in this is smart, and it would be incredibly stupid to come out to DC and harm me. The first person that Emmett would look at is Stephen since he's here.

"Blake," Emmett says, "I can't lose you again."

"I will stay somewhere else tonight, and then tomorrow, I'll start packing my things so I can come back home. I promise, I will be extra vigilant, but Keeley's parents are expecting me tomorrow afternoon, and I have to follow through."

I should've come back and met with them in person to tell them about Keeley, but I'm here now, and it's something I have to do. I'm not breaking my word.

"All right."

I walk a little farther away from Chase and Charlie. "Emmett, I know we both feel like there's something off with Stephen and the mayor, but these are just hunches. What if all they are is a diversion to keep us from looking in the right direction? I keep thinking about when we were in the desert and nothing was ever as it seemed, you know? A lot of it was smoke and mirrors. I've been so sure that it's him, but now I'm wondering if that's what it was *made* to look like."

"I know what you're saying, but all the evidence points one direction."

He's probably right, but again, it just feels off. "Maybe it's because I'm away from Rose Canyon and have time to think. I don't know, but I think you need to look at other people with connections to Portland. You know, it's always the people we least expect."

Emmett is silent for a minute. "So, who is the last person you'd expect?"

"Other than you?"

He laughs. "Other than me."

I think about all the people I met and who would have the least likelihood of being someone involved. Someone who isn't too old or has power. Someone who would blend because when you blend, no one looks at you too hard. The quiet or friendly ones. The people who you think are amazing and perfect. Really, there's only one name that comes to mind. "Tessa."

I've been in DC for six days, and I am done. I'm so over all of it. The city, the noise, the never-ending stream of people arguing. It's just . . . crap.

How I loved this place so much once is beyond me.

Now, I long for Oregon. For the quiet, the crisp mountain air, and the salty ocean breezes.

Charlie and I are meeting for lunch to discuss whatever new developments she has found. She stayed in the area, keeping watch over me until she had confirmation that Stephen and his friends left, which they did.

I met with Keeley's parents four days ago, cried for hours, and now I'm finishing up packing so I can stick my crap in storage before Emmett and I move it or sell it all.

His name appears on my phone, and I smile as I swipe it, loving his gorgeous face.

"Hey," I say, missing him so much more than I should.

"Hey, you."

I bite my lower lip, flopping onto the bed. "Miss me?"

"Tons."

He is sitting in his cruiser, outside of our apartment, in his uniform and resting his head against the seat.

"You look tired."

"I look like I am ready to have you home so I don't have to worry. Also, Sunday shit on the carpet last night and destroyed a blanket."

I laugh. "That is really why you miss me."

"Hell yeah, you make that dog less demonic."

"She's been with Brielle all day, though, right?"

He nods. "Yeah, thank God I get a break."

"You know, maybe we really shouldn't have any living thing relying on us." I laugh, but it's only funny because it's reality.

"I relied on you for years, Blake, and you didn't let me down."

My heart flutters, and I have to hold back an audible sigh. Seriously, I will not be that girl. I will not simper at his sweet words.

But then, I sigh, like a fool. "You're turning me into a girl I never thought existed."

"One with a heart?"

I purse my lips and shake my head. "That was rude."

"I'm sorry."

"You will be when I finally get home."

His radio goes off, and Emmett raises a finger to silence me while he listens and then says, "Copy."

"Everything okay?"

"Oh, it's just another boring day here in Rose Canyon."

"Have you found anything since I've been gone?"

He licks his lips. "I don't know. I wish I could explain, but . . . I can't. The Cole Security team gets here tomorrow, and I can't tell you how much of a relief it will be for Spencer and me to know you and Brielle will have extra protection."

"You do remember I am a combat medic, right?" I get that he wants to protect me, but I am not some damsel in distress.

"You remember that not even a week ago someone broke into your apartment and got the drop on you, right? I'm not saying you can't take care of yourself, but not everyone can be on alert all the time. Besides, I didn't saddle you with fifteen guards, it's two guys who can keep an eye out when we can't."

"And he was FBI, a friend, and wasn't a threat. If it really was someone trying to kill me, they wouldn't be walking around DC right now."

"Fine, but I still lost my mind."

Fair enough. I can imagine it was hard for him not knowing what happened until he got confirmation from Charlie I was fine. "Well, luckily that's not our reality. What is, is that we need to find answers. Are you going to have someone follow me around for the rest of my life?"

"If I have to."

I shake my head. "This will be a discussion to be continued."

"I figured as much."

I move up on the pillow, wishing I could be in his arms. "How is your dad?"

Emmett said he had a really bad day yesterday. They actually called Emmett to come to the facility to see if he could calm him. I hated that I was so far away and couldn't help. Not that I could have done much, but I could have been there for Emmett.

"His nurse says he's doing better today. He was still disorientated, but not belligerent."

"Has he ever been like that before?"

"No, never to the point where I had to authorize sedation. My dad has never been a violent man. He never spanked my sister or me, and he never even yelled that I can remember. It was always that implied disappointment. He was a master at that look, you know? The face that said, 'Son . . . you should do better and guilt is my best weapon.'"

I laugh a little. "My mother was a yeller. God, she would get so mad at me and my brother. I can remember as a teenager getting mouthy with her, and she would screech and walk out. If she hadn't, I think she would've wanted to punch me."

"You? A pain in the ass?"

"Imagine that. Anyway, I'm glad he's better today."

Emmett nods. "Me too. You both matter to me, more than anything."

"I'm sure Hannah appreciates that."

"Please, Hannah is quite happy to pretend this town doesn't exist—or my father for that matter."

I think Emmett's mother running off hurt Hannah in ways she can't explain. That town holds all those memories for her, and it's easier to stay away than deal with them. I understand that better than most. I'm the queen of avoidance.

As much as I'd like to suggest that, even I know this isn't something I should get in the middle of.

"Well, I want to be back there."

His smile reaches his eyes, and the blue in them deepens. "I want you in my arms, Blakely. I want to feel you, kiss you, hold you so I know that you're safe. I feel fucking empty without you."

If a heart can cement itself to another, it just happened. "Emmett—"

There's a knock on Emmett's window, and he huffs. "One second."

He tilts the camera toward his chest, but I can hear the window go down, and then there is a loud *bang* that freezes every drop of blood in my body. I know that sound. I have lived that sound so many times.

"Emmett!" I scream as the phone falls from his hand, and I can't see anything as though it's the seat of the car or floorboard. "Emmett! Oh my God!"

I am off the bed, running as though I can go anywhere. That was a gunshot. He was shot. Maybe. I don't even know.

My heart is pounding as I start to yell louder. "Emmett. Please! Please say something!"

There's nothing. No response.

I start to shake as adrenaline and fear threaten to completely take control, and I have to work to keep from panicking. He needs help. I need to do something.

Fuck. I am across the country.

Think, Blakely. Think.

I force my breathing to calm and conference in another number because I don't want to hang up.

Tears fall, blurring my vision and dripping down my cheeks unchecked. "Emmett," I say over and over. "Please, I can't lose you."

The other person picks up. "Blake?"

"Spencer! You have to get to Emmett. He was shot. Please. You have to find him."

"Where are you?"

"I'm in DC. We are on a video call. I heard the shot, and the screen is black. He's not answering me, and he was outside our apartment!"

Spencer is yelling, I'm on the verge of sobbing, and I can hear Brielle in the background. He barks out several orders, but when he comes back to the line, his voice is calm. "What did you see?"

"Nothing. We were talking, and then someone knocked on the window . . . and then the sound. God, the sound. He was in his cruiser. He was just sitting there, but I don't know where he was. There's no way—" I start to cry harder. "Emmett," I say again, begging for him to please respond.

"They're on their way to him now, Blake, they're two minutes out. I'm going too."

"What do I do?" I ask. "I need him!"

"I know. I'll call you as soon as I know something."

I sink to the floor, staring at the blank screen that hasn't moved. My mind conjures all the things that could be happening to him, none of which are good.

"Emmett," I say over and over until my voice is hoarse. Each second of silence building into a weight heavy enough to shatter my heart.

Then there are sirens. They are soft at first, but they grow louder and louder as help barrels toward him, and I start to pray.

Please don't take him from me.

Please don't make me be a widow.

Please. I can't handle it.

"He's here!" someone yells. "Get the stretcher!"

The phone lifts, my heart pounding as I wait to see something, but then the line goes dead.

CHAPTER

Twenty-Eight

BLAKELY

No one will tell me anything. Spencer isn't answering. Holden is at the hospital and can't take my calls.

Brielle at least called to say she hadn't heard from anyone yet either and to get my flight information.

There are no more flights today, but I am on the first one in the morning. Hours I have to sit here, staring at the walls and hearing that gunshot again and again.

Listening as the sirens blazed in the background, and as they arrived, someone shouting the order to get a stretcher.

Because he couldn't move on his own.

Tears come again.

There's a knock on the door, and I force myself to move. When I open it, Charlie is there.

"I know we're not what you'd call friends, but I've been where you are right now, so I thought you could use someone to just . . . drink with." She lifts a bottle of wine, and I nod.

"Do you need a glass?" I ask.

She twists the top off. "Do you?"

"No."

"Same. We'll drink like college kids. Who needs to waste time getting a glass anyway?"

We sit on the couch, feet up on the table, and pass the wine bottle back and forth. "I wish this were vodka," I say absently.

"I was worried you'd get too sloshed to fly out in the morning. This was the safer bet."

I lean my head back, my jaw trembling. "I wish I was numb."

She rests her hand on mine. "Numb will come. You have to feel it all to let it go. You know this."

I don't want to feel. I don't want to let anything go. "Why haven't they told me anything?"

"Maybe there's nothing to tell. If he's in surgery, we won't know anything until he's out. No information is better than false information anyway."

I turn to her. "I need something! I'm across the damn country, completely in the dark. I just need to know if my husband is alive or dead."

"I understand. I wish I could give you the answer. I can tell you that Liam will be here in about two hours. He is going to be your new bodyguard, and while you may not want it, that's too bad. Mark was already sending him to Rose Canyon to protect you anyway."

My chest heaves, and I don't have the strength to fight her on it. Fine. Give me a bodyguard. Give me ten as long as you give me Emmett too.

"If he dies . . ."

"What?"

I sit up, feeling overwhelmed. "Then nothing matters, Charlie! Nothing! He's all I have! I have lost everyone in my life. My father, my mother, my brother, the men I was supposed to save. I'll have nothing left . . ." I start to sob. "All I have is a puppy that he gave me because he didn't want me to be alone anymore." The tears fall so hard I can't see anymore. "God, it's like he knew I was going to be alone in the world."

"I'm not much of a hugger, but come here." Her arms are outstretched, and I lean into her. She's right. She's awkward and clearly uncomfortable, but I don't care.

All the time I spent pushing Emmett away so I wouldn't feel

this way. The time lost that I can never get back because I was so afraid of this exact thing.

I sit back up after a minute and take a long pull of wine as I stare at the boxes. My home is all packed, my shelves are bare, and my walls are blank.

"I thought I was finally going to have the marriage I dreamed of. I let my walls come down, allowed myself to be vulnerable."

Charlie grabs the bottle and sighs. "I've done that. It really sucks. Zero out of ten stars on the vulnerability shit. However, if I had never done it, I wouldn't have my kids. As crazy as they are, they're the best thing that's ever happened to me. If I lost Mark today, it would be an unimaginable pain, but I am better for the time we've had. Can you say the same?"

I think about the years we did have. Maybe not as a truly married couple, but it was ours. We ate pizza on the floor, watching horrible military movies. We laughed at ourselves as we tried to put furniture together. When my brother died, Emmett was my rock, and I wouldn't have made it through any of that if it weren't for him.

All of the nights we were huddled together in the desert, talking about the damn stars.

I wouldn't trade one second of it.

"I can, but I am not ready for this to be the end."

"I know. So, we wait."

I reach for the bottle. "And drink."

I must've fallen asleep because when I open my eyes, the sky is now black. Charlie is walking around my apartment and talking to someone on the phone.

"Nothing yet?" She's silent again. "Okay. Well, keep me posted. I'm going to stay with her. I'm watching the area, and so far, it's been quiet." She pauses. "I know, Mark. I am always careful, even more so when I know there's danger." Her laugh fills the room. "Yes, you are the most dangerous person I've ever faced. Yeah, yeah, you took me down. Idiot." I listen as her voice changes to more of a whisper. "Liam is here, yes, he'll accompany her on the plane. I'll be home tomorrow, and then we can discuss the information you're withholding from me." She pauses and then scoffs. "I'm a spy, Mark. I know when you're lying. I should go, though. I love you."

She releases a long sigh and sits at the table. I want to get up and ask her what information she thinks he's hiding, but I am too tired. Everything feels heavy. The weight of the unknown, the pit in my stomach, my limbs, and my heart. All of that I can ask her about in a few minutes. I let the heaviness overtake me and drift back to sleep, where there is nothing but darkness.

I hear Charlie moving around and then on the phone again. "Hello? Oh, good. Yes, let me wake her."

I sit up, instantly alert and praying this is news. "Is it Emmett?"

Her lips part, and her jaw moves, but there are no words. However, her hand is extended, and I take that as a sign.

He's alive and can talk.

I practically lunge for the phone. "Emmett? Are you okay?"

He clears his throat, only it's not his voice speaking. "It's Brie," she chokes a little. "I don't know how . . . to tell you this . . ."

I shake my head, unwilling to hear the words. "No." It can't be happening. "Stop."

"Blake, I am so sorry. I am . . . so, so sorry. He's gone."

"No," I choke the word out. "No, he can't. No. He isn't. You're lying." I crumble to my knees, barely bracing myself with one hand on the cold floor as pain slashes through my chest.

"They just came out to tell us. They . . . they just said he's gone."

My chest is so tight, I can't get air in or out. I thought I knew grief before. I thought I had felt the most pain there was when Dylan died in my arms.

I was wrong.

I was so wrong.

This is pain. This is agony that has no end. It's like someone has cut me open, and I can't breathe.

"Please!" I sob as the phone clatters to the floor. "Not again. Not him! No! It should be me. I can't do this again." I slam my hands on the ground, anger and devastation overwhelming me. "It should be me! Why can't it be me? Why does it have to be him?"

I want to die. I want to never feel pain again. I can't live through this. I can't lose another person. Not Emmett. Not the love of my life.

I cry harder, begging for God to make this all be a nightmare, but it's not, it's real and it's a living nightmare.

Charlie is here, her arms around me. "Breathe, Blake."

I force myself to do that, gasping for air. I try to see her through my murky vision, my watery gaze making it impossible. "He's gone."

"I know. I'm sorry."

My stomach heaves, and I rush to the bathroom where I lose whatever is in my stomach. Everything around me is falling apart. Emmett can't be dead. He can't. I need him.

Charlie is holding my hair back as my body rejects what my heart knows. "Easy. You have to calm yourself."

Each breath I take hurts, and I sink back onto my ass. "I can't be calm when everything I love is gone."

She hands me some water, and I take a small sip. Every part of my heart is shattered as I hear Brielle's words again . . . he's gone.

Gone is the loving man who made me smile. Gone is the protector who would walk in front of a bullet to save me. Gone is the loving son who combed his father's hair when he didn't think I was watching. The man who got me a puppy because he wanted us to have what we never thought we would.

I scoot back until I'm resting against the wall. I need something solid to hold me up because I have nothing left inside me.

"He's gone. He isn't supposed to be gone. We were just starting again. We were happy. We got a puppy and were going to be normal." Each word feels like another slice to my soul. "I did this."

Her hands move up and down. "No, you did not do this."

"I did. I went to him. I brought this to light. I pushed and pushed because I wanted answers. I dug into the town's secrets, and it got him killed."

Charlie shakes her head. "No. Listen to me, you didn't do this. You didn't get your husband killed. He's a cop, and he was doing his job. No one knows who shot him or why. It could have been random for all we know."

No, it wasn't random. It all happened because of me. My need to get justice for a girl I didn't know cost me the love of my life.

"How can I believe that? I showed up there, asking questions, and I clearly upset whoever is doing this."

"You are not responsible for the decisions others make. I know that's hard to hear and accept, but you didn't pull that trigger. You didn't do anything to set that into motion. Spencer wasn't going to let this drop. He had Quinn, who works for my husband, and some . . . friends . . . looking into it. It may have had nothing to do with you."

I can't hear this right now. I can't accept it. It's all too much. "I don't know what to do. I don't know if I should call his sister . . . I'm going to have to tell his father."

She rubs my back. "Let's get you back there, and then you can figure all this out."

That only makes me cry harder because when I get there, nothing will be the same.

The flight was long, and I slept a lot of it. Liam explained the plan for what we were going to do once we landed, and I was honestly too exhausted to give a shit about what he said, so I zoned out.

Apparently, they haven't discovered anything. No leads. Stephen was traveling with Ryan and Nick to a game in Texas after DC, so that's out, and the mayor has a solid alibi as well. Not that I think the mayor actually has it in him to kill someone in cold blood.

We walk out into the main terminal, and Holden is standing there, arms crossed, waiting. As soon as he spots me, he walks over.

His mouth forms into a tight line. "Hey."

"Hi."

He extends his hand for my bag. "Let me take that for you."

I nod, pushing the suitcase his way. "Thanks."

"Of course."

"Has anyone told his sister?" I ask.

"She is out of the country with her family. I didn't talk to Hank either."

That's probably for the best anyway. Hank will need a group of us, and I can't even be sure that he'll remember any of us. "Were you there? In the hospital?"

Holden shakes his head. "I was home. I had worked a twelve-hour shift, but I went back in as soon as Spencer got a hold of me. There was nothing I could do at that point."

"I've been there." My voice doesn't sound like mine. I'm just sad and can't muster enough energy.

Liam comes up behind me, pulling two bags with him. He sets one on its wheels and extends his hand to Holden. "Liam Dempsey. I'm part of the Cole Security team. You're Holden, right?"

Holden shakes his hand. "I am. Quinn is already set up at the apartment with the other team."

I'm not sure what that means. "What other team?"

Holden and Liam share a look. "Blake, Emmett set up some things while you were gone this week. He had every intention of talking to you about it when you got back, but—" His eyes cut away from me, and he clears his throat a few times before he turns back. "You aren't safe here."

"What?"

"You aren't going back to his apartment or to Rose Canyon."

My heart pounds harder, and I step back. "What do you mean

I'm not staying here? I have to go see my husband. I have to bury him, and you're saying I'm not allowed?"

Liam speaks this time. "You and I are going to make it look like we're heading there, and then, we will break off. Holden is going to take our car and continue to Rose Canyon while we head elsewhere."

"No."

I'm not doing that. I am not running away. I am not abandoning Emmett, whether he's dead or not.

"You have to."

"Says who? I have to do what is right. And that's to take care of Hank and Sunday and everything else. I have to plan a fucking funeral, not do whatever you're talking about."

Holden grips both of my shoulders. "I know you're hurting. I know you want to go to Emmett, but you can't. He loved you so much that he put this entire plan together to protect you if anything happened to him. Emmett is dead, and I will be in the ground beside him before I let anything happen to you. I won't break a promise to him, not even now."

The hits keep coming.

Now I have to run away? Now I need to hide? I am a goddamn combat vet, and I didn't make that promise. He can't dictate what I do no matter what Emmett wanted.

"I need to see my husband."

"That's not happening," Liam says, his voice stern.

"You aren't in charge of me." I stomp my foot with my fists balled. I can't take this anymore. I need to go to him.

"I actually kind of am."

I glare at him. "I don't even know you."

"No, but I am not the bad guy here. You have to go into protective custody until we can get the person behind this."

The tightness in my chest grows stronger. This is not supposed to be how this goes. None of it. "I have to see him. I have to say goodbye to him. Do you understand I just lost my husband, and you're asking me to leave him in the morgue?"

Holden moves toward me. "No one will let anything happen to Emmett's body. You will get to say goodbye to him."

"I don't even know the details." It feels like I am losing him all over again.

"What do you want to know?" Holden asks.

"Everything. I know nothing. All anyone has told me is that he was shot. I don't know . . . how or what happened. Was he in pain for a long time?" The tears fall, and Holden's eyes swim with them as well.

"This is hard. Losing Emmett right after Isaac. I'm . . . I'm struggling, and I didn't even think to talk to you about this because I am in a daze. I'm sorry, Blake."

"I don't blame anyone. I just want to know."

Holden nods and takes my hand, pulling me toward a bench. "He didn't suffer. The surgeon tried his best, but they couldn't repair the damage. The bullet hit an artery, and it was . . . it was quick."

I sniff and look down at my hands. "Thank you for telling me. I-I don't know what to say. I know you're all grieving, and I'm not so sure I can do this-s alone. I don't want to do it."

"As soon as it's safe for you to return, there is nothing we'd all like more than to be here for you. All I'm asking you to do is to follow through with the plans he put in place should something happen to him."

I turn to Liam, who is beside us. "I can't do this alone. I can't be holed up in some shack with my thoughts while his killer roams free."

"Blake, you have to think about this from what would've been his perspective," Liam tries to reason with me. "I love my wife and children more than anything in this world. If I knew there was a risk to their lives and I wasn't able to protect them, I would do the same thing Emmett has done. I would rely on the people in my life I trust the most to make sure Natalie and my kids were safe until the threat passed. I'd need her to trust that it's the right move because there is nothing more important to me than they are."

"You'd be dead, and she'd be broken. She wouldn't care about what you needed anymore because you left her." As I say the words, I can feel my anger rising. "Emmett was killed, and I am here. So don't lecture me on what he'd want because I don't care what he wants. He isn't here. I'm . . . I'm not . . ." I can't get the words to come out, and I force myself to stop for a moment. "I want my husband. I want the life he promised. I don't get that. I'm not hiding."

"Then will you protect something as important to him as you are?" Holden asks softly.

"What's that?"

"His father. Because you're both targets."

CHAPTER

Twenty-Nine

BLAKELY

I help Hank into the house where we'll be staying for who knows how long. We're on the border of Washington and Oregon on the outskirts of a town where no one knows us.

"Thank you, sweetheart. My bones are tired lately. That was a long drive."

I force a smile. "Do you need something else?"

Not that I have any idea what we have here. I arrived ten minutes before Hank did, just long enough to look over the house.

It's a quaint three-bedroom house that is surrounded by woods. It definitely has a cabin feel with wood trim everywhere and white walls. There are curtains on every window that I was instructed are to remain closed at all times. We are only allowed to access the woods on the property if we are accompanied by Liam or a Marshal.

I now only have contact with the three US Marshals that are doing surveillance, Holden, Liam, and Charlie, who called twice in the car to drive her point in about why I had to do this.

Yes, my death would be tragic.

I have no mother, father, brother, husband, friends . . . job. I'm winning at the game of life.

Sunday jumps up on my leg as my thoughts go down another

depressing path, and I sigh. I have her. The last thing of Emmett and I.

I pull her into my arms, kissing the top of her head. "I get why people love animals so much."

Hank comes into the room. "And what is this little one's name?"

"This is Sunday."

Because everything good happens on a Sunday. The tears come without warning because that statement is no longer true. Emmett was killed on a Sunday.

"Oh, don't cry," Hank says, concern etched in his voice. "Puppies aren't anything to cry over."

I laugh at that. "No, they're not."

"But something has you upset."

I haven't figured out how to tell him that Emmett was killed. It seems so cruel to do it and, at the same time, even worse to withhold the information.

"Why don't we sit?" I suggest, and Hank pulls out the chair beside me. I take a seat and then he does the same. "Hank, do you know who I am?"

He looks at me, eyes narrowed a bit. "We've met before."

"We have. Not too long ago."

"I'm not good with names."

I smile. "I'm Blakely."

Something alights in his eyes. "Do you know my son, Emmett?"

I will not cry. I will not cry.

"Yes, I did."

That word. That tense is not right on my lips. I do know him. I love him.

"He's a good boy, you know? He comes to see me all the time, talks nonstop, but I like that he comes. He spends a lot of time fussing about some girl, her name sounds like yours."

That's because I am the girl. "She must be special if he talks about her."

Sunday jumps onto his lap, and he smiles. "She is. He is in the army."

"I was too."

"With Emmett?"

I push the air from my chest. "Yes, we met there."

"He is very brave, my son."

"I know. He had this amazing ability to make me feel safe, even when our lives were in danger."

Hank smiles. "He has always been that way. When his sister was upset, he'd walk in, say something, and the room would settle. Tell me a story about him in the army."

I have so many that I want to share, but I know the one I want to share most. It was probably when I fell in love with him, only I didn't know it.

"We were on what was supposed to be a routine mission to apprehend the head of a terrorist ring operating out of this middle-of-nowhere village in the desert. The intel was valid, and the plan was to move in, grab him, and be out with no hiccups."

"But it didn't go that way?" Hank asks.

"Not even close. In fact, the whole thing went sideways almost right away. Emmett was leading the team that would breach. They went into the town unnoticed, but about two minutes before the team was set to enter, two bombs went off, everyone started shooting, and the entire mission went to hell. I did everything I could, but the injuries kept coming."

He reaches his hand over, squeezing gently, and I feel comforted for a moment. It's clear where Emmett learned his calming skills from.

I continue. "Everyone fell back, and we went to ground, trying to give me time to assess injuries while Emmett formed a new plan since the element of surprise was gone. That night, I wasn't okay."

I was so far from it. It was the first time I really thought I was going to die, and the first time I didn't know where to start. There were so many injuries that it seemed impossible to treat all of them.

Somehow, I was able to hold it together until the last person was bandaged, which happened to be Emmett.

He'd waited until everyone else was seen and then held me as I sobbed.

I wipe at my cheek and smile at Hank. "Emmett is who put me back together. He let me cry in his arms, and then we talked for hours about nothing and yet everything. Then he made me play this stupid game." I smile at the memory for a second.

"What game?"

I lean back and let the memory wash over me.

"You only get to eat a piece of granola if you have never done it."

"This is the worst version of Never Have I Ever," I grumbled. "I'm starving."

Emmett grabbed the bag from between us and thrust it into the air and well out of my reach. "Then let's hope you're not a degenerate."

"I got into the army . . . I can't be that bad."

He lifted one brow, staring at me as though I was nuts. "They let every one of us in, they have no standards."

I laughed. "Whatever, let's play so I can eat something."

I was unable to think about food for most of the day. There had been so much blood on my hands that I thought I would have to wash them for days to get it off my skin. However, Emmett calmed me down, and now I wanted to eat, only he was holding it from me with his odd game. "Never have I ever skipped school."

"Please, like you didn't?"

"I'm not eating, am I?" he taunted.

He missed the point of this game. "You're only supposed to phrase it if *you* have never done it."

"I think that rule is shit, so I'm making up my own rules."

That was great, but he needed to share those rules. "What the hell are you doing then?" I asked with exasperation.

Emmett took a few seconds while looking around at the camp we made. It had taken some time to find somewhere safe to regroup. When we did, Emmett, two other officers, and I spent hours working through what might have gone wrong and what the status of each team member was. Most of the injuries were minor, but there were two that I was concerned enough about that I requested extraction. Those who were considered non-extractable stayed to finish the mission.

"Okay, you make the statement of something you haven't done, and if the other person hasn't either, then you eat. If they have but you were lying, they get to eat. Once the other person gets the bag, they control the questions. No lying or I will down every freaking crumb in this bag, and you'll get nothing."

"How is that fair? You know things neither of us have done. I'll never get to eat at this rate."

"Well, I have the bag of granola, and this is my game. Are you scared to play?"

"You do know that we live together, and I will cut you in your sleep," I threatened.

"I'll take my chances."

I huffed. "Fine. Since your rules are completely wrong, hopefully you screw up." It was really the only chance I had.

"Never have I ever made out with my spouse."

"I hate you." We both knew that we had never made out with each other.

He grinned as he popped some of the granola into his mouth. "Never have I ever had mind-blowing sex with my spouse."

"Considering we are married to each other and haven't, you know the answer."

"This game is fun," Emmett said with smugness.

"Oh, sure, it's a treat."

"Want some?" He extended the open bag toward me, but when I reached into it, he snatched it back.

"You're an ass."

He shrugged. "You have to earn this granola. Okay, never have I ever . . . eaten sushi."

"Ha!" I finally had one. Emmett was afraid of sushi. He told me once about how the idea disgusted him. "I eat sushi all the time, and you have never because you said you thought it was still alive and would kill you."

Emmett handed over the bag of granola, and I immediately popped some into my mouth, smiling as I watched him.

"It's good, right?"

"It is very good granola," I agreed.

But, really, the granola wasn't what I was enjoying. It was this. Us. Him making me smile and laugh after having one of the worst days of my life. We'd only been married two months, and it wasn't even a real marriage. We hadn't kissed, other than at the ceremony, which was a peck before we burst into hysterical laughter. But our friendship was the best part of what I'd hoped marriage would be.

It was times when I didn't have to be afraid because I knew he'd always protect me, even when I didn't think I'd need it.

Hank clears his throat, and I give him a sheepish smile.

"Sorry," I say quickly. "I got lost in the memory."

I explain the game and how Emmett changed the rules. "As much as it drove me crazy that night, I was able to put my fear aside while he was with me and remember I wasn't alone. He was always there for me, and . . . I miss him. I don't want to be alone."

Sunday moves off his lap, jumping on mine. Her nose rubs against my chin, and Hank chuckles. "She senses you need her affection and wanted to remind you that you're not alone."

I pet my dog, nuzzling against her and fighting back my tears. No, I'm not alone because Emmett made sure we'd always have something to love. I never thought it would be a realization I had this soon, though.

Hank moves in his chair, looking around. "When will Emmett get here?"

Oh God. I breathe in through my nose, place Sunday on his lap, and then crouch in front of him. "He's not coming here, Hank."

"Why not?"

"Emmett was hurt, and you and I are in hiding right now. We have to stay here until we're told it's safe to leave."

He looks at me, his eyes full of concern. "Were you hurt too?"

"No, not physically," I say.

"Your heart is hurt."

"Very much."

My heart is broken. It's decimated, and I am trying so hard to keep it together for Hank.

"Because of Emmett?"

"Yes."

"Is he okay?" Hank asks, and I can't lie to him.

"Emmett was shot, and . . . he's gone now. He was killed, and . . . I am so sorry."

Those words seem so meaningless. Sorry doesn't bring back the son he lost. Sorry doesn't make this life-altering pain any easier to bear. And, yet, when I search for something more meaningful to say, there is nothing. I brought this to Emmett's door, and he was the one to pay for it, which is something I will never be able to verbalize my depth of regret for.

A tear drifts down Hank's cheek. I look at my fingers, trying so hard to keep my own tears from falling. Hank lifts my chin so our eyes meet. My blurry gaze finds his blue eyes, the ones that are the exact shade as Emmett's, swimming with tears. "He loved you. You made him happy."

My lower lip trembles, and I catch my breath. "I loved him."

"Then you hold on to that. Love is what makes us keep going. Even when we lose it, we can hold on to the way it felt to love someone."

I can't keep looking at him, so I duck my face as the tears roll down my cheeks. "I loved him with my whole heart, and I don't know how to go on."

"By remembering and telling the stories. I can't do that anymore. Most days, I don't have the memories, but I have the feelings. I can close my eyes and feel peace, which was because of love." Hank brushes away a tear. "I have to remember that now. The way that story made me feel about my son."

"I will tell you the story whenever you want."

"That's how he lives."

"In our hearts."

Hank nods, petting the puppy again. Something changes when his eyes meet mine again.

"Hank?"

He looks down at Sunday and then back to me. "We've met before. Do you know my son, Emmett?"

My chest aches, but I force myself to keep from falling apart. "We have, and yes, I know Emmett."

CHAPTER
Thirty
BLAKELY

The days in isolation go slower than I knew possible. I have nothing to do but think about my life. It's been six days.

Six days of nothing. No friends. No work. No phone calls. No information.

Today, I'm taking a walk in the woods, much to Liam's dismay. When I almost break my ankle for the third time, he huffs loudly. "Is this really necessary?"

"I can't stare at the walls anymore. I can't keep answering Hank's questions about when Emmett is coming. I am losing my mind, so, yes, it's necessary."

He grabs my arm, helping me onto a rock. "Fair point."

No shit it is. We continue, and then he checks his phone again. "Why is it that you get to have communication with people and I'm stuck talking to you or Hank?"

Liam shrugs. "I'm not being hunted."

"I'm being actually hunted?" I ask, pissed because this is something that no one will actually be straight with me about. "I thought it was just a possibility."

"You've had unexpected visitors at your apartment in DC and in Rose Canyon."

"I'm assuming it wasn't someone bringing a Bundt cake to offer condolences?"

He shakes his head. "No, more like a rifle."

"It's not the first time I've had that happen," I say, crossing over the stream. The forest is beautiful. Everything is lush greens and muted wildlife. The only sounds are the babbling brook as it flows toward the sea and the birds chirping. It's secluded and probably something I should relish in after living in DC for so long, but this is hell on Earth.

"Why don't you take me back to a city? It's easier to get lost when there are so many people."

"Because it's harder to keep track of who is around you. This is where the Marshals wanted you for several reasons."

"Which are?" I ask.

"You can ask them."

"Okay. Give me your phone and let me call them."

He gives me a look, and I roll my eyes. They don't talk much. Each day, they enter the home, check cameras, and scan for anything out of the ordinary. I ask questions, they grunt or ignore me, and then tell me they'll know more soon before they leave again.

I'd like to know more *now*.

"I always thought that protective custody was more like you get a new life where no one knows you. Not that you're hiding in the woods."

Liam laughs quietly. "I think that part is coming, which is when you'll lose me for good. We just need to make sure we can move you without anyone noticing. This is sort of a pre-staging."

"Great, so then I'll have the puppy, Hank, and new unsocial Marshals. Where we end up, Hank will get the care he needs?"

"Yes, it's one of the stipulations Emmett had in place. You'll be relocated to an area that has a facility capable of caring for him."

"Good, because I am not leaving him, no matter how hard it is to see his face or answer his questions. He's my father-in-law and has been abandoned enough. He's . . . well, he's the only family I have."

Emmett went to extreme lengths to care for me and Hank, and I will not let him down. His father meant everything to him, which means he's everything to me too.

"You're not as weepy today," Liam notes as we walk farther.

"Maybe I'm dehydrated."

He snort-laughs. "Grief is a funny thing, isn't it?"

I stop walking, feeling a little tired. Liam leans against the tree while I sit on a fallen trunk. "I don't know if I'd call it funny."

"I just mean that it's never what we expect. One day, we can be completely fine, thinking that life is in this new normal, and then the next day, we're a fucking mess."

"Who did you lose?" I ask.

"My mother. It's not the same as what you're feeling by any means, but I watched my dad go through it. He was lost for a while then seemed to settle in to the new normal, and weeks later, he would be a wreck again. I remember learning about the stages of grief, but it wasn't until I experienced it that I realized they aren't linear."

"No, they aren't. When my brother died, I felt like the world had just crumbled. It was this crushing heartache because I watched him take his last breath."

Liam tilts his head. "You were there?"

I nod. "Our unit had intersected with his. It was so . . . amazing. I was so happy when I saw him. It was like a scene from a movie. I called his name, he turned, and I went running toward him. We hugged for what felt like hours. Emmett and Dylan got to meet and were fast friends. I will always be thankful that they had that time to get to know each other.

"All of us were exhausted. We'd walked for-freaking-ever to reach the makeshift base. Dylan's unit was on perimeter watch that night. The Ranger team was getting much needed rest. I remember waking up to the gunfire and thinking for just one second that it was fake, which I never did because of where we were."

Liam smiles a little. "After a while, you go numb to the sound when you're out there."

I nod. "Exactly. People started screaming, and that was when I knew it was real. They were calling for doctors and medics. There was an attempted breach into the camp, and Dylan's unit held them back. It was like . . . fate led me right to him." The tears that I wasn't crying come back. My baby brother was so brave. So strong and stood his ground, sacrificing his life for his brothers and sisters who were beside him.

"You found him injured?"

I bite my lower lip, trying to stop the flood of emotion, and bob my head. "There was nothing I could do. I couldn't . . . extract the bullet there. I didn't even have my kit. I just ran out there. If I'd had my kit or was thinking right, I could've done something more. Held out until one of the surgeons could get there."

Liam doesn't offer me false sympathy. He just stays silent for a moment. "One of the things we know when we go into war is that casualty is a certainty. We know it, but we are liars who pretend we're ready for it. Losing a friend, family member, or team member is never what you prepare for. There's no manual on how horrific you're going to feel day in and day out or one that tells you which memories will haunt you."

"No, there's not," I say, my voice drifting off.

"I don't say this to make you feel better," he prefaces. "I say this because, if it were me, I would much rather the last face I see be my wife or my kid before I go. I wouldn't want it to be a complete stranger."

"And what about the pain that leaves for your survivor? What about how hard it is for me now? To have looked into my brother and my husband's eyes before they were killed?"

Liam moves to sit beside me. "That's the part I said wouldn't make you feel better. I'm coming at it from the other side, selfishly wishing I could see the person I love most in this world. Let me ask you this, Blake, if you could undo it all, take being at the camp, loving your husband, holding your brother as he died away, would you?"

A bird flies overhead, rustling the leaves as I sit and ponder his question. My gut reaction is to scream out a yes. To take all of this away, but then I would've lost still. They'd be gone, and I wouldn't have had any of these memories.

If I undid it all, I would have no memories to cling to. I wouldn't have been there for my brother when he needed me most. I would've missed knowing what it feels like to have loved. The things that make this pain so bad are all the things that made the memories beautiful. I experienced real love. I have been held and touched and kissed by a man who didn't hold back.

That would've been the tragedy in all this. To have never felt the warmth of his soul.

I turn back to Liam, feeling a small bit of peace. "No. I wouldn't. I just wouldn't have wasted a single second. That's the only thing I regret."

"Are you okay, honey?" Hank asks as I'm curled up on the couch. Tears fall in a nonstop stream. I hate that I am this sad. I hate that I reach for Emmett, only to find he's not there and he never will be again.

"I'm good." I lie to my father-in-law, who returns his gaze to the television.

A second later, he looks back to me. "What's today?"

"Sunday."

He nods. "My son comes on Sundays."

I squeeze my eyes shut. *No more crying. No more.*

"That's nice." The words have no emotion behind them.

"Do you know when he'll be here?"

Never, Hank. Never.

"I don't."

The episode of *Seinfeld* he's watching is from an early season, and he laughs at something before saying, "He'll be here. Emmett is always here on Sundays."

This time he won't, but I can't say it. I just can't.

Today has been especially hard on me because I had a dream last night. One that was so magical and perfect. Emmett and I were at the beach, walking along the rocky coast with Sunday running up and down between us. The birds were flying above, squawking before diving down to get fish that swam too close to the surface.

He was smiling, the warmth of his hand over mine made my heart race.

"I love you, Blake."

"I know," I said in return.

"And do you love me?"

"With everything I am."

It was so easy to tell him those words because they're true. I love my husband. I love the man who believes in me when I don't deserve that trust.

He pulled me into his arms, kissing my nose as the wind whipped my hair around us and Sunday jumped on our legs. We laughed, still keeping our arms around each other. Sunday barked again, and I woke up.

Alone.

Without a husband.

All I wanted was to close my eyes and never leave that dream again.

I sniff, the stupid tears not ceasing, and Liam enters.

"Blake? Are you crying?"

"I'm fine."

He raises one brow. "Come in the kitchen, let's go over our plans for the next few days."

As if I want to talk about how we will, once again, do nothing. The plan is . . . do nothing, stay hidden, and talk to no one. I find that I don't care which new and inventive way he's going to try and spin it.

But this is something to think about other than being a widow who is falling to pieces. So, I get up and follow him.

As soon as I step into the kitchen, I wish I had stayed in the living room. Akers is there, scowling at me.

"Nice to see you, Akers."

"I received word from Rose Canyon today. Holden sent over some paperwork you need to sign."

"You could ease her in a bit, man," Liam says, coming to sit in the chair beside me. "It's forms and information about his insurance policy."

I look over to Liam. "Aren't I supposed to have basically disappeared? You want me to sign documents?"

"Holden knows you're not dead. We're going to backdate them. Most of the town believes you came, handled things, and left because it was too much to bear."

So, they think I'm a coward. Great.

"What documents?"

Akers slides over a manila envelope, and I carefully remove them. The words up top make my heart plummet. Death Certificate.

Those traitorous tears come like liquid fire, burning my cheeks as they fall. None of this feels as if it's happening to me. As though I'm a spectator. As though none of it is real. I never got to see Emmett, touch his face, and kiss him goodbye. I didn't get the most basic things people need to grieve.

With Dylan, I was there, I held him as he died. I saw it happen, and while it was equally heartbreaking, at least I had the truth in front of my eyes.

I've had enough. "I am done."

"Done what?" Liam asks.

"I am done doing this. I'm done . . . sitting here while my husband rots in a cold box. You know, I don't even know if that's true. For all I know, this isn't even a real death certificate. I'm not signing it. I don't know any details on how he died or even *if* he died. For all I know, you fucking people are lying!"

I have been so naïve just going along with all of this. Not once have I questioned what they've told me, and I'm done being a good soldier. I've done it my whole life, and it's given me nothing.

"You think we're lying that your husband is dead?" Akers asks.

"How would I know? I have never seen proof. I haven't talked to anyone. No burial. Nothing. So, for all I know, this is some conspiracy to keep Emmett and me apart."

Liam laughs. "No one is lying to you, Blake. We're keeping you and Hank safe. Someone shot your husband. Someone who also made threats against your life."

It's as if he's reading from some script, and I don't have the lines. "No."

"No what?" Akers asks.

"No, I'm not signing it. No, I'm not doing this. No, no, no. I want to see my husband."

"Blakely, whatever you're feeling is normal, but you can't see Emmett's body. You can't go to Rose Canyon or you'll die."

"Then I'll fucking die! What am I living for? A life in isolation? A world where I am without any family or people I love? I didn't sign up for this, and I'm done. I am going to see my husband and bury him properly."

Akers runs his hand over his face. "You want to see Emmett?"

My eyes widen as I look at him. "What? You . . ."

Is he alive? Is he saying I can see him?

The question jars me, and I feel a spasm of hope in my belly.

He takes a folder out from his bag and tosses it onto the table. I reach for it, but Liam's hand slams on it first. "This is fucked up, Akers, and you know it."

"She asked for it," he says, clearly not agreeing.

Whatever is in that file, I want to see. I pull on it and Liam's pleading gaze meets mine. "Blake, I'm telling you not to look in this file. If it's what I think it is, I promise, you don't want to see it."

I need to see his face. I know it's insane. I know it's probably a mistake, but it's been days of questioning everything and hoping it is a lie. I need the proof.

Liam's eyes are swimming with concern as I ask, "If it was your wife, what would you do? Would you look away or would you want to honor her?"

A moment of understanding passes between us and then he

lifts his hand. Love doesn't mean looking away when it's hard, it's standing in the face of what scares you and battling the fear.

Slowly, I lift the cover open and read the report.

At 17:32, emergency dispatch received a call from Spencer Cross stating there was a possible officer in distress. Immediately dispatch attempted to reach officer Emmett Maxwell, age 39, Sheriff assigned to Rose Canyon. After one minute of no response, all units were dispatched to the corner of Maple Ave and West Shore Drive. Deputy Holman arrived on scene at 17:45 and found officer Maxwell unresponsive, having suffered a single GSW to the back of the head. The ambulance had already been dispatched and arrived on scene at 17:48.

At that point, medical aid was rendered, the officer was transported to Seaside Medical Center, and the crime scene was secured.

According to an eye witness, Sheriff Maxwell was parked in his police vehicle when an unknown suspect approached from the driver's side rear window. Witness states she heard a knock on the window, where Sheriff Maxwell lowered it, at which point a shot was fired into the vehicle, striking officer Maxwell.

It goes on to state the weather, wind and camera locations in the vicinity of the incident, along with where the single casing was found, and the transport notes.

Sheriff Maxwell was still alive when he arrived at Seaside Medical Center.

The police report then references the coroner's report.

It repeats a lot of the same but uses complex medical terms, thankfully my medical background makes it easy to understand.

Basically, he was still alive, but as soon as they started surgery, he died.

I look at Akers, who is watching me closely. He clears his throat. "There are photos in there, Blake. I warn you, they aren't . . ."

"I understand."

I do my very best to detach myself and be the medic I was trained to be. Dead bodies don't bother me, but this isn't a dead soldier, it's Emmett. My Emmett.

I push the paper to the left, and then I see him. In the photo, there is a sheet over his face, probably because it's gruesome, but it's him. The tattoo on his chest, the Army Ranger one I spent time touching. My finger traces the lines of it, and I wish I could feel his heartbeat, but I can't.

My hands tremble as I move to the next photo, knowing it'll be the final one.

Slowly and then all at once, a sob is ripped from my chest.

He's gone and there's no more questioning it. Emmett is dead, and I will never see him again.

CHAPTER
Thirty-One
BLAKELY

Days pass like molasses. I spend my time crying, hiking, or plotting revenge. Each one is equally frustrating. So, today, I'm going for anarchy.

"All I want is to talk to Brielle, Spencer, or Holden. I don't understand why that's not possible."

Of course, I don't have a cell phone. No, we have a freaking landline, which I didn't know was still a thing.

So, I picked up the receiver to call Holden first, and the line went dead. Then I tried Spencer, same thing. Finally, on the third call, Nelson's voice came down the line, telling me to stop it. When I kept trying, he came inside, ripped the cord out of the receiver, and glared at me as he stomped back out.

He's such a dick.

I proceeded to walk outside and scream at him through the car window he refused to roll down.

I have had it.

"It's been two weeks! Two weeks of no communication with anyone. I need to know what's going on. I am losing my shit."

"No," Nelson replies.

"No?"

"No," he says again. "You are in protective custody."

"Then protect me in Rose Canyon! I have to go back. I have to . . ." I need to lay my husband to rest. "I can't stay here."

"Blake, get inside," Liam says from the door.

"I'll leave without you."

Liam gives me a look of disapproval. "You can try, but I'm not giving you keys, and you're not going to walk there."

Nelson exits the car, crossing his arms over his chest. My inner teenage girl wants to rail. I hate being told what to do and especially like this. "I am pretty sure this is kidnapping."

Nelson snorts. "I promise, none of us want to be holed up here, waiting for someone to make our lives interesting."

"Oh, that's reassuring," I scoff.

"Get inside, please," Liam tries again.

That please is the only reason I consider it, but then I remember how over this I am and refuse to take a single step. "Not until I can talk to Holden."

"You can't. If you call him, what do you think is going to happen? I'll tell you," Liam continues without allowing me to speak. "I will have to save your ass because the bad guys will swarm this house like a military exercise. They are waiting for someone to slip up. Someone will get killed, most likely Nelson, so you'll have to explain to his family why he died because you wanted to make a phone call."

I cross my arms over my chest. "I'd like to hit you right about now."

"Yeah, but that's not exactly getting us all killed. You know I have a daughter, a son, and a wife I love, so you would probably have considerable guilt if you end up getting me killed."

"I would, but . . . I'm losing my fucking mind here!"

Nelson steps forward. "You need to go inside and pack a small bag. We're going on a field trip."

"I am not going anywhere unless it's to Rose Canyon."

Liam laughs. "Get inside, Blakely. Have a mega pint of wine while you glare at me and I tell you the plan for today."

"What is a mega pint?"

He shrugs. "I'll let you find out."

I walk inside because, really, what am I going to do? There is no one around for miles, and I am not in the mood to walk to Oregon. Regardless that I could be fueled solely by anger and sadness. The reality is that I am being hunted and that wouldn't be the smart decision.

When I get inside, Hank waves as he and the other US Marshal start their daily routine of taking the dog on a long walk. He's usually gone almost two hours as they move at a snail's pace, but it's nice for him to get out and get some exercise. He and Sunday have become best friends, and I try not to let the fact that *my* dog has adopted him bother me.

I sit at the table in the kitchen, and Nelson and Liam enter a few seconds later. The two of them are complete opposites. Nelson is uptight, walks almost like he has a stick up his ass, and never smiles. Liam is laid-back, confident but not arrogant, and seems to always have a smile on his lips. The two of them have this odd friendship that I've given up trying to figure out.

"So, where are we going on this field trip?"

"Fishing on the lake. It's a nice day out, and maybe the fresh air will help."

I sigh. "I don't want to go fishing. I want to talk to my friends and plan a funeral to mourn the loss of the man I love. I don't want to sit on a lake and think about how much I miss him. I need to *do* something. Do you get that? I have to do *something* because sitting here or on a lake or in the middle of the woods isn't working."

"Blakely, I understand this is hard," Nelson says.

"Dying is probably harder," Liam offers before turning to me. "You're being selfish, and you know it."

I gasp. "Selfish? I'm being selfish?"

I used to like him.

"There are people looking for you who want to kill you. I don't know what you and Emmett stepped in, but there's a target on your back."

"I'm aware of that."

"Are you? Because you're acting like you aren't. You know how this works. Your husband was killed. You watched it, and you're acting like they won't execute you the same way!" Liam runs his hand through his hair as he paces. "All we're trying to do is keep that from happening."

Nelson grunts in agreement. "You're in pain, and we understand that. I wish we could do more, but we could all use a break. I think the lake will give you some peace."

I don't think there's anything that can give me peace at this point. While I get what Liam is saying, it doesn't change the fact that I want to go home. I want to get out of this cabin and this area. I can go back to the FBI, beg for my old job back, and start doing some actual investigating into what insane bullshit is going on here.

"I don't want peace. That's what neither of you seem to understand."

"You want answers," Nelson states because he's heard me say it a thousand times a day since we got here.

"Yes. And I want to say goodbye to him. I want to see him, touch him, have a final moment . . ."

"You don't," Liam cuts in. "You don't want to see him in real life, Blakely. You don't want that memory, and you're lying to yourself if you say otherwise. We're leaving in fifteen minutes for the lake."

"Why? Why can't I stay here?" I ask.

"Because you can't, goddamn it. We're going fishing, and you're coming with us because we all need some fresh air."

"And you say that I'm being selfish?" I toss back at him.

I've come to love Liam like one loves a brother. He doesn't pull punches. He has been a shoulder for me to cry on—most days. We have become friends, and for some reason, he is not handling the isolation very well today.

"Are Natalie and the kids okay?"

His head jerks up. "What?"

"You're being an ass. Did you get into a fight?"

"Go get ready. We're leaving."

"I'm not going," I say defiantly.

Now I'm doing it out of spite. I am fully aware I'm being ridiculous, but my days are filled with television, Hank, Sunday, and that's it. I have nothing else, and maybe it is selfish to fight with him about all of this, but I have no more accommodation inside me.

"We're going fishing."

Nelson clears his throat. "Blake, it'll be good for all of us."

It's the softness in his tone that throws me. Typically, it's Nelson who is a prick and Liam who is soothing with me. I glare at both of them. "Are we having a good-cop, bad-cop moment? Because you both really fucked up if that's the game. The role reversal isn't believable."

Liam chuckles. "You're in rare form."

"I'm done with this false reality. I feel like nothing is real. This life isn't real."

"Well, it is *very* real," Nelson says. "It's my job to protect you, even if it's from yourself."

"Which is a task we're all finding extremely fun today." Liam's sarcasm is thick.

"You all act as if I have never been in danger before. I was a combat medic! I literally ran into gunfire. I have the medals to prove it."

"So do I, pumpkin. We all do. You, me, Nelson, Akers, we were all that way. We're built differently, and I get that. The isolation or the appearance of running from danger grates on us. However, this is the job right now. It's for Hank, and it's for your husband who lost his life and did everything he could do to protect you."

"I don't run from a fight."

Nelson shakes his head. "It's not running. It's allowing the people who need to do their jobs to do it without worrying about you. That's what we're doing."

That may be true, but it doesn't erase the fact that this is all precautionary. I'm in some freaking cabin in the woods and not even allowed to use the internet or a phone.

I haven't gotten the things I need, like a damn hug.

"Maybe not, but this isn't going to work either."

Nelson grumbles as he walks to the refrigerator and grabs the glass milk jug. He's lifting it to his lips, and I'm getting ready to tell him to use a damn glass when the window glass shatters, and the room erupts in gunshots.

The rounds come one after another. In what feels like a millisecond, I'm thrown to the ground. Liam is on top of me, shielding me as he and Nelson shout orders to each other.

Nelson grabs the table, flips it onto its side, and moves it so it acts as an additional shield between us and whoever is trying to kill us.

The sounds of gunfire popping off doesn't relent.

"We have to move!" Liam yells. "Stay low, Blake. Crawl to your bedroom."

I nod, my adrenaline pumping through my veins. I have been here before, and all I can think is how grateful I am that Hank is not home.

We move, low and slow, to the back of the cabin with Nelson in front and Liam behind me. "Keep your head down," Nelson orders.

It's already so low it's almost brushing the carpet, but the ingrained response of, "Yes, sir," falls from my lips anyway. I don't know what the plan is, but I know they have contingencies upon contingencies, so I trust them to get us all out without being shot.

When we get to my room, Nelson yanks up a floorboard and pulls out a rifle, which he hands to Liam. Then he pulls out another one, which he slings cross-body over his chest. Then he starts unloading handguns.

Nice to know there was an armory in my bedroom.

"Give me one," I say, knowing there are more beneath there.

"Blake . . ."

"Give me a fucking gun, Nelson. Now."

Liam hands me the rifle Nelson gave him and an extra magazine. "Here. Get in the closet, close the door, and stay there." He points to the closet and takes the gun Nelson hands him. "It has reinforced steel plates around the sides. Go in there and wait for us."

"How many do you think?" Nelson asks.

"At least two, but it could be as many as six. That was a lot of rounds from a lot of different directions."

"I heard one reload," I say. The cadence of the gunshots changed while we were crawling.

Nelson nods.

The gunfire comes to a stop for a second, and the three of us pause. While some may think that's a good thing, I have seen this play out before, and it's usually not. They're either regrouping and reloading or going to enter the property.

"We have to get out of the house," he says, echoing my concerns.

"Yes, but we need to know what we're facing when we do," Liam says.

"What if they found Hank?" I question, fear for my father-in-law's safety mounting.

Nelson doesn't look concerned. "Akers will have directed Hank to a secure location on their walking route. He'll double back to offer us support if he thinks Hank can stay put."

I shake my head. "You need to make sure. We have to protect him before me."

"We're the ones in the worst position right now," Liam says. "I need to look to see if I can get an idea of what we're dealing with."

"Okay. I'll go around the back of the cabin and do the same. Blake, you stay here, shoot anyone other than Liam, me, Hank, or Akers. When we are going to enter the room, we'll make a bird sound. Do you understand?"

"Yes. Go because I don't think we have a lot of time before they come in or smoke us out."

The two of them share a look, and then they drop low to the ground as they leave me here. I check my weapon, making sure it's loaded and there's a round in the chamber. Once that's set, I shove my extra magazine in my back pocket, press my back to the wall so I'm facing the open doorway, and bring the butt of the rifle to my shoulder. I will not do anything stupid or against what I agreed to. Right now, I'm a soldier following orders.

I hear people talking, but it's so faint that I can't understand what they're saying. As the seconds tick by, their voices grow a little louder, and eventually, I hear two different voices.

"Get the girl, that's the mission."

"What about the father?"

"Follow the fucking orders. We get her and bring her to him."

Who is him?

"This is a fool's mission."

"I know he wants her alive, but we can just say we had no choice but to shoot her. Makes it much easier."

I want to laugh. Not only do I think Liam and Nelson will protect me, but also, I am not some simpering woman. They're going to have to kill me if they want me.

The first guy talks again. "Let's go around the back, take out anyone in your way."

They must keep going because their voices are gone.

I hear the bird sound, and then Nelson enters, silently crawling toward me. "I counted at least three guys, fully loaded."

"Two are walking around the back now," I tell him.

"I secured the back door. It'll buy us a few minutes."

"We can go out the front then and hide in the woods," I suggest.

He shakes his head. "There are people in the front, and we need to get to the vehicle, which is parked about a hundred yards into the woods at the back of the house. There's no way we can get there undetected from the front of the house."

"What about Akers, Hank, and Sunday?"

"We'll pick them up as we leave. He'll know where to meet us."

Another bird whistle sounds a second before Liam is army crawling back into the room. Before he can say anything, another barrage of bullets begins. He practically dives into the closet, and Nelson pulls a shield from behind me, which I hadn't even known was there, and places it in front of us.

"I think this is just round one. The cameras picked up another car about a half mile away."

"We're sitting ducks," I say.

"We were supposed to be gone when this started," Liam says.

I turn to him. "Fishing? I guess we weren't really going fishing?"

"Not now, Blake," Nelson cuts in. "There is a drop in the floor beneath Hank's room. We can go out there."

"That's the first place I'd look," Liam says.

"They don't seem all that smart," I explain.

Liam pinches the bridge of his nose. "We can't take any chances. They may have the blueprints, and we have to think two steps ahead."

I have spent weeks here and never thought to do any of this. I feel like such an idiot.

"We go out the back," I say with confidence. "They just checked there and hopefully they're moving. No doubt they'll find the hole in the floor where they can enter the house. We go out, we move carefully, and we get to the vehicle."

Nelson looks to Liam. "She's right. We have to go that way if they're going to be under the house."

"We have no idea if they're going to do that."

"What does the camera on the house show?" I ask.

"They took them out first."

Of course, they did. I try to slip back into being a soldier. It's been a while since I've thought that way, but it's going to be what helps us all survive this.

Liam moves, his shoulders straight, and nods once. "We go now. We have no choice. If I were them, I would either enter through whatever trap doors I knew would be in a safe house or set the place on fire."

He's right. I would set the house on fire too.

At least I don't have anything here that I care about.

"Okay."

Liam crouches low, moving on the balls of his feet in almost a duck walk. "Stay low when passing the windows, run when you can, and keep your head on a swivel."

I follow behind him, the same position, and Nelson falls in behind me. The three of us move like a well-trained military unit, sweeping the perimeter as we move to ensure no one can shoot at us first. Liam starts to work on the back door, removing the security bar that Nelson must've put there. I keep my gun pointed to the left while Nelson covers the right.

Once the bar is lifted, Liam moves to the side and Nelson goes through first. I follow, and Liam's hand rests on my shoulder, bringing up the rear.

As we open the back door, Nelson grabs someone, his arm wraps around his neck and the man's arms fall limp. The body drops to the ground, and Nelson waves two fingers forward, and we begin again.

When we get out of the house, the gunfire starts up again, but it's concentrated on the front of the house. The three of us stay steady at our pace, nearing the edge of the woods.

Liam taps my shoulder twice, I do the same to Nelson, letting him know to step it up. We go a bit faster, keeping our hand-on-shoulder connections as we move, ensuring no one gets left behind.

My heart is pounding so loudly, I have to work to keep myself calm as we go. Every instinct in my body is saying to run, but that is just fight or flight, and I ruthlessly smother it and demand my thoughts remain calm.

The tree line is right there. It's so close.

My thighs start to burn a bit from walking in a half-crouch, but I ignore it, focusing wholly on getting to the underbrush where we will have a bit of cover.

We just have three more yards to the trees and then we can make our break toward the vehicle.

One more yard.

"Move!" Liam yells and starts to fire his weapon.

Nelson turns around, pushing me behind him, and the two of them fire at whoever is chasing us while trusting me not to let them back into anything. We keep moving toward the woods, but more people are headed in our direction, all of them moving in quickly.

I fire as they approach, as do Liam and Nelson.

We have cover, but there's no way we can outrun them. My count is eight hostiles, and we're going to die here.

Liam's eyes find mine. "Get to the car! Go!"

I won't leave them. No fucking way. "No. We fight together."

He shakes his head and fires two more shots, dropping one of the eight.

Down to seven.

I am crouched behind the tree to the left, so I lean, fire, and then pull back. One more falls, leaving us with six. Liam and Nelson fire more.

"I don't have many rounds left," Nelson warns.

"I have one mag full, but I have maybe two left," Liam replies.

"I have ten. We have to pull back into the woods and split up," I tell them.

I know they won't like it, but it's our best shot. "If I can get high, I can pick them off," Liam says, clearly not liking the plan.

"We stay together," Nelson reiterates.

"I am not untrained. We have to do it this way, and you know it," I say to Nelson.

He nods. "We meet at the vehicle. You wait no more than fifteen minutes, and then you go to Akers, no matter what. You don't wait for us. There's a house a half of a mile to the north, when you see the trail, turn left. Akers will be waiting."

"I'll see you all in fifteen."

Nelson stands, firing three more shots, and Liam and I move. He goes to the right, and I go deeper into the woods.

We will all make it back. It can't end this way. No one else can die because of this piece of shit who is trafficking girls. It's all tied to that, and I am done allowing them to wreck my damn world.

I run, every few seconds finding somewhere to duck and assess if anyone is following me. So far, it looks clear. Moving faster, I find the area where the car is hidden with a green tarp and branches. I have hiked these woods for weeks now and never saw this here.

My breathing is labored, and I inhale slowly to regulate it. Being quiet for the next fifteen minutes is my goal.

The distant sounds of gunfire tells me that at least one of them is alive. I hate myself for being such a bitch today. We should've gone fishing like they wanted. If I hadn't been so spun up, we would have been long gone before the party crashers dropped in. That makes me think that Liam, Nelson, and Akers might have known this was going to happen and were trying to get Hank and me out of the house.

We're going to discuss all of that later.

I lean my head back against the car and a second later, a branch snaps over to my left. I pull my rifle up, waiting for the bird sound to let me know it's them.

Another branch breaks, and I close my eyes, listening and waiting. There's some scuffling noise, but not a single bird sound like the ones I heard inside the house. When I open my eyes, there are two men there, one on each side of me, pointing their guns directly at my head.

"Hello, Blakely."

My rifle is pointed right at one of them, if I am going to die, that asshole is coming to hell with me. "I don't have the pleasure of knowing who you are."

"You will."

They're both masked, and I don't recognize their voices. "Are you sure you want to die this way?"

The one to my left moves to press the barrel of his gun to the back of my head. "Are you sure you want to? Put the gun down, and we won't hurt you."

"I'd rather not."

The guy in front of me smirks. "He'll shoot you, sweetheart. We can bring you in alive or in a body bag, just like your husband."

These are the assholes who shot Emmett. My breathing accelerates as rage bubbles up. "You killed him?"

"I didn't pull the trigger, but my friend behind you did."

The gun pushes harder. "He shouldn't be sticking his nose into other people's business."

"It's a trait she shared with him." The asshole in front of me laughs.

"Then we should kill her now so she'll die wondering who we are."

"Or we could fill her in and watch her eyes fill with fear as she discovers what kind of world she's living in."

The guy behind me leans in and whispers, "You want to know all the secrets, Blake? You want to know which of the friends you made recently weren't really friends?"

I want to shoot them both, end this ridiculous bullshit, but the longer I keep them talking, the more time I buy. Liam and Nelson should be here soon, and they'll kill them both. I'll get the answers then.

"I think you're both bluffing," I say back.

The guy in front of me shakes his head. "Put the gun down, and we'll find out."

"You both put yours down."

"That's not possible."

I shrug. "Then neither is me putting mine down without a fight."

The guy in front of me inclines his head. "Then I guess we'll just shoot you now."

He raises his gun higher, and I know this is it. He is going to execute me. The man behind me moves out of the way. I have no out.

But, like I said before, if I die, one of them is coming with me.

I love you, Emmett. I'll see you soon.

I go to pull the trigger, but a split second before the hammer pushes the firing pin, another shot goes off, and the guy to my left falls. I don't hesitate. That moment of surprise was all I needed. I fire, and the guy who had been behind me falls. I rush over and kick his gun away, keeping the rifle aimed at him, but he's not moving.

The shot came from in front of me, not from behind, which

would have been where Liam and Nelson should have been coming from.

I wait for one of them to appear, but the man who steps from the trees isn't either.

It's Emmett.

My knees give out, and everything goes black.

CHAPTER
Thirty-Two
EMMETT

That was too close. Much too fucking close. I saw my life flash before my eyes when that piece of shit had his gun pointed at her.

I knew he would shoot, and I couldn't wait. While the plan was to remain concealed until we knew more, there was not a chance in hell I would let anyone hurt Blakely.

"Blake," I say, tapping her cheek, waiting for her to come to. "Blake, wake up."

Her eyes slowly flutter open, sunlight breaking through the trees and dancing across her skin. "No. No, please no."

"You're okay, love. You're safe."

"You're dead," she whispers, disbelief in her eyes.

I help her sit up and take her face in my hands. "I'm not dead. I had to pretend to be dead for this to work."

"No."

"I'm sorry. I promise you can hate me later, but right now, we need to get in the vehicle and get to the other safe house."

She just keeps shaking her head. "You're not real. I'm dead."

"Blakely, I didn't die. I am here, and we have to get you out of here now. Are Liam and Nelson on their way here?"

Her nod is slow, and then it seems to hit her at once, her jaw clenches and she takes a swing at me, clocking me in my jaw. "You—"

Fuck, that hurt. "Jesus, woman!"

"You son of a bitch! I am going to kill you for real this time." She rears back and throws another punch, but I duck before she can make contact.

Definitely not how I envisioned our reunion, but I guess I should have known better. I deserved that. "We're in danger, we have to move."

Her eyes flare. "You're the only one in danger at this moment."

As much as she wants to argue, we don't have the time.

"Get in the car!" Liam yells, crashing into the small clearing as gunshots sound from somewhere behind him. I move quickly, pulling the tarp off in one motion and then thrusting Blakely toward the back.

"You're not driving. You've been dead for two weeks." She tries to push past me, aiming for the driver's door. Always a pain in the ass, this woman. "Get out of my way, you asshole."

Then Liam is there, picking her up and folding her into the backseat before following behind her. I barely have time to close the driver's door before he's yelling, "Go!"

I put the car in drive. "Where is Nelson?"

"We'll grab him on the way, he knows where to go."

Blakely slaps at Liam. "Get off me, you liars! All of you!"

"I would've thought she'd be happy to see you."

"One would think."

She grunts. "No, I'm not, and you're going to wish you were fucking dead when I'm through with you."

"I look forward to it," I say, navigating through the woods. "Do we know if Akers is at the right location?"

"No idea, but he should follow protocol."

"Is any of this real? I mean, maybe this is a dream. A bad one where everything I knew in life was a lie," Blake mutters to herself.

I turn the wheel quickly, avoiding the tree that must've fallen in the storm two days ago.

"It's not a bad dream," I say.

"No? Because today, I've been shot at, had guns pointed at my damn head by psychos, and found out my lying husband, who I've spent the last two weeks mourning, is actually alive and well while I've been stuck in this hellhole!"

"Sounds like a good time to me." Liam chuckles. "Ouch!"

"Idiot." Blakely crosses her arms over her chest.

I want to laugh, smile, pull the car over and kiss her until she can't speak, and cry all at the same time. These two weeks have been hell. I've been hiding out in a hunting cabin not too far from the house. Liam has come out to meet me once everyone was asleep because he's one of only six people who knew I was actually alive. Spencer, Quinn, Holden, Liam, Nelson, and the surgeon, all sworn to secrecy and working different angles to draw out the people responsible for the hit on me and Blake for getting close to the trafficking ring.

Once we had a clear idea of who was involved, we fed them this location and put a plan into place to get Blakely and my father out of the house. It was all planned, but well, my wife is not known for her accommodation skills.

"To the left," Liam says, and I slow as we approach the secondary meeting spot.

"If he's dead . . ." Blake says.

"He'll be here."

"You don't know that because we left him, Liam," she says with a snark in her tone.

I'm going to assume that attitude is multiple layers of her aggravation right now, none of which I blame her for. I'd be full of piss and vinegar too if I were in her shoes, but I'd grovel once we were out of here.

I park the car, continuing to scan the area. "I didn't leave him."

"You're here, my not-so-dead-soon-to-be-ex-husband is here, I'm here . . . we're missing, oh, that's right, Nelson!"

"I'm not going to be your ex-anything," I correct.

"Ha!"

It wasn't a complete denial. I'll take it.

"He was busy doing something else. Relax."

"You can say the word," Blake says, throwing her hands up. "I understand what an interrogation is if that's what you mean."

Liam huffs. "Fine, he was taking photos and interrogating one of the men we shot. Happy now?"

"Elated." She turns to look out the window instead of at me in the mirror.

"Blake," I say, but she doesn't move. "Blake, I know you're upset."

Now she looks. "Do you? You know that I'm *upset*? Whatever would I be upset about?"

Liam chuckles and then mashes his lips together.

Yeah, I'm so fucked.

"I promised you a chance to be angry later."

Her eyes narrow. "You promised to love, honor, obey me, and not be dead."

"I'm *not* dead."

"And that's a boon from the universe. Now, I have the chance to kill you myself."

"You could at least admit you're a little happy."

She shrugs. "I'm glad that Hank will have his son back, there you go."

"And what about Sunday?"

"Fine. I'm happy for Hank and Sunday."

I fight back a grin. "Anyone else you're just a little happy for?"

Blakely looks out the front of the car, the sides, and then shakes her head. "Nope. No one else comes to mind."

"Okay," I say with a chuckle.

"Don't laugh at me, Maxwell. I'm not being funny. I am so angry and hurt."

"I know."

Liam sighs. "Can you two save this for when I am not stuck in a car with you? You're both giving me a headache."

Blake turns to face him. "Oh, am I making things uncomfortable for you? Did you know that he wasn't dead?"

"Yes."

Bad move, Liam.

"And you just thought, hey, I like watching a grown woman sob every night? I should keep this a secret because . . . why would I want Blakely to stop making herself sick? Why would I want to offer her some comfort? Or . . . brilliant idea . . . include her in the plan so that when the house is getting shot up, she is aware of what's going on? No, no, I wouldn't want you to feel bad at all."

He looks to me through the mirror. "Looks like I'm the bad guy now."

"You all are each equally loathed by me," she corrects. "If Nelson isn't dead and he knew about this, he goes on the list too."

"He's not dead," I tell her.

"You would know since you have all the information."

Getting out of hot water with her is going to be a load of fun.

"There he is," Liam says.

I throw the car in drive, moving extremely slowly, but if we are moving, the car can accelerate a little faster, and there is less chance of us getting stuck in the mud.

Liam reaches forward, opening the passenger door, and Nelson hops in. As soon as it's closed, I push down on the gas.

"What did you find out?" Liam asks as Nelson tries to catch his breath.

"He said he was a low man on the totem pole and answered to Bill for a long time."

"So, Bill was higher up than I thought," I say, approaching the clearing where my father and Akers should be.

"Seems so."

"Did he tell you anything else?"

He nods. "They weren't here to kill you, Blake. They had very strict instructions that they wanted you alive and brought back to who they work for. I have no idea what they think you have, but they want it."

"Well, I overheard them talking, and they clearly weren't going to follow that plan because two said to just kill me and not take me."

My jaw tenses. "They can't have her."

"Well, they're not going to stop until they do. There is another group coming, they were arriving as I started to head to our meeting spot."

Blakely sighs heavily. "Get to the good stuff. Did you find out anything else? Anything about who is taking the girls or running the organization? Anything about who they work for?"

"I got a name."

"Who?" we all ask in unison.

Nelson turns. "Ryan."

CHAPTER
Thirty-Three
BLAKELY

There he is, laughing as Sunday runs around him and jumps up on his leg. She greeted him with joy and love.

I have yet to do that.

We arrived in the clearing where Hank and Akers were safely waiting with a guy named Quinn, who Liam was very happy to see.

I have stayed back by the car, watching this scene like an outsider in my life. All of these people knew Emmett was alive. All of them lied to me. Yes, to some extent, I understand why, but it's still unfair, and I'm hurt.

I was so broken over losing him. My heart felt as though it would never beat the same. The rhythm of my life had faltered when he died, and it felt as if it would never be in sync again.

The second my eyes found his in the woods, it came back. I was whole again.

And I am not ready to admit that.

Emmett glances over at me for the fiftieth time and claps Liam's shoulder before walking toward me.

Great. It's time for this talk.

"Hey."

I rub the back of my neck. "Hey?"

"I'm not sure what to say."

"I'm not sure there's anything you can say."

"I'm sorry," Emmett says, his voice filled with regret.

It's probably the only reason I haven't kneed him in the balls. "For which part?"

"All of it. I didn't want to lie to you, Blake. I wanted to tell you a thousand times, but we had no idea who was behind any of it. I didn't know how to protect you, and we both know that if I asked you to do this, you never would've."

"We will never know the answer to that because you *didn't* ask me. You made a choice and then just let me believe I had lost you. You . . . you let me cry my fucking eyes out, thinking you were dead. God, do you know how much I've ached?" I slam my hands against his chest. "Do you know how many times I wished for you back? How I had to tell your father you were dead every single day?" I hit him again, feeling so overwhelmed. The stupid traitorous tears come again, dripping down my cheeks. "How I laid in bed at night, curled in a ball, sobbing because I would never lay beside you again?" His arms come out, but I slap his chest again. "No. You don't get to comfort me now. You broke me, Emmett. You broke my fucking heart. You took away *you*. You . . . died. It's the one thing I fear most in this whole damn world, and you made me believe it was my reality, and I don't forgive you for it."

He steps toward me anyway, his hands coming to my face, my neck, then my shoulders. "I never wanted to break you. I only ever wanted to come to you, to hold you, to lie beside you, and wipe those tears. I stood outside your window almost every night, wishing I could close the measly four feet between us. I ached knowing I could be near you, but not near enough. I had to protect you, Blakely. I knew they would kill us. They shot me in that goddamn squad car, and if I didn't die, I knew they'd try for you next. You are my weakness. You are the *only* thing in this world that means more to me than my own life. If they took you from me, I'd fucking die."

I stare into his blue eyes as he says every word. I see the dark circles under his eyes, the dark scruff on his face, and the anguish in his voice threatens to rip a new chasm open inside me. I don't want to forgive him.

I want to be so angry, but there's only relief in my heart.

He's alive, and he's touching me.

I wished this, and now he's here.

"You will never lie to me again. I don't care if an army is marching upon us, you don't lie to me."

Emmett shakes his head. "Never. If an army is approaching, I'll stand with you."

"We're a team, Emmett. And we have been to battle before. I am not afraid of a fight, but I don't want to do it alone."

"I love you, Blake. I love you more than anything in this world. I made a split-second decision, and the only thing I could think was that I needed to make sure you were safe. It was the best way I could think to make that happen." He presses his lips to my forehead before leaning his forehead there. "Forgive me. Love me. Let me make this up to you."

I melt because, as much as I want to chop his balls off, I also just want to kiss him.

So, I lift my face to his and rub my thumb along his scratchy cheek. "Not yet. I love you more than I should. And yes, you can make it up to me, you have a lot of work to do."

Emmett smiles. "I can do work."

"Good."

"I'm going to kiss you, and you can grumble about it later."

"I will."

He leans down, and I push up at the same time. My arms wrap around his neck, and my body is flush against his as his lips crash against mine. We kiss, our tongues meeting and brushing together, exactly as they were meant to do. The minty taste is like home, and the gaping hole in my chest starts to close. Emmett is alive, and he's kissing me.

His strong hands are splayed against my back as I arch more into him.

Someone coughs behind us, and Emmett breaks the kiss,

rubbing his nose against mine. "Tonight, I am going to do a lot more than that."

I smile and pull my head back. "Is that so?"

"Yes. It is."

"While we are all enjoying you two love birds making up," Liam says from the edge of the clearing. "We have work to do that includes the both of you."

"We'll be right there," Emmett says. He takes a step back, holding both my hands. "Are we going to be okay?"

I have spent the last few weeks living in a world where I didn't think he existed. It was cold and dark. It was miserable, and I don't have any desire to stay there. "We will be, but you're going to hear about this again."

"I look forward to it." He winks and pulls me along with him to the group.

"Who is Ryan?" Nelson asks.

"It could be a few people. I don't know if Ryan is a first or a last name."

"Emmett, we both know who it is," I say, squeezing his hand.

"It doesn't make sense."

I look up into his eyes, which seem to be miles away. "Why not?"

"Ryan Wilkinson is like the fucking nicest guy."

"Oh, and nice guys can't be psychopaths?" I ask and then sigh. "I mean, psychopaths aren't actually nice. They are just good at acting like they are. However, I was thinking of the mayor's stepson, Paul Ryan. He has the connection to everyone in this town, and while Stephen was our main suspect, I can't help but think Paul Ryan fits better."

Liam asks, "What if you're wrong, though?"

"I'm not," I say with confidence.

"That's great you think that, but all we know is a name of Ryan. We don't have enough information to go into Rose Canyon, guns blazing, and arrest someone by the first—or last—name of Ryan."

Emmett continues with his agreement of Liam. "I don't know. Either Ryan could've killed either of us several times once we started snooping around. Ryan, Stephen, and Nick were all in DC, and they didn't harm you then. We don't have enough information here."

Nelson nods. "I sent the photos in to my boss, and they're going to run facial recognition."

Quinn speaks then. "I'll have answers very soon. Cole Security is already working on the background searches as well as pulling everything they can on both those guys."

Akers looks up at the gray sky. "We can talk about all this later, but no matter what, we can't stay here. At least no one else knows Emmett is alive. That's one thing that didn't go sideways today."

Thank God for that, I guess.

"I agree, we're sitting ducks here. So where do you want to take her and Hank now that the safe house location is blown?" Quinn asks.

Oh, that's not happening.

"What exactly did you geniuses plan to do once this location was burned?" I ask, one brow raised. "I mean, you did have a plan, right? You wouldn't just tell them where we were without having an idea of where to move us."

Liam claps Quinn on the back when he grumbles under his breath. "She's going to be your responsibility next."

"Next what?" I ask.

"Next safe house."

I stand there, looking at him like he's lost his damn mind. "I'm not going to another safe house. I am not hiding while you guys go off doing God knows what. No."

"Blake . . ." Emmett starts but stops when he sees my face.

Yeah, that's right.

"You are not going to go with them and leave me again. I am not sitting on the sidelines again."

"I never said I was," Emmett corrects. "You and I are going to the next safe house together. We have to stay hidden."

Oh. He's coming too. I can handle that, kind of. It's not that I want to be involved in this, but I can help. Whoever this Ryan is tried to take my husband from me.

I turn to him. "Were you even shot?"

He at least has the decency to look ashamed. "I . . . was . . . I could've been."

"Emmett Maxwell! You weren't even shot? You made me watch that, for what?"

"Dramatic effect," Quinn says. "We needed it to look real. There was an actual hit on Emmett and you. Charlie was in DC, she made sure you were safe, and I handled it here. You're welcome."

My mouth opens, and I want to punch him. "You are so not thanked."

He steps toward me. "I truly feel for you, Blake. I know you don't know me and probably think I'm a prick, but if we didn't do it, he would've been killed. We needed everyone, most of all you, to think it was real so you would go into hiding. We needed the town to panic and cry. It was the only way that the people involved would feel safe enough to drop their guard. If they believed he was dead and you'd disappeared, then we could investigate it much easier. I am sorry."

I'm slightly mollified. "Okay."

"I'm married, and if I did that to Ashton, she would've done a lot more bodily harm to me than you did to Emmett," he says with a smile.

"I think I'd like her."

"I know you would, and you both scare me a little, so we'll make sure that doesn't happen."

I make a note to ask Charlie about her.

Liam claps his hands. "Back to the plan part."

"I am going to take Blake and Sunday out of state until the second phase is in play," Emmett says.

"What? We're not going to stay close?"

He shakes his head. "We need a honeymoon, and the team needs to do what investigating they can without worrying about me being spotted. Right now, they're only hunting you."

That's reassuring. "What about Hank?"

He looks over at his dad. "He is going to stay with a friend in California."

"Emmett, this is a lot for him. He was taken from his nursing facility he's been at for years and has gone through a lot in just the last two weeks. I worry—"

"I know, and I love you for it, but it will be okay, and we'll work through it with him once this has passed."

I glance over to where Hank is sitting on a tree stump while Sunday chases the ball he tosses. "That dog loves him."

Emmett smiles, wrapping his arm around me, pulling my back to his chest. His low voice is soft against my ear. "Maybe we should let her go with him while we go away? A stay with Grandpa while Mom and Dad get some alone time."

"I would love that, but I think she needs you."

"As much as you do?"

I turn my head to peek at him. "Maybe not that much."

CHAPTER

Thirty-Four

EMMETT

We can't go anywhere that requires flying on a commercial plane, but we have to go somewhere neither of us have been.

I figured we would play heads or tails and see where the road led.

I'm an idiot for thinking it could be that simple with Blake.

"Why can't we go to Mexico?"

"Because we use our passports."

She pulls her map out. "This is dumb. Fine, I'll close my eyes, swirl my hand around, and wherever it lands, we go."

"I wanted you to decide between two places you've wanted to see, not some random spot on a map."

Blake lifts one shoulder. "I am who I am."

She is, and I love her no matter what. "All right, let's pick a place."

Her eyes close, and she waves her finger around dramatically before stabbing it onto the map. "Here."

We look to see where she landed, and I'm actually relieved. I am completely fine with heading to Idaho. Neither of us have been there, and it's close enough that we can get back here in under a day.

Another Ranger was from Idaho, and he always talked about how remote everything was and how many outdoor things there were to do. Not that I plan to do much other than my wife, and it'll give us some time to work through the residual anger I know she still has.

"All right." I take her hand in mine and bring it to my lips. "Let's have our honeymoon."

After about fifteen minutes, we were able to secure an a-frame cabin out in the middle of nowhere. The area of Garden Valley has a lot to do, but the population is small, which is perfect. Plus, the cabin is owned by a celebrity who works with Catherine Cole. No paperwork means we are off-grid completely.

The drive out there is long, but Blake and Sunday nap for most of it. Blakely is holding Sunday against her chest, the two of them lightly snoring.

The last few weeks have been hell on all of us, but more so on Blakely. I will never be able to express how much I hated the choice I had to make. How badly I wanted to go to her, but Quinn, Liam, Spencer, and Holden were adamant that I see it through. I had to protect her the only way I could—by staying away and letting her grieve.

But when her eyes met mine and she realized I was alive, the betrayal I saw in them was enough to convince me she'd never forgive me.

I drive the windy road, being extra cautious as we hug the freaking cliff. Once we get to the house, I gently wake her.

She sits up, and Sunday falls forward a bit before Blakely can catch her. "Jesus! You scared me."

"We're here."

Blake rubs her eyes and hands Sunday over to me as she exits the car. "Don't worry, I'll take the dog," I say with a grin, holding the puppy up. "Mommy almost tossed you and then left."

"I can hear you."

"I wasn't whispering," I say back.

I get out and walk over to where she stands, looking up at the cabin that sits on the edge of the land. "Wow," Blake says, and while it's dark and we're in the middle of nowhere, I can't help but agree with her.

It's a tall a-frame building that looks as though it grew out of the ground. The tall roofline isn't obnoxious because it sits at the same height as the trees around it and rocks almost cocoon the building.

"Let's go inside."

She looks to me and nods. Sunday walks beside us, smelling everything on the way to the door. The owner gave me instructions on how to get the key, which is the super-secret hiding spot under the mat.

Once it's unlocked, I grab her arm and stop her from entering. "Let me do this right."

"Do what?"

I smile and then lift her into my arms. "Emmett!"

"This is our honeymoon, Blake. It's our new beginning to the life we are going to have. I know danger is still in front of us, but today marks us being a team again, taking it on together."

Her hand moves to my cheek. "You and me against the world."

"Until the end."

Her lip quirks up. "And the end better not come anytime soon."

We cross the threshold, and I kiss her softly before putting her on her feet. Her eyes scan the cabin. "Why the hell didn't I stay here to begin with? This place is amazing."

The cabin is beautiful. The interior is bright white with warm Earth tones everywhere else. There's a large, camel-colored leather sofa that breaks up the kitchen from the rest of the house. It faces the back of the house, which is completely made of windows. It is nothing but a one hundred and eighty degree view of the woods and mountains.

Just off the back deck, the house has its own private hot spring. There are lights around it, making the water look almost iridescent.

"We have our own hot spring?" Blake asks.

"We do."

"This is amazing." She grins.

"This is what we should've had when we got married years ago."

Instead, our honeymoon was being re-deployed to the desert.

"Well, this is truly spectacular, and I love it here."

Sunday barks at the deer head on the wall before running back to us, barking again, and then running in circles.

"If I ever have to hide you away again, I'll be sure you have upgraded accommodations like this one."

Blakely turns, the joy that was in her eyes is gone as she looks at me. "Emmett . . ."

I know it's coming, the next part of this is where she will tell me everything she couldn't in the clearing.

"Say what you need to, baby."

She sighs, turning away. "That's just it. I don't know what I need to say. I'm angry, fucking elated you're not dead, and sad that you don't trust me."

"I do trust you."

"You don't! You let me watch you die, Emmett. Do you have any idea how distraught I was?"

"I do. I watched you cry every night."

She runs her hands through her dark hair. "I know you did what you thought was right, but it wasn't. Not when you know how I feel about losing everyone. That is my biggest fear, and you let me stay in the dark."

"I hate that I put you through that, but you have to know that if there were another way, I would have taken it. Spencer and Quinn caught wind of the assassin on his way to me two minutes before I called you. We had very little time to make a decision, and I didn't want to do it with you on the video. I swear to God, I didn't, but I wasn't sure how else you'd ever believe it. Quinn shot out the window, and we had no time to adjust the plan." I step toward her. "I knew that if you had a sliver of doubt, you'd never let it go. You would've run away or pulled a damn gun on them to get to me."

"Yeah, no shit I would."

Another step closer. "And that's why. I almost lost it on the fifth night. I was just outside your safe house, and I heard you sobbing. I sat there, my back against the wall below your window, and tried to talk myself out of going to you. It was too hard, so I stood, fully intending to walk into that house and hold you until you stopped crying, but Liam was there."

Blakely watches me. "To stop you?"

I nod. "He . . . had to walk with me for miles before I could calm down. I was a fucking wreck listening to you in pain because of me. I hated myself and this situation. I hate you for making me love you again and want this life. I hated the town, the people, the goddamn world."

"You should've come to me," she says.

"I couldn't, Blake. Please understand that I was doing what I thought I had to."

She turns to me, her eyes filling with tears. "I mourned you. I cried and begged God to give you back or take me with you."

I reach my hand out to rub her cheek. "He did. He gave me back to you."

She grips my wrist. "I don't think God did that, but . . ."

"Listen, I can imagine to some small extent how you felt. When you left me years ago, I was broken over it. Not in the same way, but I thought I lost you forever. Somehow, we found our way back, and I knew, this time, it wasn't because of love that we were apart. I love you more than anything in this world."

Sunday makes a noise, and we laugh. "She takes offense to that."

I rub my thumb against her lips. "She'll survive. What I won't survive is losing your love, Blake. I don't want to go backward because of this. I want to build our life together, buy a home, start a family." Her eyes widen, and I laugh. "In a few months, we can talk about it, but you're my wife. You, me, and Sunday are a family."

"I wouldn't mind a baby at some point. I'm getting old, so if it's what you want . . ."

I never would've thought those words would come out of her

mouth. "Good, then maybe one day we'll be fortunate enough to have one."

She lifts onto her toes. "I spent the last two weeks mourning the fact that I would never kiss your lips again. Never feel your touch or hear your voice."

My hands move to her hips, and I pick her up so she can wrap her legs around my hips. "I'm going to take you to that bed now, and I'm going to worship every inch of you."

I do exactly what I said, walking us to the bed that looks out the wall of windows. There's no one around us for miles.

After placing her on the bed, I take a second to look at her. Really look at her. To see the flecks of gold in her brown eyes, memorize the way her hair frames her face, and watch the way her long lashes brush the top of her cheeks. She's so beautiful—so perfect, and she's mine.

"What?" she asks softly.

"I love you, Blake."

"I love you, Emmett."

"No, baby. I love you. In a way I didn't know that love could exist. I think what I feel surpasses love. It fills my chest to a point I think I'm going to explode because I can't contain how much I feel for you." I sink to my knees in front of her. "You deserved a man who felt this way before he married you. You should've had the ring, the proposal you dreamed of, and the husband who stood before friends and family and pledged his love. Not some half-assed ceremony where we asked two people we don't even talk to anymore to be our witnesses."

She moves forward. "I didn't need the big proposal or the wedding. I never would have been able to open my heart to you any other way than how we did this. Us working backward in some ways is what gave me the ability to love. I didn't think I ever could."

"You were never unable to love, you just didn't know how to give it without fear."

A tear falls down her cheek. "You showed me how, which is

why losing you was the worst pain I've ever felt. I don't want to be in a world where you aren't beside me."

"You are stuck with me forever now, Blakely."

She smiles. "I think I'm okay with that."

I lift her hand and kiss the finger that a ring will sit on soon, then her palm, wrist, and move up her arm. Her brown eyes watch me as I move until we're face-to-face. "I'm going to put a ring on that finger. I want to give you everything."

"Just give me love."

"You have it."

Blakely lies down, and I move over her, kissing her neck and pulling her shirt up. She moves so I can remove it easily and throw it to the floor. Neither of us says anything as we continue to kiss and slowly tug piece after piece of clothing off.

Her hands fumble at my pants, and I help her with the buckle before sliding them off. Then we're both naked, kissing and exploring each other as though we never have.

And maybe I haven't. Not this way.

Not without restraint or fear. Not without wondering if she truly wants this.

We are bare to each other. Open to love and each other.

She runs her fingers along my chest. "I never knew I could feel this way."

"What way?"

"Like I have everything in the world, but it came with the most intense fear. Love is . . . well, it's terrifying."

I brush her hair back. "It's also freeing. It's knowing that I have you beside me."

"And I have you."

"In every way, baby."

I want her in another way right now, so I bring our lips together. I want to make love to her and make her feel everything in my heart.

The kiss goes deeper, and then I move my mouth down the slim column of her neck and down to her chest. I kiss the valley between her perfect tits, running my tongue to the right one first.

Blakely's hands grip my hair as I trace my lower lip along her nipple before taking it into my mouth. I suck softly, flicking it before blowing air against the puckered skin. "Emmett."

"You taste like sweetness and sin. I can't get enough."

"I want you so badly."

"I want you too, baby, and I promise, I'm going to have you."

She arches her back, and I move to the other breast, giving it the same attention as the first. After I've lavished each to the point where Blakely is panting softly, I move down her stomach, kissing my way to where I really want to taste.

Her legs fall open for me, and I lift them, resting her feet on my shoulders. I stare at her, dark hair on the pillow and a saucy grin on her lips. She is a siren, and I will never be able to resist her call.

"Do you want me here, Blakely?"

"You know I do."

I grin. "Mmm, and do you want me to make you come, wife?"

That word shatters in the room around us. The meaning isn't used as a weapon anymore. It's a benediction to the woman I love.

"Do you think you can?" Blake issues the challenge.

"I know I can."

"Then, please, put your money where your mouth is."

I lightly nip the inside of her thigh for that one and then move my mouth to her clit. Her hips lift, and I repeat the motion, loving the sound of her moan filling the room. I could stay here all night, loving this woman, making her feel good. That's all I have ever wanted anyway.

Since the day we met, my goal has been to make things better for Blakely, to give her whatever she needed, be it my friendship or more.

I have loved her for a long time, and I am going to continue forever.

"Yes," she pants, so I increase the pressure. I flick her clit a bit faster, varying the degrees and moving my face to create different angles.

Her taste on my tongue is fucking perfect.

I don't stop as her moans become louder. I want her to blow the roof off this house. The way her fingers wrap around my hair, pulling tighter, spurs me on.

"Emmett. I'm so close."

I move my tongue lower, pushing inside her before going back to the bundle of nerves she wants me at. I push two fingers in and suck her clit harder.

"Yes! Don't stop. Please don't stop!"

There's nothing in this world that could make me stop now. I want to drown in her moans and feel her come apart beneath me.

She cries out louder, her body going tight before falling lax. I keep up, making sure it goes for as long as I can make it.

Only after her body stops pulsing around my fingers do I lift my head and climb up her body.

"You're so beautiful when you fall apart."

She turns her head, and her eyelids flutter open just enough for her to see me. "I'm happy to let you do it anytime you want."

"Well, good thing we're up on this mountain with no one around for miles, and I have nothing else I'd like to do . . ."

Blakely's eyes sparkle with excitement. "Yes, that is a good thing. Now, make love to me."

Her hips cradle me, and I move myself in place. This woman is everything to me. She's brave, smart, sexy, fierce, and so much more. I want to give her everything, most of all my heart.

As I push into her, the pleasure is indescribable. Our eyes lock and something changes around us. It's as though everything is right again. All the shit we went through for this moment is gone, and it's just us.

Tears fill her eyes, and her lower lip trembles, so I kiss her softly.

"Blakely—" My voice cracks, making me pause for just breath. "I vow that I will always love you." I push deeper into her. "I will protect you, cherish you, hold your heart in my hands and always be gentle with it." A tear falls down her cheek. "I promise to be true to you, forsaking all others because there's no one else in this world for me." I move again, giving her everything of me. "I will honor you with my body and soul. You are my wife, my heart, my entire reason for living." A sob breaks from her chest, and she grips my arms as she cries. I lean down, kissing the tears away. "Don't cry, my love."

She takes my face in her hands. "I love you. I vow that I will love you until the day I die. That I will always be faithful to you, honor you, and cherish you because you are the only person in this world who could break through my walls. You are my heart and soul, Emmett Maxwell. I am crying because you are making love to me as you're marrying me, aren't you?"

I nod and move my hips. "I married you already, but these are what I vow to you now and always."

She moves quickly while I'm slightly off guard, flipping our positions. My eyes widen, but it only takes one movement of her hips to stop my protest.

Her hands rest on my chest, right above my heart. "You are my husband in every way. Now let me make you feel good."

And she does without another word being spoken.

S unday is in absolute doggy heaven here. The last three days, we've done very little besides playing with the dog or cuddling on the couch watching movies, or soaking in the hot springs.

This trail we're walking Sunday down is supposed to lead to a larger hot spring that is more of a creek. I'm excited because it's the first time we're really leaving the house.

No one has heard from anyone in Rose Canyon, which Emmett doesn't think is a good thing or a bad thing, just what it is.

I wish I could share his nonchalance about it. I'm half tempted to buy a burner phone and make some calls. Only, I know that would put a target on our backs since people still think he's dead. So, here I am, walking in the woods.

"This reminds me of deployment," Emmett says.

"What does?"

First, it's kind of cold here. We're in the beginning of summer, but the temperature only gets to the mid-sixties. Second, there were no trees like this on any of our deployments. We spent our days sweating our asses off, carrying fifty pounds of gear, and sleeping in caves.

"The walking."

Okay, that part is true. "We walked miles each day."

He nods. "Also, the danger part."

"Yeah, I could've gone without that too."

"I wouldn't have let anything happen to you then, and I still won't now."

I huff out a laugh. "I'm not the one who had to fake my own death to avoid getting actually shot."

Emmett gives me a look that shows he's not amused. "You would've been if you'd stayed in Rose Canyon."

"But I didn't."

"Because I sent you back to DC for some bullshit reason."

I stop walking as my jaw drops. Well, isn't that a kick in the head. "You *sent* me back?"

"Don't act so surprised. You probably thought it was a lame attempt and knew all along."

Of course I did. I knew the second he agreed with me about the whole outfit thing. I just didn't *know* it was a ploy to get me out of town. But now it makes a lot more sense why he was so paranoid about some of the people from the town being in DC.

"I thought maybe you were just eager for me to move to Oregon."

"I was that too."

That makes me feel marginally better.

"But you had ulterior motives, dear husband."

He keeps moving with the puppy and shrugs. "Yes, to keep you safe."

Emmett has always been protective of me, and to some extent, I appreciate it. At least I allow him to think I need the protection because it seems to make him happy since he's . . . such a big strong man. However, I have never been one to not call someone to the carpet either.

"Lot of good that did as I almost got executed four days ago, and we're hiding out off the grid in bum-fuck Idaho."

Emmett walks backward, a sly smile on his face. "Honeymoon with lots of sex and your own hot spring. You're really suffering."

"I didn't say the sex or location was bad, but you can't tell me this was your plan."

"No, it definitely wasn't. We were getting close to finding who was supposed to be the shooter hired to take me out. As soon as we found that, I was going to confess everything to you. We thought we'd have it wrapped up in a few days, but nothing has gone our way, so I had to lay low and hope they'd make a move."

He's not kidding that nothing has gone our way. "What do your friends think?"

He reaches out for my hand as we walk. "What do you mean?"

"Holden and Spencer know, but what about Brielle? And what is the story going around town about me?"

"Brielle thinks I'm dead," he admits, and I almost smack him. Does he have any idea how upset she was when she had to tell me? "Spencer and I will have a hell of a time making it up to her once she finds out I'm alive. As for your cover story, the town thinks you're in hiding for protection. No one is supposed to know where you are, so everyone will have to keep up that rouse."

I stay quiet, absorbing how many people are impacted by all of it.

"I don't like any of this," I tell him.

"I am not all that fond of it either."

"Then what the fuck are we doing here? You wanted to draw the killer out a few days ago, so why are we in Idaho?"

Emmett shakes his head. "I'm not following."

"Why are we here instead of in Rose Canyon, taking stock of what's going on? Brielle, your friends, the town, Mama James, none of them deserve this, Emmett. The town just mourned Isaac, and now they all assume you're dead. It's unfair to them and to us. We did nothing wrong, and we are all stronger together."

"You think we should go right back into a situation where there is someone literally trying to kill us?"

"I never chose to leave, and I didn't get a vote. Besides, what's the alternative? We live out the rest of our days here without our friends?"

He sighs. "We can't even do the honeymoon thing right."

The sad part is that he's not wrong. We are really bad at conventional, but I wouldn't have it any other way.

"I think we need to be there, that's all."

He brings my hand to his lips. "Okay. I'll call Quinn tonight and see where they're at with this."

<hr />

"Absolutely not," Quinn says over the car speakers as we are nearing Rose Canyon. "You're not coming here. You'll fuck it all up."

I roll my eyes. "How are we going to fuck it up?"

I am so tired of being sidelined. I love being in this place with Emmett, but we need to be smart here. One of the biggest surprises we have is that Emmett isn't dead. We can use that to our advantage.

"Because we believe we know who it is. We just don't have enough to make charges stick or to get an arrest warrant."

"Wait, so you know who ordered a hit on Emmett?" I ask, the knot in my stomach growing as we enter town limits.

"Yes, and there's an order to abduct you because they no longer believe Emmett is dead. We're assuming they want you so they can draw him out into the open. Someone relayed that Emmett wasn't dead back at the house. You being back is a big fucking mistake, so don't get all joyful," Liam says.

"Aww, you miss me," I say with a laugh.

"Not even a little."

He's lying, but it's fine. I am very missable.

Emmett cuts in before we bicker more. "Who? Who put the hit on me and ordered people to take my wife?"

"Our office was able to do facial recognition on two of the guys who came to take Blakely at the safe house. One had close ties to the mayor's stepson," Quinn says.

"Ha!" I yell. "I knew it! If you have this information, why haven't you grabbed him?"

"All right, Columbo, before you get all excited," Liam says. "No one has seen or heard from the stepson in weeks. And you thought Stephen this entire time, so you knew nothing."

"I'm honestly a little shocked," Emmett says.

"Why?" Quinn asks.

"He has never been in trouble or even been around much. What everyone knows of him is that he's quiet and . . . well, chill."

"And you don't think he's capable of it?" I ask.

"I didn't say that. It's just that out of all of them, he would have been the last one I pinned as a human trafficker."

Quinn clears his throat. "I know nothing of the guy other than what headquarters told me. The facial recognition came back to a Landon Henkle out of Portland. We were able to run his financials, and he had a deposit of fifteen thousand dollars right after Emmett was shot from a company owned by Paul Ryan."

"So Paul ordered the murder of my husband and me," I say, feeling a rage like I've never known.

Emmett takes my hand in his, squeezing gently. "And do we have anything tying him to the girls?"

"That's the thing, nothing about this company, these guys, or anything else leads to anything else. It's almost as though Paul Ryan is being framed, at least that was our tech guy's initial response. He felt it was odd that someone who committed murder for hire would be that obvious. I'm slightly inclined to agree, but at the same time, people never believe they'll be caught," Quinn adds on.

"I agree, it's a little stupid to just transfer money from your company," Emmett adds on. "Why wouldn't you at least try to hide it? It makes me wonder if he's not being set up as well."

That causes something to click in me. The evidence we have of the photo and the app connecting to Bill talking to the girl is misleading too. He's dead, he couldn't have spoken on an app to a runaway. Then we know someone is drugging these girls, wants

Emmett and I dead, and is most likely setting up Paul to appear as though he's involved. Wouldn't someone else named Ryan from Rose Canyon stand to benefit from that? Ryan is a nice guy who everyone loves, a paramedic with knowledge of drugs and how to get them, and has ties to Stephen as well, who we suspected all along.

He travels. He does well for himself based on his clothes and car, but isn't flashy. He's charismatic, smart, and no one would ever suspect him.

"I think we were wrong," I admit.

"Wrong about what?" Emmett asks.

"I don't think it's Paul Ryan. I think it's Ryan Wilkinson."

Quinn cuts in. "Where are you guys?"

Emmett gives our location.

"Just sit tight until we can get there," Liam says.

"No one knows we're here," Emmett adds because the silence over the line is deafening.

And then, not even ten seconds later, four cars fly into the parking lot and box us in.

"Blake, get the gun," Emmett instructs. "Quinn, we have four cars surrounding us. Unknown headcount since all of the vehicles have black-out windows. One vehicle is white, Oregon plates." He reads off the rest of the plates and vehicle descriptions. Two men in each car open the doors with guns pointing at ours. "They're armed, guns are pointed at us now. They're either going to kill us or take us hostage."

Not us. It'll be me.

I hand Emmett the gun, and he looks at me. "Don't get out of this car."

Two guys start to walk toward the car with a barrel aimed at one of us. Emmett's hand is gripping the wheel. "I can drive forward, but . . ."

"We'll die."

"We might die anyway. If Quinn is right, they want to take you, and I'd rather give you a chance to get out of here."

"There's no way out of this, we know it."

I have to be strong now. I have to put my brave face on and make this easier for Emmett. This is the exact thing he has spent the last two weeks trying to avoid, and now it's happening because I talked him into coming back to this town.

Now he'll have to watch them take me, or I'll have to watch them kill him. If there's a choice, I know which I'll choose.

I move the kennel to the floor to protect our baby. "I love you, Sunday. You stay here and take care of Daddy," I whisper to her with tears in my eyes.

If they're smart, they'll use me as leverage to get whatever information Emmett and Quinn have dug up. That means I'll be safe-ish for a while. I hope.

"Emmett." I sigh his name, and his mouth presses into a thin line.

He'll come find me.

He always does.

"Don't get out of this car."

"It'll be okay."

"Blakely."

I lift my hand to his lips, not wanting the last moments we might have to be spent arguing. "We both know how this is going to go. It'll be okay. You'll hunt them down, and I'll stay alive until then."

"No."

"Baby, I love you, but our choices are we get shot or I let them take me without a fight. Promise me that you'll come get me."

"I'll fucking die trying."

I nod, tears running down my cheeks. "I love you."

"I love you." The two men take another step forward, and Emmett's hand tightens around the gun I handed to him. "I can't do this."

"You have to. Get what they want and get me back."

He leans in, his lips touching mine in the most tender kiss we've shared. A few nights ago, we said our vows, the ones we should've had from the beginning. We loved in a way I didn't know possible. Now, once again, we're going to have to part, but I know we'll find a way back to each other.

Before I lose my nerve, I open the door and step out with my hands raised. They all start to yell different things, but all I hear is Emmett when he yells, "Don't fucking die, Blakely! I am going to find you!"

CHAPTER
Thirty-Six
EMMETT

"Fuck!" I scream, banging my hands on the steering wheel over and over again.

Less than thirty seconds after she stepped out of the door, she'd been restrained, stuffed into a trunk, and the car had peeled out of the lot, followed by another car.

The other two vehicles are still here, and the two men are still holding me at gunpoint. "What do you want?" I ask loudly.

"The file."

"What file?"

"Get the file, and you'll get your wife back, you make the choice." The man yells as he backs toward his car without lowering his gun.

"Bring what file where?"

"We'll be in touch. Find the file before he loses his patience."

As soon as they get in, I open my door, roll out, use the engine block as cover, and fire my weapon until it's empty. I strike the first car, blowing out the back windshield. The other has some bullet holes in the trunk, but they get away.

Then I stand, feeling despair the likes of which I can't describe. They have Blakely, and I have no idea where they took her.

I can't move. I should head to Holden's house or maybe

Brielle's or maybe do anything other than standing here frozen. However, I can't seem to do anything but stare at the last place I saw her.

Sunday's barking like crazy, and I rush to her, opening the kennel. It takes a second, but eventually, I get her to settle down. "I'll find her, baby. I'll find her."

At the same time that Holman comes around the corner, Quinn and Liam do from the opposite direction. Liam is out of the car, rushing to me before Holman even parks. "Where is she?"

"They took her," I say, feeling like the biggest piece of shit.

"Tell us everything."

I run down the entire story from start to finish, filling in small pieces I didn't think about until they ask. They deconstruct the entire thing, writing notes while on the phone with Mark and Charlie in Virginia.

"You did the right thing," Quinn says, his hand resting on my shoulder.

"I let them take my wife, how is that the right thing?"

"They would've killed you both. Blakely knew it, which is why she went."

Doesn't change a goddamn thing. All it does is make me feel helpless again. I saw the tears in her eyes and heard the resolution and trust in her voice. She believes I will find her, and standing here going over this story isn't doing anything to make that happen.

"What file?" I ask the group. "What file do they want?"

And then, like a piece snapping into place, it makes sense. They want the missing file from Brielle's office. The one with documents about Bill and his family. Only, what could she possibly have in there that would be so important to these people.

Quinn looks to me. "The file."

I'm behind the wheel in a heartbeat. It has to be what they want. I ride hell for leather through the streets, Holman behind me with lights and sirens. I pull up to Spencer's house, and he's already at the door, no doubt having heard the commotion.

"Where's the file?" I ask, not sure if I put the car in park as I rushed out.

"What?"

"The file. Brielle's file. The file she had on Bill."

Brielle rushes outside. "Emmett? Emmett is . . . you're . . . I—" She launches herself at me, throwing her arms around my neck. "Oh, God, you're alive. You're alive, and you're here." She releases me and turns to her husband. His lips are set in a thin line, and after a second, she releases a sigh through her nose. "Why don't you look surprised to see him?"

"Oh, I'm surprised, all right," Spencer says.

"We can argue and talk later, they took Blakely."

"Who took Blakely?" Brie asks. "She disappeared . . . oh, God, what the hell have you two done?"

Spencer moves to her side. "Do you know who?"

"Not for sure, but whoever they are, they want a file—Brielle's file," I reply. "They said they'll be in touch, and if I don't have the file, then . . . I need it."

Quinn and Liam pull in behind me. "You're reckless!" Quinn yells.

"Quinn? Is that you? What the fuck is going on here?" Brielle throws her hands in the air.

"Brie, we'll explain later," Spencer says. "Right now, we have to deal with this." He is in a load of trouble with that girl. "They want a file?"

Quinn shoves me. "I get that you're upset. I get that your wife was taken from you, but Jesus Christ, you need to think. This is a chess game, and you're playing Tic-Tac-Toe."

"I'm not playing games! I want my wife."

Liam steps in front of Quinn. "We get that, I care about Blakely too. But we're on defense, and I don't know about you, but I'd much rather change that up. You should've never come back here, but you did. Then, instead of working through the issue, you take off. Did you stop for even a second to consider that they might have people watching you? That you coming directly to Spencer and Brielle's house after you've been told to find a file makes it look like they have the damn thing? That it puts them in danger too? We all need to calm down and look at the situation and make better moves."

I wish I could calm down. All I see are her eyes as she made the choice to go with them. There was no other option. I couldn't shoot my way out or plow the car through without us both dying. She has faith that I will find her, and that's my goal. My only goal.

"You didn't see . . ."

"No, I didn't, but if you want her back, we have to have a damn plan that's more than speeding through town and drawing attention to yourself. People here think you're dead."

"Speaking of," Spencer cuts in, "can we move this inside to avoid more people knowing."

We enter Spencer's house, but my world feels dull and sluggish. If this is even an ounce of what she felt, I regret ever faking my death because this is agony.

Quinn gives Spencer the details of what happened, and then he walks over to me and nods once. "We'll find her."

"If they want that file, then we know they'll keep her alive until they get it. It gives us the upper hand."

Spencer gets up and heads to the back room before emerging with the file. He lays it on the table, and the four of us go through it, taking photos of everything so we have a record in case anything happens to it. Quinn also sends the contents to his guy at Cole Security.

And I sit here, waiting for someone to contact me so I can get my wife back.

CHAPTER
Thirty~Seven
BLAKELY

I have been in some pretty shitty places in my life, but this one is really up there on the craphole meter. It's cold, that's the first thing I don't like, and it has the worst damn odor I've ever freaking smelled.

I'm afraid to even look around because it could be coming from a dead body, and that is where I draw the line.

Not that I haven't been around dead bodies, but this wouldn't be fresh.

So, I lean my head against the wall and focus on breathing through my mouth.

Once I was in the car with the idiots, which is what I refer to them as, they put a bag over my head. We drove for what felt like an eternity, no one saying a word. I did my best to focus on the sounds, the length of time we drove, and the way the car moved, but . . . it's not like I'm going to have a chance to use it.

Still, it allowed me to focus on something other than Emmett's face as I left him.

We drove until I counted to 1,998, the road was windy, I didn't hear much of anything, and the car seemed to pull a bit to the right. I'm pretty sure we got on the highway and off it at the next exit. That's all I got.

There are blankets over the window in this horrible room, so I have no concept of time. And my hands are zip tied, so I can't even get out of them.

There is someone talking outside the door, and it kind of sounds as if the person is pacing, but I can't be sure. Either I have a visitor, or they've abducted someone else, and I'll have a room-mate. Shit. I don't want to think about that possibility. That they will sell me.

I wonder how much I'd go for . . .

I shake that thought out and go back to focusing on what's going on.

More whispering and then the door flies open, the light behind the person is blinding, and I can't see a face.

"Hello, Blakely."

That voice.

I know that voice.

I wait for my eyes to adjust, slowly trying to open them. After blinking a few times, the silhouette becomes clearer. He's tall, but not quite as tall as Emmett. I try to make out anything else, but I can't see. He steps deeper into the room, and I fucking knew it.

"You."

He smiles. "You're surprised that it's me?"

My heart is pounding, and I stare up at the man who saved my life. I hate that I'm right. I hate that this man ever spoke to me, and I thought he was *nice*. "How? How could you do this?"

He shrugs. "There's not a lot of money in being a paramedic, is there?"

"And money is more important than the welfare of young girls?"

"Girls who have already lost their way," he tries to correct. "I rescue girls off the streets who are addicted to drugs, lost, or want to escape their lives."

"And you think this is a better life?"

"I'm not one to say what is better or worse, but they have purpose."

My eyes widen. "You took an oath," I remind him. "You're supposed to help others."

"I help people in a way that actually allows me to live above the poverty line. You can judge me all you like, I really don't care. I have made my peace with my life."

So happy for him. Asshole. Also, my chances of getting out of here alive have just jumped from a plane with no parachute. He has just shown himself, and there's not a chance in hell that he would do that if he intended to let me live. But I have Emmett, Quinn, Liam, and the US Marshals looking for me. Surely, that will give me a slim chance—I hope.

"How does it work? How are you able to take girls from all over the country? It doesn't make sense."

He squats in front of me with a smirk. "You think too small. That's usually the problem with law enforcement. I had hoped you would see it differently, but you were so sure it was the mayor or Stephen, who, of course, has a role, just not the one you assume."

"And what role would that be?" I ask. "I don't think too small. I just allowed my personal feelings toward you to cloud my judgment. I won't make that mistake again."

Ryan laughs. "I like you, Blake. I really do, and I didn't want this to be your story, but when things started to unravel, it became the only option."

"Killing Emmett and abducting me became your last choice?"

I blow at the piece of hair that keeps falling in my eyes. Ryan tucks it behind my ear, and I restrain myself from trying to bite him.

"You got closer than anyone else."

"Why, because we assumed Stephen was involved?"

He stands and walks to the window, pulling the blanket back. I practically break my neck trying to look out, but he moves before I can see anything.

"Hardly. Stephen cares too much about his father's opinion to step a toe out of line, which is ridiculous because that man can do no wrong in his father's eyes. So, your assumption on him being involved is wrong. He never wants to disappoint Daddy." He nearly spits the name. "I couldn't give two fucks about that. I want money and power. And . . . I have it."

This still makes no sense. "So, again, how are you doing all this?"

Ryan sighs. "People don't think outside the box anymore, you know?"

I know that he's a few crayons short of a full box, but I can't say that. "Enlighten me."

"Since you'll never make it out of here, I don't see why telling you is a bad idea."

"Good to know you're planning to kill me."

"It is regrettable, but it's how it has to be. Or I could send you somewhere, but there's a chance you'd make it back."

Oh, he could bet his fucking life on it. I would die trying to make sure this piece of shit suffered.

"Yes, we wouldn't want that," I mutter, my hope draining. Hope is a bullshit word we use when we are in despair. Right now, I'm trying to find a way out of this, but I don't think anyone has a clue where I am.

How could they? We drove for over a half hour, and before they showed up to ruin my damn day, I don't know how they can find me. Ryan was never our main suspect so we don't have much on him.

Might as well go down with false bravado.

"My point is, you living stopped being an option the moment I walked through that door."

I glance up at him. "I have another option."

"What's that?"

"Since you're sort of a douchebag who is abducting young girls and killing them, maybe you should kill yourself. Then, the world would be a better place all around."

He gets low, his nose almost brushing mine. "And here I was being nice. It's why I didn't drug you or do all the things that I could've. Let's try to remember that and maybe show some respect."

My limbs start to tremble. I'm not sure if it's from the cold or fear, but I turn my head away and inhale, and then count as I exhale to try to reclaim a bit of calm.

I steel my voice. "I would love to do that, Ryan, but I am struggling here. You have me in some horrible place. The smell is . . . disgusting, and I'm being told I will die in these horrible zip ties. Could you swap them out for handcuffs? At least then I can move my elbows a bit."

"I imagine that's not easy for you." He whistles three times, and someone rushes forward. "Can you get the metal handcuffs? The lady requests it. Also . . . a blanket."

"Thank you," I say softly.

Guys like Ryan have a hero complex, no one becomes a medic without wanting to save lives in some way. We want to be that person, the one who allows someone just one more minute or another chance. Somewhere, deep inside of his sick mind, that has to exist. I need to appeal to it.

"I'm not a monster," he says.

Right.

"How did you go from paramedic to this? I'm just struggling to see the connection. I like money just as much as the next person, but it's not the same as going on a call or being the person to hold a heart in their hand while they race to get someone help."

"I'm still that person."

"Okay, then what brought us here?"

He looks around the room and shrugs. "I was a traveling paramedic for years. I wanted to see the world, treat different kinds of people, and the company my uncle owned allowed me to do that. I trained, worked insane hours, went all over the US, and was fucking broke."

"But you helped so many people."

Ryan's eyes find mine. "For what?"

Oh, I don't know, to help people. It's not like people who want to be rich join the military. There is no money. Even as an officer, I lived paycheck to paycheck. Emmett and I watched these eighteen-year-old kids join, thinking they'd get free food, lodging, health-care, and a chance at a better life. They were met with food you didn't want to eat and barracks that were built in the sixties, had mold, and smelled like feet. Healthcare consisted of . . . here, take a Motrin and advice to suck it up. Even though the reality of military life was not what we thought, we did it because it felt good.

Not in the wallet.

But in our hearts.

Soldiers, sailors, marines, and airmen fight for our country without complaint. We weren't trying to get rich, we just wanted to make a difference in this world.

"I don't know, only you can answer that. I know why I became a medic."

The assistant comes back in the room, halting our conversation. He hands Ryan the metal handcuffs, the blanket, and a bottle of water before he leaves again.

"I want to hear about that, but first, I'd like to get you out of the zip ties. If you try anything, I'll make your death painful. Understand?"

"I understand."

Not that I am not a little tempted to do something stupid, I just know better. If I make a move, I better know what the next one is, and right now, I don't. I have no idea where I am or how many people are here. It would be suicide to risk running now. Ryan doesn't seem to be in any great hurry to kill me, so I am going to take that as a win.

He helps me up, turns me so my face is against the cold, concrete wall. Then he removes the plastic tie, closes the metal handcuffs around my wrists, and turns me back to him. "Better?"

"Yes. I appreciate the gesture."

"As I said, I'm not a monster."

No, you're definitely a monster, but I have enough self-preservation to keep that to myself.

"You were saying what led you to this change in your career."

I sit back down, my legs feeling weak from stress and anxiety. He wraps the blanket around my shoulders since I have no arms, which works fine for me. I always keep my paperclip in my back pocket, so I'll be out of these cuffs as soon as he's gone.

"You want to know how I went from answering emergency calls to this? Okay. I was on a call in Florida, it was around spring break and there was this girl in an alleyway. She was around fifteen, clearly hungry, dirty, and definitely high. I brought her some food, started talking to her, and she begged me to get her somewhere safe."

I listen, imagining Keeley in this same situation, thinking this man, this paramedic, would protect her. I hold back the bile threatening to rise.

Ryan moves around the room, kicking random objects as he talks. "Anyway, I got her loaded into my rig, fed her, and cleaned her up the best I could, but when we started to head to a rehab center, she lost her mind. She kept saying she couldn't go there, she needed drugs, she needed a different life. She offered things no fifteen-year-old should offer, and I was horrified. I tried to get her name, anything to get her true help, but she didn't want that, just the drugs."

"I'm not following," I admit.

Maybe it's the smell or the cold, but none of this equals abducting girls.

He turns, his eyes finding mine in the hazy darkness. "I brought her to that facility, even though she didn't want it. I offered her a chance at a new life, and when I was checking her in, I met *him*."

"Him?"

"Yes, he offered her something I wouldn't—the drugs and the truth about what she'd need to do to get them. You'd have thought he offered her a million dollars."

"Who is him?" I ask.

"It doesn't matter. He offered me a whole new life that day. He gave me a chance to get these girls off the street and give them a choice."

I feel sick. Absolutely fucking disgusted over this. He's acting as if what he did to them was a choice? There was no choice. Dear God.

"He told me to bring any runaway who needed a choice to him, so I did. I brought three more that week, and then I found out the money that I could make."

"So, you think you were helping them?"

"I do help them. I give them the options. They know full well what they are going into."

I keep my lips together so I don't scream at him about what a sociopath he is and look away. To think this man touched me to save my life. Once I feel a bit less nauseous, I meet his gaze again.

"You judge me," Ryan says, his voice even.

I'm not sure how to answer this. "I judge the choice you made. The fact that you walked those girls into a life of drugs and sex."

"They were already in that life. I found a way to get them off the street."

There is that savior complex I was looking for earlier. Too bad it's twisted and vile. "So, that was Florida years ago, how did you get Keeley?"

"Ahh, yes, the girl you came all the way back here for thanks to Bill and his mishandling with that fucking app. Well, it's simple, we have paramedics all over the country who offer choices to runaways."

My breath hitches, and I can do nothing to process this. There is a network of paramedics who he has indoctrinated into this? I seriously want to cry. How anyone can do something so horrifying is beyond anything I could comprehend. I know there is evil in the world. I'm fully aware of the sick and disgusting things that people do, but this is up high on the list of fucked-up things I wish I could forget.

And I want to know who the boss is.

Who is the mystery person Ryan and the other paramedics bring these girls to? That is the thread that needs to be unraveled.

"And your benefactor, does he keep his hands clean?"

Ryan stops in front of me, dropping on his haunches. "You ask a lot of questions for a dead girl."

"What can I say? It's the investigator in me. I won't lie, I'm impressed. Not that you steal young girls off the streets and sell them into whatever it is, but that you have a well-organized system. There's no trail to you or the other paramedics who are getting their hands dirty, you avoid police scrutiny while also appearing to be wonderful and caring people." Flattery mixed with loathing is all I can muster at this point. "It's a dangerous game, though. Look how quickly we were able to find out about Bill."

He laughs. "Bill was nothing."

"Then why did you order a hit on my husband? Why go through the dog and pony show of abducting me?"

"Bill had only one tie to me. One. And it's in that file your husband should be working on getting."

"A file?"

He smirks. "Yes, something you didn't know about."

"And that tie would be?"

"The house."

Then, seemingly done with the conversation, Ryan walks out, closing me back in the darkness. Only the next time someone comes, I'll be out of these cuffs, and I'll fight until my last breath. If I die, I'm going to die on my own terms.

CHAPTER
Thirty-Eight
EMMETT

"**Y**ou're sure this is the right location?" I ask Quinn, who is on the phone with some tech guy in Virginia.

"This is where he used his phone last."

We're on the outskirts of a small town on the coast. There's nothing around but a shipping yard that looks like it's been closed down forever. What the hell did he come here for?

"There's no one here," Spencer says, looking through his binocular.

"We wait. This is our only lead," I instruct.

Thankfully, no one is pushing back on anything I've said so far. Liam and Quinn were both leaders of their SEAL team, and I ran my Ranger team. Then there's Spencer, who went through eighteen months of training so he could write the piece that ended up earning him a Pulitzer Prize. The four of us work together well. I appreciate that they've given me the helm because it's forced me to slow my thinking and focus on strategizing instead of my wife being in danger.

It's not just about me or Blake. It's all of us who need to go home at the end.

Liam, who is about a half mile down on overwatch, radios in. "I have nothing so far. If he's here, he's hiding pretty well."

I take a very slow look at everything, searching for any sign that someone is or has been here. There are no tire marks visible from this side. No one is walking around, and I don't see any lights.

Quinn taps my shoulder. "Ben says the signal is pinging again, and it's definitely here."

It's been nine hours that they've had her without contact.

We all poured through the paperwork, trying to find a connection to the mayor, his son, or anyone in power, and we couldn't find a damn thing.

It wasn't until I went through Sonya's information that it clicked. There was a deed on a house in Portland. Ryan Wilkinson had owned it, and then it was placed in Bill Waugh's name about a year before Keeley's disappearance. Brielle had it listed in Bill's previous addresses list and was the only tie to Ryan.

If it weren't for knowing the name to look for, I never would've given that information a second glance.

I nod. "Then we watch."

We relay that information to Liam, and then we settle in to wait and watch. As much as I want to focus on the job, I can't stop thinking about Blake. I wonder if she's okay or if they've hurt her or are hurting her. All these thoughts go in circles.

After about an hour, we finally see something.

A reflection in the window, just a small flick of a curtain, but it means there's life in there.

"Did you see that?" I ask Spencer and Quinn.

"I saw, what do you want to do?" Spencer asks.

"We keep watching. There's no way for us to know how many people are in there, but he doesn't know we're looking for him or that we suspect his involvement. If we don't see anything in the hour, we move. I can't leave her in there or risk her being moved."

They both nod.

While we do that, Spencer works on getting the building layout, Quinn is running everything on Ryan Wilkinson, and I continue to watch along with Liam.

There's very little activity, and the clock keeps moving as adrenaline continues to build.

I need to get to her before anything goes wrong.

Finally, after another three minutes, we get movement.

I lift my hand, but Spencer and Quinn are already beside me. We all watch as someone walks onto the dock.

Then my phone rings.

Quinn nods, indicating it's recording and transmitting to Ben at Cole.

"Hello?" I ask, trying to inject enough fear in my voice.

"So, it's true," the voice that is being put through a scrambler says. "You live."

"Who is this?"

Quinn gives me a thumbs-up that Ben is getting the information and the team is working with it. I need to keep the call going for as long as I can.

"I'm asking the questions."

"Not until I know who I'm talking to and if my wife is alive."

"Such a romantic you are, Emmett. Your wife is fine. She's enjoying staying cool in this heat."

Sloppy of him to give away so much information in an innocent comment.

"I want proof."

The voice makes an audible sigh. "We're going to have to have a little trust here, Sheriff."

"That was thrown out the window the minute you took my wife and left me sitting here for hours without any information."

"I can see how that would trouble you." There is a pause. "Fine. I'll go get Blakely."

My eyes widen, and I turn to the guys, who adjust their positions. This is it. This is going to be the moment.

I hear the door click, indicating they went inside. Then another door opens. I count the seconds, trying to map out where they're holding her based on the blueprints.

There are some hushed murmurs, and then I hear her voice. "Emmett?"

"Blake!" I yell. "Are you hurt? Are you okay?"

The voice with the scrambler comes back on. "You heard enough. Now, I'll give you a location, and you're to go there, drop the folder, and we'll release Blakely from our care."

They're going to kill her as soon as that drop happens.

"If you hurt her," I warn.

"Bring the file, Emmett. I don't have time for anything else."

"If she's not at the drop, I'm not bringing the file," I call his bluff. More than anything, I want however many guards he has with him to leave, giving us less resistance when we go to extricate her.

Quinn nods at what I said. "No Blakely, no file," I repeat.

"You're not really in a position to negotiate. I could kill her right now."

"And if you did that, I would have no incentive to ever bring this file to you."

"You go alone. If I see anyone near that location, she dies . . . and you die. Understand?"

"Understand."

He disconnects, and I let out a shaky breath. "You did well," Spencer says. "We have Ben compiling a map based off where he moved through the building."

I look to Quinn. "We need to move. She can't leave here, and if they decide to take her, it'll be impossible."

"Then we go now."

I give them a rundown of my plan, and a few suggestions are thrown to make sure this goes off without injury. There's not a lot of time, so we all have to rely on each other's training. Since these are some of the best men I've ever met, it's comforting to know they have my back.

I pull my rifle over my shoulder and adjust my vest. Once we're all geared up, I signal to the group to start the descent toward the building. We move in tandem, keeping low to the ground to avoid anyone seeing us. When we reach the bottom of the cliff, we halt. Wherever the vehicles are will be our best shot.

Liam's com comes on. "I don't see a vehicle on the south side."

"Nothing to the East," Spencer says.

"West is clear," Quinn says.

I look around, and then I see the building with a loading area. "Come around the North."

As we start to move, I hear gunfire inside.

I crouch low, my heart pounding harder as my worst fears start to come to life. They killed her before I could get to her. I knew it was a possibility.

"Get against the wall, we'll enter together," I say, the three of them coming in around me.

Quinn, who is at my back, taps twice.

I kick the door open, move to the left, and he enters. As soon as he's through, Spencer goes, then me, and then Liam. The four of us go through, clearing the area as we walk. Another gunshot sounds down the hall.

Quinn lifts his fist, and we pull to a stop as footsteps start to move our way. Whoever it is, they are moving quickly. We are going to have seconds.

He's on his one knee, gun facing forward as the three of us cover him.

Closer.

Closer.

And then a person with long brown hair billowing behind her comes into view.

"Blake," I say, all of us lowering our weapons.

"Hey, boys. You're a little late to the party. I shot Ryan in the shoulder, paltry wound but it got my point across, and then I cuffed him."

I blink. "What?"

"The guy he had with him was a cocky asshole. He made a big mistake when he decided to take me out of the zip ties and put me in cuffs. As soon as I heard their big plan, I got out and killed the first fool with his own gun. Then I waited for Ryan, shot him, and tied him up until I could get help. Here you are."

Liam laughs. "This girl."

"That's pretty badass, Blake." Quinn's admiration is thick in his voice.

"Ballsy," Spencer agrees.

"Mine." I walk to her, taking her face in my hands and kissing her. "All mine."

She smiles up at me. "Forever. Lucky you."

I am lucky. I'm so damn lucky I found her and married her before I knew I loved her.

CHAPTER
Thirty~Nine
BLAKELY

"Anything else you want to add to your statement, Mrs. Maxwell?" the district attorney asks.

"Nope. I told you everything. Now what?"

She looks down at her file. "Now the waiting begins. We have all the information, and we'll hand it over to the state law enforcement to complete their investigation. After that, we'll see what else he'll be charged with. As of now, we're looking at kidnapping, assault, battery, as well as solicitation to commit murder for the attempted assassination of your husband. There's a long list, but as for the other part, regarding the runaways, I can't answer that. I am going to hand it over to the FBI, though."

That's something, I guess. "He has a very organized operation. Whoever he answers to is big, and this isn't going to stop."

"I understand. If we can tie Ryan Wilkinson to the girls in Portland, that's going to be a large investigation. Believe me, I am not going to just let this go. I'm absolutely sickened by what you told me, and we will do what we can to ensure he pays for his crimes."

I guess that's all I can really ask for at this point. "Okay. I just worry we aren't safe."

"Would you like to go back into protective custody?"

"Not a damn chance," I say. As fun as it was to spend some

alone time with Emmett, I really don't want to hide. "We have no idea what this mysterious *him* knows. If we stay exposed, maybe he'll be lulled into thinking we know nothing."

"You're very brave, and I understand what you're thinking. The offer stands. My office will do whatever you need."

"Thank you."

As she leaves, Emmett enters and rests his hand on my shoulder. I can feel the energy between us changing. We've been through so much, and this has been hard on us.

I look up at him, placing my hand on his. "I want to go home."

The way his blue eyes shimmer with emotion is enough to make me cry. "Let's go home."

He helps me up, and we walk to the car, not saying anything. When I open the door, a fluffy baby comes flying up in the front. "Sunday!" She licks my face, and I giggle, holding her tight. "Hi, sweet girl. Did you miss your mommy? Yeah? I missed you too. Did you take care of Daddy like I asked?"

Emmett chuckles as he gets into the car. "She stayed with Brie while we worked things out. I think she wanted to keep her."

"She can't. She's our baby."

"She is. I will always protect you both."

Sunday starts to settle, and I reach for Emmett's hand. "We're going to be okay, babe. We are stronger together."

"Watching you get in that car, Blake. It took ages off my life."

"Watching you die in front of me wasn't any easier, but when I got in the car, I knew you'd come for me. You have always been the one person I could count on."

He snorts. "Please, you had four special ops trained men looking like a bunch of idiots as you saved your damn self and came walking out."

"I didn't say I needed you, I said I knew you'd come. I was just faster."

"Don't do that again, okay?"

I smile. "Do what?"

"Be the fucking hero."

"Oh, is that your role?"

His lips flatten into a thin line. "One, yes, it is. Two, you could've gotten yourself killed. We were there to make sure that didn't happen."

"I didn't know you were there, Emmett. I saw an opening and took it. You could just say: thank you, Blakely, for being a badass who did my job for me."

"Did my . . . woman!"

I grin and lean in. "Say thank you."

"I'm not saying it."

"Say it."

Emmett rolls his eyes. "Shut up."

"You shut up."

"I could make you."

I like the sound of that. "With a kiss?"

He laughs. "Only you would go through getting kidnapped, shooting someone, and finding out about an organized trafficking ring and still want to be a pain in my ass."

"It's a gift," I say with a shrug.

I don't try to be annoying. It just comes naturally at this point.

He moves toward me, and I meet him halfway, letting him kiss me. Emmett pulls back, resting his forehead to mine. "How about we have some time without anyone trying to kill us?"

"That sounds nice, are you planning to retire?"

"Retire? Why the hell would I retire?"

"I don't know, you're bound to get shot at again," I explain since he clearly forgot.

"I didn't get shot at until you showed up."

"Oh, sure, blame me."

We laugh, and then we laugh harder. Before we know it, we have tears running down our faces. All the tension and stress leave us as we lose it in the car. Sunday is barking, moving back and forth between us as she tries to figure out what's happening. She must think we've gone nuts, which we have.

My stomach hurts, and I struggle to get control. By the time we stop, I'm gasping as I put my head against the headrest.

Emmett looks to me and smiles. "I love you."

"I love you too."

"Home?"

I nod. "Home."

Home is where we belong.

Emmett's lips touch mine, and I smile against his mouth. "Go to work."

"I'd rather stay here and kiss you." He does it again, and I laugh.

"You're going to be late."

"Let them fire me." Emmett's arms are tight around me as he brings us together again.

Silly, amazing, sexy, caring man.

"Then we'll both be unemployed."

He squeezes my butt. "That would be an issue."

"It would. I need my sugar daddy to keep me happy."

Emmett bursts out laughing. "You must be talking about someone else."

"I am."

"Oh? And what's his name?"

I roll my eyes. "Daddy, duh."

He kisses my forehead. "Walk me to the door."

Today is his first day back at the station. We've spent the last week curled up in bed, walking with Sunday, and visiting his dad, who settled back into his facility as though he never left. The staff was happy to see all of us back and find out that Emmett was alive.

That was the main reason we've sequestered ourselves in the house, we weren't ready to deal with the million questions about what happened and why.

However, today is a day to venture out, and it's causing him no small amount of anxiety. I understand why he doesn't want to leave me alone, but we have to rip the Band-Aid off.

When we get to the door, he stops and shifts. "Emmett, we have to live. I am completely capable of taking care of myself."

"I know that, but you shouldn't have to worry about this shit."

"I'm not worried. He's in jail, you can get to me in minutes, and Liam is still camped out in Brielle's apartment."

Him still being here is probably the only reason he's considering going back to work.

"All right. You call me if there's anything that feels off. Don't go getting your gun and trying to fix it on your own. You call for help, you get Liam, and you stay in this damn apartment."

"Okay," I agree, but we both know I don't mean it. If there's danger, I have no intention of shrinking away. Whatever or whoever is after us isn't going to force me into hiding.

"Liar."

I shrug. "I could listen."

"You won't."

"You never know."

He leans in and gives me a kiss. When he opens the door, he stops and turns to me. "I almost forgot."

"What?"

Emmett reaches into his pocket and then drops to one knee. Oh. Oh, he's . . . proposing?

He lifts the ring between his fingers, holding it up in the sunlight. I gasp as the prisms dance across the walls.

"We're already married, twice really. I've given you every promise and every part of myself. I don't kneel before you to ask you to be my wife, but to be my partner in this world. I ask you to wear this ring as a symbol of what we are and all we will be. I want this to be the token they speak of, the representation of how much you own me, Blakely. You are my heart and soul, and I ask you to take this, wear it, and always know that you are the most precious jewel in the world."

Tears leak down my cheeks, and I nod. "Of course."

He smiles and places the ring on my finger before bringing my hand to his lips. But then I'm pulling him back to his feet and kissing him, pressing as close as I can get to him. I pull him inside, walking backward toward the bedroom. "Blake."

With my lip between my teeth, I wink. "You need to call Holman."

"Oh?"

I drop his hand and remove my shirt, tossing it on the floor. "Yeah, you're really going to be late now."

Next goes my bra. He makes an audible moan. "Killing me, baby."

I shimmy out of my shorts, letting them fall, and then I shake my hair out. "For the rest of your life."

"I am a lucky man."

Yeah, he is, but I am also one lucky woman.

Epilogue
EMMETT

~Two months later~

"**P**ut that box over there," Blakely says, pointing to the side of the room.

"Yes, dear."

We are moving Blakely into her new office on Main Street. It's a single-story building right across from the police station.

"Do you think people will see the sign?" she asks.

How could they miss it? She painted the entire front window. After everything she went through, she couldn't get the missing girls out of her mind. She and Addison decided to put their talents to work and open an outreach program to help reunite runaways with their families. For those who don't want to return home, she provides safe and effective housing, meals, healthcare, and rehabilitation options so they hopefully don't end up in a trafficking ring.

A month ago, we received an extremely large donation from Keeley's family, which enabled Run to Me to be completely operational on two coasts. Our first office is here, in Rose Canyon, and in two weeks, we head out to Sugarloaf to open Addison's location. When she believed I was dead, it was too much for her, and she decided to move to Sugarloaf permanently.

I can't blame her. None of us can, but Blakely found a way to give her a purpose in memory of Isaac. How she managed to open two offices across the country from each other in such a short time is nothing short of amazing, but that's Blakely.

She turns to Holden. "What's the hold up on building the desk?"

"Nothing."

"Do you need instructions to put the thing together?"

He scoffs. "I'm a fucking surgeon. I can put a desk together."

I love my wife. The fact that she bosses Holden and Spencer around like Brielle does makes me so happy. It's nice to watch them cower a little because she can be scary as hell. After she freed herself from the people who kidnapped her, I think Spencer fell a little in love with her, not in the sexual sense, of course. She just has that effect on people. You want to be around her, and you can't help but love her.

"Then do it already. Sheesh," Blake says with a smirk.

She's totally egging him on.

Brielle walks in, stops next to Holden, and asks, "Do you need the directions?"

Both Blakely and I laugh.

He throws the screwdriver down. "Hey, peanut gallery, if you two could do it faster, why don't you try?"

Brie lifts her hands in surrender. "I didn't say anything. You're moody."

"Yes, yes, I am. Hey, Blake, are you open to doing any kind of investigating on the side?"

Oh, God, this again. I sigh heavily. "You're so dramatic. Seriously."

"I'm dramatic? Mr. Fake-My-Own-Death-And-Make-Everyone-Lie." He tilts his head with a raised brow. "Even better, how about when Blakely went with the psycho and you were unglued."

"I'd love to see how you would've handled it," I counter.

I don't think I was unglued. I was determined. My wife had been ripped away from me, and I wanted her back.

"My point is that you don't get to give me shit, buddy."

Spencer enters the fray. "What are we arguing about?"

Blake replies. "Holden asked me for help on investigating something, and Emmett is butthurt he didn't ask him."

"I did ask him!" Holden throws his hands up. "I went to him about it the first time, then the second, and now I'm asking Blakely since he's unwilling to help."

He acts like the notes and trinkets he's getting are threatening, they aren't. I understand it's stalking, but there has been different information that has made it difficult to piece together. The only consistent things are that the packages come to the hospital and always have Holden's license number. Other than that, nothing else makes sense.

The first thing he received was the Eiffel Tower figurine and a postcard of the Grand Canyon. The second gift, which showed up after the fiasco with my shooting, was a Las Vegas postcard and a small statue of an Egyptian pyramid with the exact same wording from the first postcard.

"What was this one?" Spencer asks.

Holden pulls the postcard out and hands it to him. He reads it and gives it to Blake.

"'Your package is arriving, and you need to pick it up.' What do you think it means?"

"Maybe it's a bomb," Brie unhelpfully suggests.

I laugh. "Or maybe it's his mail-order bride."

Blake glares at me. "Not funny, considering where we're standing."

"I didn't say that he was getting her illegally." I shake my head and bring the conversation back on track before my wife skewers me. "You've gotten three strange postcards and weird statues of iconic places. No idea what any of it means, but nothing about them is threatening."

Spencer taps his foot, which means he's trying to unravel this mystery. "All three came with postcards from the Vegas area."

"We know you boys and your love of Vegas," Brie scoffs.

"No one loves Vegas. We survived Vegas," I remind her.

She turns to Blake. "They barely survived my brother's bachelor party. It was a mess, to say the least, and Addison almost called off the wedding."

"Did anyone ever think that we took the fall for some of the shit he did?" I say, crossing my arms. "Your brother wasn't a saint."

"No, but from what I heard, you were the worst of them."

Spencer grins. "You were. Admit it."

"I don't remember shit."

Holden claps his hands. "Focus, fuckers. It's me who remembers nothing about Vegas. I blacked out."

I laugh. "Yeah, we found you with your dick out in that bathroom."

Spencer nods. "The *women's* bathroom."

We drank an ungodly amount of alcohol that weekend. It started on the plane and didn't stop until the third night because we were so drunk that we couldn't remember our names. Isaac tried to sing at a drag bar, Spencer ended up lost for a period of time, I ended up locked out of the hotel room naked, and Holden banged some girl in the bathroom at a club and then passed out.

After that, we all promised never to return to Vegas without adult supervision because, clearly, we weren't capable of behaving.

Blakely steps toward me. "I can't wait to hear your part in this."

I clear my throat. "What happens in Vegas stays in Vegas."

She smiles, running her finger along my collarbone. "And we were married during that."

"We were, and I didn't sleep with anyone."

She eyes me curiously. "Good."

"I like when you're jealous," I tease.

Holden groans. "You two need to go on a real honeymoon."

I pull my wife to my side. "Or you need to find a girl willing to marry your ass and finally be happy."

"Yeah, that's not going to happen. I have no desire for a woman or kids. I'm perfectly happy living a single and stress-free life."

Just then, someone knocks on the door. A petite woman with blonde hair stands in the threshold, holding on to a toddler.

"Excuse me? I . . . I was hoping someone could help?" she says in a British accent.

Blake steps out of my embrace and walks over. "Hi, I'm Blakely, the director of Run to Me. That's my husband, Sheriff Maxwell, and this is Brielle, Spencer, and that's Holden, he's a doctor if you need help. What's your name?"

Her eyes go to his, something flashing in them. "Holden?"

He moves toward her, his steps careful and deliberate. "Yes, my name is Holden James. I'm a surgeon, and I can help if you're hurt."

She shakes her head. "No, I'm not hurt. Not . . . physically at least."

The girl looks terrified, and it's clear she's been crying.

Blakely's soft voice steps in. "Is this your daughter?"

The woman glances at the child. "Yes, this is Eden."

"Hello, Eden, my name is Blakely. Would you like something to eat?"

Eden's eyes go to her mother and then back to Blakely before she smiles a little. Blake takes that as a yes and walks over to the cabinet and grabs a granola bar. When she returns, the little girl twists her body a little and then grabs her mother's leg.

"Sorry, she's normally rather chatty, but it's been a very hard few days, and when I got into town, I was told to come here to find Holden James."

His eyes move from the little girl back up to the woman's face. "You were looking for me? Do I know you?"

"My name is Sophie Pearson. We met a few years ago, my name then would've been—well, it doesn't matter, we didn't exchange names that night."

"We have met then?"

"Yes, and while I wasn't quite sure why I was sent here, now it's a bit clearer." Sophie hoists Eden up into her arms.

Blake moves back to my side as she realizes this isn't a runaway seeking refuge. She takes my hand and brings her lips to my ear. "Did you know Holden had a kid?"

She sees it too. I shake my head, wanting to catch all of this, and consider pulling out my phone to record it.

He clears his throat. "And when did we meet?"

"It would be a little over three years ago."

He looks over at Eden. "Where?"

"Las Vegas."

Oh shit. Looks like my friend is a father, and we found the girl who left him passed out after having sex in the club.

Blakely steps forward, her hand resting on Holden's shoulder. "Why don't you three go in the back room where there's some privacy."

"Thank you," Sophie says.

Holden doesn't move for a minute. He just watches them follow Brielle to the conference room in the back. Then Blake taps twice, urging him to follow. "Don't worry about the desk, Holden, we'll figure it out. You have another problem to disassemble."

Looking wholly shellshocked, he moves back into the room, and the rest of us just stare.

"Well," I finally say, needing to break the tension. "I guess what happened in Vegas didn't stay there."

Blake throws something at me, and we all laugh. I open my arms, wanting her near me because I can't get enough, and she tucks her head under my chin.

"I won't ever have to worry about that, will I?"

I lift her chin up, wanting her to see my eyes. "Since the day we got married, you have been the only woman I have wanted. I will never want anyone else but you. There's nothing to worry about. The only child that will ever come from me is a child we have together."

She lifts onto her toes and slides her arms around my neck. "I can live with that. Maybe after the trial, we can discuss it further."

"I would like that."

"Who would've thought this would be our life?"

I kiss her nose. "I hoped it."

And now I get to live it—for as long as I draw breath.

Thank you so much for reading Give Me Love. I can't tell you how much I loved Emmett and Blake. They were fun, heartbreaking, and a little crazy.
And we aren't done yet!
Next is Holden and Sophie and … what exactly happened in Vegas?

Keep This Promise is next and I hope you're ready for another swoony, suspenseful, and beautiful ride that will leave you breathless!

Preorder Here!

However, I wasn't done with Emmett and Blakely yet!

There is access to an epic bonus scene on the next page. I hope you enjoy!

Dear Reader,

I hope you enjoyed Give Me Love. I fell so hard for Emmett and Blakely and I wanted to give just a little more of a glimpse into their lives, so ... I wrote a super fun scene. I have an EXCLUSIVE bonus scene as a thank you!

Since giving you a link would be a pain in the ... you know what ... I have an easy QR code you can just scan, sign up for my newsletter, and you'll get and email giving you access!

Books by Corinne Michaels

The Salvation Series

Beloved

Beholden

Consolation

Conviction

Defenseless

Evermore: A 1001 Dark Night Novella

Indefinite

Infinite

The Hennington Brothers

Say You'll Stay

Say You Want Me

Say I'm Yours

Say You Won't Let Go: A Return to Me / Masters and Mercenaries Novella

Second Time Around Series

We Own Tonight

One Last Time

Not Until You

If I Only Knew

The Arrowood Brothers

Come Back for Me

Fight for Me

The One for Me

Stay for Me

Willow Creek Valley Series

Return to Us

Could Have Been Us

A Moment for Us

A Chance for Us

Rose Canyon Series

Help Me Remember

Give Me Love

Keep This Promise (Coming 2023)

Co-Written with Melanie Harlow

Hold You Close

Imperfect Match

Standalone Novels

All I Ask

You Loved Me Once

About the Author

Corinne Michaels is a *New York Times, USA Today, and Wall Street Journal* bestselling author of romance novels. Her stories are chock full of emotion, humor, and unrelenting love, and she enjoys putting her characters through intense heartbreak before finding a way to heal them through their struggles.

Corinne is a former Navy wife and happily married to the man of her dreams. She began her writing career after spending months away from her husband while he was deployed—reading and writing were her escape from the loneliness. Corinne now lives in Virginia with her husband and is the emotional, witty, sarcastic, and fun-loving mom of two beautiful children.